Secrets

Enid Blyton

The Mystery that Never Was
The Secret of Moon Castle

·PARRAGON·

This edition published in 1996 for
Parragon Book Service Limited
Units 13–17 Avonbridge Industrial Estate
Atlantic Road
Avonmouth, Bristol BS11 9QD
by Diamond Books
77–85 Fulham Palace Road
Hammersmith, London W6 8JB

First edition published 1992 for Parragon
Book Service Limited

Printed and bound by Caledonian International
Book Manufacturing Ltd, Glasgow

Conditions of Sale

The Mystery that Never Was

First published in this edition in a single volume in 1976 by
William Collins Sons & Co Ltd.
First published in Armada in 1983

CHAPTER 1

News At Breakfast Time

Nicky Fraser came down the stairs at top speed, his dog Punch at his heels barking in excitement. The little terrier flung himself against the dining room door and it flew open, crashing against the wall.

The family were at breakfast. Nicky's father gave a roar of anger. "NICKY! What's the matter with you this morning? Take that dog out of the room!"

Mrs Fraser put down the coffee jug and fended off Punch who was leaping up joyfully at her. Grandma smiled at Nicky, and tapped his father on the hand.

"*Just* like you used to be when you were his age!" she said.

"Hallo, family!" said Nicky, beaming round as he went to the sideboard to help himself to scrambled eggs. "I can see you've forgotten what day this is!"

"I told you to take that dog out of the room," said his father.

"Day? Well, what particular day *is* it?" said Grandma. "Not a birthday – that I do know!"

"No, Granny! It's the first day of the hols! Ha – four glorious long weeks to do just what I like in!" He began to sing loudly. "Hey derry, hey derry ho, hey . . ."

"Stop that row," said his father. "And take that . . ."

"Dog out of the room!" finished Nicky. He put his plate down on the table and turned to give his father a sudden hug. "Oh, Dad – it's the first day of the hols. Come on, Dad – I bet *you* used to sing for joy, too!"

"Sit down," said his father. "*I'll* sing for joy – I hope – when I see your report. Punch, get off my feet."

Punch removed himself and went to sit on Grandma's feet. He gave her leg a loving lick. He loved her very much. She *never* shouted at him!

"I suppose you and Kenneth have plenty of plans for these holidays?" said the old lady. "It's lucky he lives next door."

"Jolly lucky!" said Nicky, buttering his toast. "Actually we haven't any *definite* plans. We thought we'd teach Punch a few more tricks – like fetching shoes or slippers for people. Granny, wouldn't you be pleased if Punch fetched you your slippers to put on, when you came in from a walk?"

"Good heavens!" said his father. "Don't tell me we're going to find slippers strewn about all over the place!"

"What's that dog eating?" said Mrs Fraser, as a loud crunching noise came from under the table. "Oh *Nicky* – you've given him a piece of toast again."

"I bet it was Grandma who gave it to him," said Nicky. "Punch, stop eating so rudely. Dad – are you going to give me my usual ten shillings if my report's good? And a pound if it's super?"

"Yes, yes, yes," said his father. "Now be quiet. I want to read the paper, and your mother hasn't even read her letters yet."

Mrs Fraser was reading a short letter. Nicky's sharp eyes recognized the handwriting.

"I bet that's from Uncle Bob!" he said. "Isn't it, Mother? Has he had any exciting jobs lately?"

"Yes – it *is* from my brother Bob," said his mother, putting down the letter. "He's coming to stay with us for a while, and . . ."

8

"CHEERS!" cried Nicky, putting his cup down with a thump. "Did you hear that, Punch?"

Punch barked joyfully, and came out from under the table, his tail thumping against Mr Fraser's leg. He was promptly pushed back again.

"Mother! I say, Mother, he isn't coming down here on a *job*, is he?" asked Nicky, his eyes shining.

"I bet he is! Mother, will he do some sleuthing here? I'll help him, if so. So will Ken. What's the job? Is it something we . . .?"

"Nicky! Don't get so excited!" said his mother. "No. Uncle Bob is coming down here because he's been ill and wants a rest."

"Oh, blow! I thought he might be hunting a murderer or a swindler or a – a kidnapper or something," said Nicky, disappointed. "You know, Mother, I'm the only boy at school whose uncle is a detective!"

"A private investigator," his mother corrected him. "His work is . . ."

"Oooh, I know all about his *work*," said Nicky, taking another piece of toast. "They've got plenty of investigators on television. Last week one had a frightfully difficult case to solve. It ended up in an aeroplane chase, and . . ."

"You watch television too much," said his father, gathering up his letters. "And now listen to me – if your Uncle Bob is coming here for a rest, he will NOT want hordes of gaping schoolboys coming here to listen to his adventures! Bob is not supposed to talk about them, anyway – they are private. Nobody is to be told that he's the uncle you've been boasting about."

"Oh Dad – can't I even tell *Ken*?" said Nicky, in dismay.

"Well, I suppose you can't *possibly* keep anything from Kenneth," said his father, going out of the room. "But ONLY Kenneth, mind!"

"I shall tell him immediately after breakfast!" said Nicky, passing another bit of toast under the table. "Did you hear the news, Punch? Whoops – we'll have some fun with Uncle Bob. Mother, have you ever seen him in any of his disguises? Can I telephone him and ask him to come in disguise tomorrow, to see if Ken and I can spot him?"

"Oh don't be so ridiculous, Nicky," said his mother. "And listen – there's no going over to Ken's until you have tidied up your room. All your school books seem to be spread over the floor!"

"Right, Mother!" said Nicky. "Gosh, to think it's only the *first* day of the hols! Come on, Punch! You're going to be busy the next few weeks, learning a whole lot of new tricks! That's the time to learn, you know – when you're young! And you're hardly a year old yet. Scram!"

Punch scrammed. He shot out into the hall, sending the mat flying, and up the stairs, barking. He thought it must be a Saturday as Nicky was not going to school. He raced into Nicky's room and raced round and round the bed at top speed, barking madly. Oh what joy to have Nicky all day long!

Nicky picked up all his scattered books, and decided to stack them in the fireplace, out of the way.

"All my bookshelves are full," he told Punch. "So the fireplace is the obvious place. They'll go half-way up the chimney, I expect. Then I'll slip downstairs and phone Uncle Bob. Shut up barking now, Punch – you'll have Mother shouting up to us."

He slipped downstairs to the study after his bout of tidying. No one seemed to be about. He went in, shut the door and sat down by the telephone. He rang his uncle's number and waited impatiently, Punch sitting as close to him as possible.

His uncle's secretary answered. "Oh, is that you, Mr Hewitt?" said Nicky. "Well, listen. Uncle Bob's coming to stay with us tomorrow. Tell him I'll meet him with my friend Kenneth – and we'd like him to come in disguise just to see if we can spot him. You won't forget, will you?"

"I'll tell him," said the voice at the other end of the phone. "That's if I see him before he leaves but it may be that I . . ."

Nicky heard footsteps approaching along the hall, said goodbye hurriedly, and put down the receiver. He

11

couldn't help feeling that his father would consider it a waste of the telephone to ask Uncle Bob such a thing. Luckily the footsteps passed the study door, and Nicky crept out unseen.

"Come on, Punch! We'll go and find Ken and tell him Uncle Bob's coming!" he said to the excited dog. "Race you out into the garden – GO!"

CHAPTER 2

Down In The Shed

Punch took the short cut that the boys always used – out of the back door, through the yard, down the garden to the hole in the hedge. Mrs Hawes, the women who came in to help each day, shook her broom at Punch as he flew past, almost tripping her up.

"You and that boy!" she said. "Sixty miles an hour and no brakes! Give me a cat any time!"

Punch and Nicky squeezed through the hole in the yew hedge, and Nicky gave a piercing whistle. It was immediately answered by Kenneth, who was down in his garden shed. Punch arrived there before Nicky, and flung himself on Kenneth, whom, next to Nicky, he adored with all his heart. He licked him from top to toe, giving little whines all the time.

"You'll wear your tongue out, Punch," said Kenneth. "Stop it now. I've already washed twice this morning. What a dog! Hello, Nicky! I see Punch is his usual fatheaded self. Hope you are too!"

Nicky grinned. "Hello, Ken! I say, isn't it grand, no school this morning! First thing I thought of when I woke. How are your guinea pigs?"

"Fine. I've just finished feeding them," said Ken. "Look at this tiddler – the youngest of the lot, and the cutest. Get down, Punch. He's an awfully *nosy* dog, isn't he, Nicky? Nosy would be a much better name for him than Punch."

"Listen, Ken – I've a bit of news," said Nicky, pulling Punch away from the guinea pig cage. "Wait a minute though – where's that nosy sister of yours? She's not anywhere about, is she?"

"She might be," said Ken, cautiously, and went to the door of the shed to see if his sister Penelope was in sight. "No – all clear," he said, and came back.

"Penny's just about as nosy as old Punch here," said Nicky. "Listen, Ken – you know my Uncle Bob – the one who's a sort of detective?"

"Yes. What about him? Has he solved some mystery or other?" said Ken, interested at once. "I say, did you see that detective play on TV last night – where nobody could make out who stole the . . .?"

"No, I didn't. Do listen, Ken. Uncle Bob is coming this morning – and I phoned him and asked him to come in disguise, so that we could show him how good we are at tracking people and seeing through any disguise. Uncle Bob's a wow at disguising himself – he showed me his Special Wardrobe once – bung full of all kinds of different clothes – and hats! You should have seen them!"

"Gosh!" said Ken. "I say – do you think he's come down to do a spot of detective work here in our town? Can we help him? We're pretty good at disguises ourselves, aren't we? Do you remember that time when you dressed up as a guy and I wheeled you down-town on Guy Fawkes Day? If you hadn't had a coughing fit nobody would ever have seen through *that* disguise!"

"My mother says he hasn't come to do any sleuthing here," said Nicky, mournfully. "But, of course, he might *not* have told her, if anything was up. He's supposed to be coming because he needs a rest."

"*That's* a likely story, I *don't* think!" said Ken, scornfully. "I never in my life saw anyone so bursting with health as your Uncle Bob. The way he made us walk for miles, too – do you remember? Personally I'm quite glad to hear he needs a rest!"

"Well, anyway, he's coming today," said Nicky. "And, as I said, I asked if he'd come in disguise. He's always one for a game, you know – so what disguise do you think he'll wear?"

There was a pause. Ken scratched his head. "Well – he might dress up as an old man," he said.

"Yes, he might," said Nicky. "Or as a postman. I saw a postman's uniform in his wardrobe. Anyway, there's one thing he *can't* disguise, and that's his big feet!"

"Would he disguise himself as a *woman*?" asked Ken.

"I don't *think* so – the voice would be difficult," said Nicky, considering the matter. "And the walk, too. Uncle Bob's got a proper man's walk."

"Well, so has Penny's riding mistress," pointed out

15

Ken. "And her voice is jolly deep. Like this!" And to Punch's alarmed surprise he suddenly spoke in a curious, deep-down, hoarse voice. Punch growled at once.

"It's all right, Punch," grinned Nicky, patting him. "That was a jolly good effort, Ken. Well, what we'll do is this – go to the station and meet the London train with old Punch here, and . . ."

"But that wouldn't be fair," objected Ken. "Punch would recognise him at once by his smell. We'd better leave him behind. He'd do what he always does when he sees or smells anyone he knows – go round them in circles, barking his head off."

"Yes, you're right. We won't take old Punch then," said Nicky. "He'll howl the place down," said Ken. "Lock him in *yours*."

"Right," said Nicky. "Do you hear that, Punch, old thing? In the shed for you, see, while we go walky-walkies – and if you don't make a sound, I'll give you a great big bone."

"Wuff!" said Punch, wagging his tail violently at the word "bone." The boys patted him, and he rolled over on his back, doing his favourite bicycling act with all four legs in the air.

"Ass," said Nicky. "What shall we do till midday, Ken? The London train comes in about five past twelve."

"Sh!" said Ken, as the sound of someone singing came on the air. "There's Penny. Pretend to be tidying up the shed in case she wants us to do anything."

At once the two boys began to pull boxes about feverishly, and straighten up things on the dirty shelves. A face peered in at the door.

"Oh, so there you are," said Penny, and came right

into the shed. "*You've* been a long time feeding your guinea pigs, Ken! Mother wondered what you were up to."

"You mean *you* did!" said Ken, busily brushing a great deal of dust off a shelf, all over Penny. "Look out! We're busy, as you can see. Like to help – though it's a pretty dirty job, cleaning out this shed."

"*Well*! I've never seen you clean out this shed before!" said Penny, sneezing as the dust flew around. "I wondered if you'd like to mend my bicycle brake for me. It's gone again."

"Penny – we're BUSY!" said Ken. "I'll do it tonight. Or you can ask Gardener. He's good at bikes."

"Well, I certainly don't want to stay here in *this* mess and muddle!" said Penny. "Get down, Punch. *Now* look how he's dirtied me with his paws!"

"Oh, for goodness' sake, go away," said Ken, and swished another cloud of dust from a nearby shelf. Penny sneezed and hurried out. Nicky looked at Ken.

"Shall *I* go and mend her brake?" he said. "She just *might* have an accident, you know. We've plenty of time."

"I can hear her asking Gardener," said Ken, climbing down from the box he was standing on. "She's a Nosy Parker – only came down to see what we were doing! Why *are* girls so nosy? You're lucky not to have a sister."

"Oh, I wouldn't mind a *little* one," said Nicky. "It's not much fun being an 'only', you know. It's a lucky thing for me that you live next door. Still – I've got old Punch!"

"Wuff!" said Punch, and licked his hand. Ken looked round the shed. "We might as well clean it up properly now," he said. "We've nothing to do till midday, when the London train comes in. Shan't we get filthy!"

They worked hard, and quite enjoyed themselves. "My word – we're a sight!" said Nicky. "I'd better go in and change – and hope I shan't bump into Mother on the way! Meet you outside my gate in a quarter of an hour – and then we'll just show Uncle Bob that we can see through *any* disguise he's put on! Come on, Punch – you've got to be locked up, old fellow, till we come back!"

CHAPTER 3

Which Is Uncle Bob?

The two boys left a very angry Punch locked up in Nicky's shed. "Hope Penny won't hear him howling and let him out," said Ken. "I say, I'd better come in with you while you put on something clean, and give myself a brush. I'm pretty filthy too – but if I go into my own house and Mum sees me I might be sent on all kinds of errands."

"Well, come on in, then," said Nicky. "Back way, then we'll only see Mrs Hawes, our daily woman."

Mrs Hawes stared at them in surprise, as they tiptoed through the kitchen. "Well, there now – I never knew the Missis had ordered two sweeps for the chimneys this morning!" she said, as they went by her, grinning cheekily.

Nicky put on a clean sweater and washed his face, while Ken brushed himself vigorously, sending black clouds of dust all over the bedroom. Through the open window came woeful howls from the garden shed. Poor Punch!

"Now to slip out without Mother seeing me," said Nicky. "I don't want to have to stop and do odd jobs just as we're off to meet the train."

They crept down the stairs and made for the kitchen again. An astonished voice called after them. "Oh! *There* you are, Nicky! Where have you been all morning? I wanted you to . . ."

"Sorry, Mother – we're off to meet the London train!" shouted Nicky. "Uncle Bob, you know!"

"Yes, but wait, Nicky, you silly boy, you won't be . . ."

began his mother, coming out of the sitting room after them. But the boys had disappeared, and the kitchen door banged.

"Narrow escape!" panted Nicky, racing round to the front gate. "Come on! We'll just get to the station in time."

The train was signalled as they ran on to the platform. "Now you keep a watch on the people coming from the back of the train, and I'll watch the front," said Nicky. "And remember to look for BIG FEET!"

Ken remembered quite well what Nicky's Uncle Bob looked like – an upstanding fellow with keen eyes, determined mouth, and clean-shaven.

"Still, he might wear a false moustache or a beard this morning," thought Ken. "And stand bent over like an old man." He stood waiting as the train came in by him and pulled to a stop.

Six people stepped down from the carriages. Two were women, both small. They could be ruled out at once. One was a boy, who went whistling down the platform. That left three. Nicky and Ken looked at them closely.

An oldish man with a beard – shuffling along, head bent forward – glasses on his nose – and large feet! Nicky brightened at once. "Might quite well be Uncle Bob!" he thought, and fell in behind him at once.

Of the other two, one was a postman with a large bag. He too had large feet, and was bent under the weight of his heavy bag. He had a small moustache, and mopped his face with a handkerchief as he went, giving a large sneeze as he passed the boys. They nudged one another.

"Bet that's him!" whispered Ken. "You follow him

20

and I'll follow the old chap – just in case! I don't think that other person's any good. Small feet!"

Nicky nodded. He followed close behind the postman, wishing he could get a better look at his face. Gosh – he certainly had large feet! Nicky tried to peer into his face as he walked past him, but the man was still mopping his nose. He slung his bag from one shoulder to the other, and it knocked against Nicky.

"Hey!" said Nicky, almost bowled over by the weight of the bag. "Got a cold, Uncle Bob?"

"What you following me about for?" growled the postman. "Think you're being funny calling me your uncle? Clear off!"

His voice was not deep, but rather hoarse as if he had a bad cold. Nicky decided that it was decidedly a false voice. He gave the postman a nudge with his arm. "Come on, Uncle Bob! Own up! I'd know your voice anywhere, even though you're making it as croaky as an old crow's. But it's a jolly good disguise!"

The postman put his bag down with a thump and glared at Nicky. "Now if I have any more funny business from *you*, me lad, I'll talk to that policeman over there, see?"

The postman was now staring straight at Nicky, and he could see the man's whole face very clearly – good gracious, it was nothing like his Uncle Bob's face – and the little moustache was certainly real! Nicky began to feel most uncomfortable.

"Sorry!" he said, awkwardly. "I just thought you were – er – in disguise, you know. I was looking for someone else!"

"Now you clear off, see? And if my voice sounds like an old crow's, so would yours with a cold like mine,"

21

"Come on, Uncle Bob! Own up!"

said the angry postman, and sneezed again so violently that his postman's cap almost flew off.

"It was a mistake," said poor Nicky, red in the face. "I apologise!" And he raced off after Ken, who was still following the old man. Ken was lucky, thought Nicky – *that* must be Uncle Bob, shuffling along, pulling at his beard and mumbling to himself.

He caught up with Ken and raised his eyebrows, muttering, "Any luck?"

Ken nodded. "I think so. Haven't said anything yet, though. Look at his feet!"

Nicky looked. Yes – they were just about the same size as Uncle Bob's – and so were his hands. That beard was clever – hid half the face! The old man suddenly stopped, pulled out a cigarette case and lit a cigarette, holding the match with trembling fingers. He flipped the match away with finger and thumb. "Just like Uncle Bob always does!" thought Nicky. "Aha, Uncle Bob! I'll have a little fun with you!"

So he fell into step beside the old man and began to talk. "Do you know the way to Mr Fraser's house?" he asked, and Ken gave a grin, for that, of course, was Nicky's home. "I'll take you there myself, if you like."

"Don't play the fool," grunted the old man in a husky voice. "What are you two boys following me for?"

"What big feet you've got, Uncle Bob!" said Nicky. "And do let me feel your nice thick beard!"

The old man looked angry and a little frightened. He walked on, saying nothing, then suddenly crossed the road to where the town policeman stood, stolid and burly.

"Constable, will you take these boys' names, and tell their fathers they have been molesting me?" said the old man. The policeman stared in astonishment at Nicky and Ken, whom he knew well.

"Now what have you two been doing to old Mr Holdsworth?" he demanded. Then he turned back to the old man. "All right, sir," he said. "I'll deal with this for you. Young rascals!"

"I say, Constable – is he *really* an old man?" said Nicky, taken aback, as he watched the old fellow go off, mumbling. "I thought he was my Uncle Bob in disguise. Is he *really* a Mr Holdsworth?"

"Now look here, Nicky Fraser, *you* know he's an old man all right, and no more your Uncle Bob than *I* am!" said the policeman. "Don't you start getting into trouble like some of the youngsters in this town! Playing the fool and making fun of old people isn't the sort of thing your parents would like to hear about."

"It was a mistake, really it was," stammered poor Nicky, and Ken nodded his head too, scared. "You see . . ."

"Go home," said the policeman, impatiently. "I've no time to waste on silly kids that don't act their age. *Next* time I'll deal with you properly."

He marched out into the road, and began sorting out a small traffic jam. The two boys, red in the face, hurried home. They felt very foolish indeed.

Nicky saw his mother in the front garden and yelled to her. "Mother! We went to meet Uncle Bob, and he wasn't on the train."

"Well, no wonder!" said his mother. "Didn't you hear what I called out to you, when you left in such a hurry? I said he was coming by *car*!"

"BLOW!" said both boys at once. Nicky groaned. "Gosh – what asses we've been! What time *is* Uncle Bob arriving, then?"

At that very moment a sports car drew up in front of the house, and the horn was blown loudly. The boys swung round.

"It's Uncle Bob! Goodness, Uncle Bob, we've been meeting several of you at the station! What a smashing car! Come on in, you're just in time for dinner!"

CHAPTER 4

Good Old Uncle Bob!

Uncle Bob was just the same as ever, except that he was a bit thinner, and rather pale. Nicky's mother, his sister, made a fuss of him.

"Oh Bob, dear! Whatever have you been doing to yourself? You've gone as thin as a rake!"

"Now Lucy, don't exaggerate!" said Uncle Bob, and gave her such a bear hug that she gasped. "I'm a bit overdone, that's all! If you can put up with me for a week or two I'll soon be as fit as a fiddle! Hello, boys – what's this about meeting several of me at the station?"

The boys told him, and he roared with laughter. "You're a couple of idiots! I can see you need a few lessons in detective work! Come on in and help me to unpack my bag."

It was grand to have Uncle Bob staying with them again. Punch was thrilled too. When the boys let him out of the shed, giving him a bone as they had promised, he ignored the bone completely, and tore up the garden, barking loudly. He had already heard Uncle Bob's voice, and not even a juicy bone could tempt him! He flung himself on Uncle Bob, and licked every bit of him that he could.

"Here – be careful of Uncle Bob – he's rather frail at the moment," said Nicky, grinning. "Isn't he pleased to see you, Uncle! You've come on a good day – it's the first day of the Easter hols!"

"Good for you!" said Uncle Bob, clapping Nicky on

the back. "You'll be able to take me for some walks – and maybe we can do some bird-sleuthing together – you're still keen on birds, I suppose?"

"Oh *yes*," said Nicky, pleased. "Ken and I mean to go out bird-watching as usual. We've heard there's a sparrow hawk somewhere on the hills, and we'd like to find his nest. Not to take the eggs," he added hastily, knowing his Uncle's strict ideas about egg-collecting. "Ken's got an old pair of field-glasses. Wish *I* had!"

"Well – I might lend you *my* pair," said his uncle, who was by this time up in his room, opening his bag. "I always have a pair with me – useful in my work, you know – and as I shan't be needing them this time, I'll lend them to you. That's if you'll promise to care for them as if they were made of gold! They're jolly fine ones."

"Oh, Uncle Bob! Thanks most awfully!" said Nicky, overjoyed. "It's not much fun sharing a pair, you know. Ken always wants to use them when *I'm* longing to – but it's jolly decent of him to lend them to me, anyhow. Now we'll each have a pair. I *say* – are these the ones you use? What *magnificent* field-glasses! I bet Mother'll say you're not to lend them to me!"

Everyone liked Uncle Bob, and as for Mrs Hawes, she was, as Nicky said, "quite potty on him."

"We always get smashing cakes when *you* come, Uncle," said Nicky, at tea time, when a grand new fruit cake appeared on the table. "And I bet we'll get heaps of rissoles now, because Uncle Bob likes them. Shan't we, Mother?"

"Bob always was spoilt," said his mother.

"I wish *I* was," said Nicky. "How did you manage to get spoilt. Uncle Bob?"

27

"Let's change the conversation," said his Uncle. "Actually, when we were kids, *I* always thought your mother was the spoilt one. Well – what sort of a report did you get for last term, youngster?"

"It hasn't come yet," said Nicky. "Two of the teachers were ill at end of term, so the reports are held up. Horrible! It means I have to shiver in my shoes longer than I need. Don't let's talk about reports! Let's talk about Punch. We're going to teach him a lot of new tricks, Uncle. Will you help?"

"You bet!" said Uncle Bob, helping himself to a second piece of the fruit cake. "My word, Lucy, if Mrs Hawes goes on cooking and baking like this, I shall get so fat I'll have to buy new clothes!"

Punch was sitting as close to Uncle Bob as he could. He liked his smell. He liked his voice. He liked the firm way in which Uncle Bob patted his head. How wonderful to have his two best friends together – Uncle Bob *and* Nicky!

"I thought I'd teach Punch to fetch people's slippers for them, Uncle," said Nicky. "Think how pleased Dad would be to find his slippers by his armchair each night! And I could teach him to fetch you your outdoor shoes, Granny! Then you wouldn't have to go and look for them."

"Hm!" said Granny. "If Punch is going to be as clever as that, he *will* be a busybody! I think it would be better to teach him to wipe his feet on the mat when he comes in from a walk – that really *would* be something!"

"Wuff!" said Punch, sitting up straight, proud that he was being talked about. He gave Nicky's hand a lick, and then Uncle Bob's. He did so like this family of his!

He gave a happy sigh, and laid his head down on Uncle Bob's foot.

"He's getting a bit soppy," said Nicky, amused. "Biscuit, Punch?"

Punch stopped being "soppy" at once, and sat up, barking. "Beg, then; beg properly!" ordered Nicky, and waited for Punch to sit up on his hind legs, front paws waving in the air.

"Not very steady, are you?" said Nicky, and gave him a biscuit.

It really was good to have Uncle Bob in the house. He was always ready for a joke, always ready to give a hand with anything, and full of funny stories about his work, though, of course, he never gave any secrets away. He took Punch for long walks, he went shopping for Nicky's mother, and was quite one of the family.

But there were times when he sat silent by the window, drawing on his pipe, hardly answering anyone who spoke to him. He puzzled Nicky and Ken one rainy morning. They were full of high spirits, and wanted him to join in the fun – but he seemed somehow far away, and didn't even notice when Punch tried to leap on to his knee.

Nicky went to his Mother. "Mother – is Uncle Bob all right today? He's hardly spoken a word."

"Well, I told you he's been overworking," said his mother. "He's been forbidden to do any of his work for some time – and the days must sometimes seem empty to him now that he has no puzzling cases or problems to work out. With a brain like his, he must often be bored to death, not being able to use it. I only wish something interesting would happen, so that he could have something to think about."

"What sort of thing do you mean?" asked Nicky. "Burglaries – or kidnappings – something like that? I bet our policeman would be proud to have Uncle Bob's help if anything happened here. But nothing ever does – unless you count things like Mrs Lane's washing being stolen off her line – or somebody breaking the grocer's window!

"No, of course I don't mean things like that," said his mother. "I don't really know what I *do* mean – except that Bob needs something to take his mind off himself. It's not like him to sit and mope at times. I think the doctor's wrong. Bob doesn't need time on his hands like this – he wants something to *do* – something to set those brains of his working again, instead of rusting."

This was a long speech for his mother to make. Nicky

stared at her, worried. "Would he like to go bird-watching with us?" he said, hopefully. "Or shall I ask him to help me to teach tricks to Punch? He'd do anything for Uncle Bob."

"Well – you ask him. See what *you* can do," said his mother. "He can't bear me or Granny to fuss round him – and *I* can't bear to see him sitting there not taking any notice of anything, as he's doing today! Maybe you and Ken can help him more than anyone else can."

Nicky went off with Punch, looking thoughtful. Poor Uncle Bob! He certainly must miss the exciting life he usually had – tracking down criminals – perhaps hunting a murderer – finding stolen goods! But what *could* he and Ken do to help?

"Come on, Punch – we'll find Ken, and see if he's got any good ideas," said Nicky. Off they went to Ken's shed, little knowing what good ideas Ken would have – and what extraordinary things would come of them!

CHAPTER 5

Ken Has An Idea

Ken was down in his guinea pig shed as usual. Penelope was there too, cleaning some garden tools. "Hello Ken!" said Nicky. "Hello, Penny!"

Penny didn't answer. "She wants to be called Penelope now," explained Ken. "She won't answer to Penny."

"Oh," said Nicky, astonished. "But, why? Penelope is rather a silly sort of name – Penny's much nicer."

"Well, if that's what you think, I'll go," said Penny huffily, and promptly threw down the hoe she was cleaning, and went.

"Good!" said Ken, with a sigh of relief. "She's been reading an old Greek story about some wonderful person called Penelope, and she rather fancies herself now. Any news?"

"Yes. A bit," said Nicky. "I want your help, Ken. Stop messing about with those guinea pigs."

Ken looked solemn at once, and shut the door of the cage. "What on earth's up?" he said. "You look as solemn as Penny!"

Nicky began to explain about his uncle. "Mother thinks he's moping now," he said. "You know – misses his work. Hasn't anything to sharpen his brains on. She said that perhaps you and I could think of something interesting to brighten him up."

"He might like my guinea pigs," said Ken at once.

"They're *really* interesting. This one, now, he washes his whiskers just as if . . ."

"Don't be an ass, Ken. Who wants to sit and watch guinea pigs washing their whiskers? I'd go potty if I'd nothing better to do than that! No – I mean something really *exciting* – something to take the place of all the interesting and thrilling puzzles and problems that Uncle Bob has to solve for people, when he's in London."

"Well, let's make up a few for him," said Ken, half-joking. "Let's see now – the 'Mystery of the Lights in the Empty House!' or 'Who is the Prisoner in the Cave?' or 'What made those strange Noises in the Night?' It would be a bit of fun for all of us! We'd lead him properly up the garden path!"

"You really are rather a fat head, Ken," said Nicky. "You *know* we couldn't do things like that." He drummed his heels against the side of the box on which he was sitting. Then he suddenly stopped, and sat up straight. He gave Ken a delighted punch, and stared at him with bright eyes.

"*Now* what's up?" said Ken, quite surprised. "Well – it's just that I think you've got hold of a good idea," said Nicky. "It sounded too silly for words when you said all that – but, you know, there *is* something in it!"

"Wuff!" said Punch, feeling Nicky's sudden excitement, putting his paw up on the boy's knee.

"You don't mean we *could* make up a mystery for your uncle to solve, do you?" said Ken, disbelievingly. "He'd be wild when he found out! Anyway, he'd never believe in it. He'd smell a rat at once."

"Wuff!" said Punch again, hearing the word "rat".

33

Penelope was there too . . .

"Don't interrupt, Punch," said Nicky, feeling more and more excited. "Ken, it would be *fun*! We'll work out something between us. Let me see – how could it be done? I'll have to think."

"Look – we can't deceive your uncle like that," said Ken, really alarmed now. "He'd be furious. Anyway, he's so jolly clever he'd see through it at once. We can't pit our brains against *his*!"

"We can try!" said Nicky, red with excitement. "Look – something like this, Ken. We'll get him to come out bird-watching with us – taking our field glasses, of course. And we'll put clues here and there, see, for him to find."

"You're barmy," said Ken, disgusted.

"I'm not. We could let a piece of paper blow in the wind, and when he picks it up, it's a message in code! Ha – very mysterious! And we could get him to train his field glasses on something peculiar, and . . ."

"Peculiar? What do you mean, *peculiar*?" asked Ken, puzzled.

"Oh – someone signalling out of a window or out of that old tower up on the hills!" said Nicky. "I'm sure Uncle Bob would think that peculiar, and he'd want to find out what was going on."

"Yes. But actually there wouldn't *be* anything going on," said Ken. "And he'd soon find that out."

"Oh shut up finding fault with everything I say," said Nicky, drumming his heels angrily against the box, and making Punch bark again. "I thought you'd be glad to help. Mother said we might think of something together – and here you've come up with a perfectly splendid idea, that would be fun for all of us – and now you pooh-pooh it! I only wish *I'd* thought of it!"

35

Ken began to think he must have been very clever after all. He stopped making difficulties. "Oh well – if you *really* think I've had a brainwave, I'll help. But it's all got to be worked out carefully, mind – this pretend mystery, whatever it is. And what will your uncle say when he finds it's all a hoax?"

"He'll laugh like anything," said Nicky. "He's got a terrific sense of humour, and he never minds a joke against himself. We'll be giving him a bit of excitement, something to puzzle him and take him out of himself, as Mother says. And what's more, *we* shall enjoy it too! Shan't we, Punch, old thing?"

Punch hadn't the faintest idea what the boys were talking about, but he heartily agreed with everything. He ran round the shed, barking loudly, and nosed excitedly into every corner.

"He's looking for a deep, dark secret, a hidden mystery that only Uncle Bob can solve," said Nicky, in a hollow, dramatic voice that made Ken laugh, and Punch look up in surprise.

"All right," said Ken. "You think up the clues. I thought of the idea, so I've done my bit. Is all this to happen in the daytime or night-time? I'm quite game to wander about at night, if you want me to. Only it's no good asking Mum if I can – she'd say 'no'."

"For goodness' sake! You mustn't say *anything* about this to your mother!" said Nicky, in horror. "She'd go and tell *my* mother at once, and that would be the end of it. We're doing this to help my Uncle Bob, remember, and NOBODY except you and me must know about it. And Punch, of course."

"When will you think out the clues we're to spread around?"

"I think I'd better think about them in bed tonight," said Nicky, sliding off the box. "That's when I get my best ideas. What a laugh we'll have! By the way – I'm teaching Punch some tricks. Like to come and help? I'm teaching him to fetch people's slippers for them. He's already got the hang of it."

"*Really*? Isn't he a marvellous dog?" said Ken, twiddling one of Punch's alert ears. "Yes, I'll come. And listen, Nicky – don't say a word of our plan in front of Penny – Penelope, I mean – you know how snoopy she is."

"As if I would!" said Nicky, scornfully. "Come on, Punch. Come and show what a clever dog you are!"

And, for the next half-hour, Nicky's house echoed to sounds of "Fetch it, then, boy! Grandma's shoes! Up the stairs, Punch! That's right. He's gone to get one, Ken! Buck up, Punch! GRANDMA'S SHOES!"

Down the stairs came Punch at top speed, carrying one of Uncle Bob's bedroom slippers in his mouth. He put it down at Nicky's feet with a look of pride, his tail wagging nineteen to the dozen.

"Ass!" said Nicky. "I said 'GRANDMA'S' not Uncle Bob's. Try again." And up the stairs went Punch, tail down now. He appeared in a few seconds with one of Nicky's football boots, tripping over the laces as he came.

"He's not really very clever, is he?" said Ken. Nicky was puzzled. "I don't understand him. He fetched Grandma's shoes after breakfast all right."

A voice came down the stairs – Grandma's. "Nicky! Please STOP Punch scratching at my door. He can't have my shoes – I'm wearing them!"

"There!" said Nicky, relieved. "I *knew* there was a

good reason why he didn't bring them. Good dog, Punch. You shall help us with our secret plan! You're as clever as a bagful of monkeys!"

CHAPTER 6

Nicky Makes Some Plans

For once in a way Nicky went off to bed without voicing his usual strong objections. He really was longing to think up some wonderful mystery for his Uncle Bob! His Granny was surprised when he kissed her so early in the evening.

"My, Nicky – you're going early tonight!" she said. "Are you feeling all right?"

"Yes. I'm fine," said Nicky. "I just want to think out something in bed, that's all. 'Night, Mother, 'night, Dad. Come on, Punch."

Punch leapt up, gave everyone a goodnight lick, and disappeared out of the door with Nicky.

"Well! *They're* early to roost tonight!" said Grandma. "Nicky must be tired."

He wasn't! He was very wide awake indeed, and his mind was already busily thinking out plans, as he undressed. Punch was surprised that Nicky said nothing to him, for usually he was very talkative. He whined, wondering if he was in disgrace for something, but still Nicky took no notice!

Punch wondered what to do. Why didn't Nicky talk to him as he usually did? Was he in disgrace? The little terrier suddenly barked and ran out of the room, his tail wagging. *He* knew how to please Nicky and make him talk to him, he was sure he did! He came back with a shoe of Uncle Bob's. Nicky didn't even notice! Punch ran out again, and came back with Mrs Fraser's bedroom slippers, and set them down beside the shoe. Then off he went again for more!

But Nicky was still lost in thought. He had cleaned his teeth, washed, done his hair – and then by mistake he cleaned his teeth again without even noticing! That really did surprise Punch!

Nicky leapt into bed, and was just about to put out his bedside lamp when he caught sight of the seven or eight slippers and shoes that Punch had been fetching to try to please him. There they were, all set out on the bedside rug, Punch lying forlornly with his head on two of them.

"Oh *poor* old Punch!" said Nicky. "I've not said a word to you for ages! I've been thinking hard, Punch, and all the time you've been rushing about fetching shoes to please me. *Dear* Punch! Did you think I was cross with you, or something? Well, I'm not. I think you're the best dog in the world!"

Punch went quite mad with joy. He tore round and round the room, sending the shoes flying, barking madly – and then with one final enormous leap he landed on top of Nicky, and licked every inch of his face.

"Oooh, Punch – that was my tummy you jumped on!" groaned Nicky. "Lie down, you ass. No, you can't get into bed beside me. You know Mother would find you when she came up, and you'd get a smack. Gosh, look at all those slippers and shoes – honestly, you're a mutt. Now just you take them back!"

But that was a trick that Punch had not yet learnt, and he lay still, licking Nicky's hand every now and again, glad to find that his beloved master was not angry with him after all.

"Now just keep absolutely *quiet*," said Nicky. "I'm going to have one of my THINKS, and I'll push you off the bed if you so much as wriggle your tail."

Punch lay so still that Nicky forgot all about him, and was soon lost in thought. Now then – a smashing mystery was what he wanted – complete with clues, strange goings-on, and all the rest of it – a mystery in which he could make Uncle Bob so interested that he would forget all about being bored and miserable.

Where should the mystery *be*? That was the first thing to think out. At once a picture of an old burnt-out building up on Skylark Hill came into Nicky's mind. Yes – that would be a fine eerie sort of place for a mystery. He thought about it, remembering the blackened, half-fallen walls – the one old tower still standing – the curious spiral stairway of stone that led down into the old cellars, which he and Ken had so often longed to explore.

41

"My word, yes – *that's* the place for a pretend mystery," thought Nicky, beginning to feel excitement welling up inside him. "Now, what next? – yes, clues. They'd better be in code – an easy code, so that Uncle Bob can decipher it and read the message. And there shall be lights flashing from the tower at night – I'll make Ken go up there with his torch and flash it – and what about noises? If I can get Uncle up to the burnt house, Ken can hide and make awful groans. Gosh, this is going to be super. If only I could tell Ken this very minute!"

He debated whether to put on his clothes again and slip over to Ken's. No – he'd probably be in bed, and if he was asleep nothing in the world would wake him, not even stones rattling against his window!

Nicky became so excited as he thought of the wonderful Mystery that was lying in wait for Uncle Bob, that he couldn't keep still. He turned over and over in bed, and Punch was soon tired of continually being bumped, and leapt down to the rug, landing on the slippers and shoes.

"We'll begin the Mystery tomorrow," thought Nicky, sticking his hot feet out of bed to cool them. "Ow – stop it, Punch – those are my toes you're biting! Sh – here comes Mother. Get under the bed."

Punch disappeared at once. Mrs Fraser opened the bedroom door, and the landing light shone into the room, showing her Punch's surprising collection of shoes. "So *that's* where my slippers went to!" she thought, and picked them up. "Good gracious – this is quite a shoe-shop! I'll have to stop this new trick of Punch's, I can see!"

She laid her hand gently on Nicky's forehead, for she still felt puzzled about his going off to bed so early. But it was quite cool – Nicky was obviously all right! Picking up a few more shoes she crept out of the room.

Punch came out from under the bed, and climbed carefully up beside Nicky. He gave his face the tiniest lick, heaved an enormous sigh of love, and settled down to sleep.

Nicky gave Punch a pat, and then slid off into his Mystery once more. But now he was getting sleepy, and his thoughts became muddled. He was at the old burnt house – he was climbing up to the tower – a light was flashing there – good gracious, *two* lights – but no, they weren't lights after all – they were the brilliant green eyes of Ken's cat – and now the cat grew simply enormous, and Nicky fled down to the cellar, where immediately some frightful, bloodcurdling noises began that made poor Nicky's hair stand on end!

He was so scared that he tried to scream – and immediately found himself sitting up in bed clutching at a growling, most surprised Punch.

"Oh, it was a *dream*, thank goodness!" said Nicky, thankfully. "I suppose those awful noises I heard in my dream were you snoring or something, Punch. Gosh, I was scared! If our Mystery's going to be anything like as thrilling as my dream about it, we're going to have some fun! Get off my feet, Punch. No wonder I found it difficult to climb up to the tower in my dream – you must have been lying on my feet all the time!"

Punch obligingly slid off Nicky's feet, and lay at the bottom of the bed. His ears twitched as an owl hooted somewhere in the trees at the bottom of the garden. They twitched again, and a small growl came from him when he heard a cat miaowing below the window. Nicky turned over and buried his head in the pillow. He felt wide awake again, and longed for tomorrow to come so that he might tell Ken all his plans.

"Ha, Uncle Bob – you don't know what thrills I've got in store for you!" he murmured. "I'll write out that code message first thing tomorrow and show it to Ken – I bet *he* won't be able to decipher it! And we'll go up to that old burnt-out house and snoop round. I wonder what will come of my Plan for a Mystery – I DO hope it will be a success!"

Success, Nicky? Well, you're certainly going to be *surprised*! It's a wonderful plan of yours – but it may not work out in quite the way you think. So watch out, Nicky, watch out, Ken!

CHAPTER 7

A Mysterious Message

As soon as Nicky woke up the next morning he remembered his wonderful plan of the night before. He sat up in bed, excited, and Punch began to pull off the blankets and sheet, trying to make his master get up and dress.

"All right, all right, Punch – I'm in just as much a hurry as you are!" said Nicky. "If Ken's up I could go and tell him my plans before breakfast. No – *don't* drag the pillow on to the floor. Bring me my shoes – SHOES, idiot, not boots."

Nicky was soon dressed, and leapt down the stairs with Punch just in front. They almost bowled over Mrs Hawes, who was sweeping the hall.

"Are you two catching a train or something?" she demanded. "Stop it, Punch – leave my broom alone! Nicky, he's got my duster now – if he goes off with it, I'll . . ."

"Bad dog," said Nicky, sternly. "Drop it, sir! There – see how obedient he is, Mrs Hawes. What's for breakfast? I've got time to go and see Ken, haven't I?"

"It's kippers for breakfast, and you've about ten minutes," said Mrs Hawes. "Bless that dog – he's gone off with my floor cloth now!"

Nicky grinned and shot off at top speed after Punch. He ordered him to take back the floor cloth.

"And then come down to Ken's shed," he said. "But DON'T bring any shoes with you. I'm sorry I taught you that trick now."

He squeezed through the hedge and went across to Ken's shed. He could hear him chanting his favourite tune – good – he was there then. He whistled piercingly and Ken at once appeared at the shed door, holding one of his smallest guinea pigs.

"Hello! *You're* early!" he said. "Anything up? Get down, Punch, you are *not* going to have guinea pigs for breakfast."

"Ken! I've thought out a smashing mystery!" said Nicky. "Where's Penny? Not in hearing distance, I hope?"

"No. She's with Winnie – our cousin, you know. She's come to stay again."

"Not that Winnie who wants to tag on to *us* all the time?" said Nicky, in dismay.

"The very same," said Ken, gloomily. "She arrived last night, fat as ever. We'll have to look out, or we'll have the girls spying on us all the time – especially Winnie. But I say – why are you up so early?"

"Because I wanted to tell you about the Mystery I've thought out – the one we're going to pretend is a real one, so that Uncle Bob can have something exciting to think about," said Nicky. "Honestly, Ken, it's really *good* – I tell you, we're going to have some fun. Shut the door, and listen. Punch, sit by the door and bark like mad if you hear footsteps or whispering."

Punch at once sat down by the door, and cocked his ears. "Now we're safe," said Nicky. "Listen, Ken."

And he told his surprised friend all that he had thought of during the night. Ken listened, gaping, taking in all the details, but when Nicky came to the bit where he, Ken, was to go to the old burnt-out house at night and flash a torch, he shook his head firmly.

"No. If anyone's to do that, *you* can. I'd be scared to do that on my own."

"Oh don't make things difficult," said Nicky. "Anyway, we can decide all the details later on. I just HAD to let you know what I'd planned. The first thing to do is to write out a secret message – in code, of course. Then we'll take Uncle Bob for a walk up the hills – and let him find the paper with the message on – and – oh BLOW, there's the breakfast gong. You be thinking out a good secret message. I'll be back after breakfast."

He tore off with Punch barking at his heels, and just managed to be sitting down at the breakfast table before his father arrived.

"You seem out of breath," said his mother, surprised. "Have you been for a walk?"

"No. Just to see Ken about something important," said Nicky. "Do you want me to do anything this morning, Mother? I thought I'd ask Uncle Bob if he'd like to go for a walk up on Skylark Hill with me and Ken. We want to go bird-spotting, and Uncle Bob said he'd lend me his field glasses."

"I'm sure he'd *love* to go with you," said his mother pleased. "It's such a beautiful morning, it will do him good – and he's always been so fond of birds."

Uncle Bob arrived down a few minutes later, looking rather gloomy.

"Hello, everyone!" he said. "No, no kipper for me, thanks. I don't feel too good. Couldn't get a wink of sleep because of the owls hooting all night."

"I never heard them," said his sister. "Poor old Bob – you do look washed out."

"Uncle – come for a walk up Skylark Hill this morning!" said Nicky, eagerly. "Ken's going too – bird-

47

spotting. We might see the sparrow hawk. You said you'd lend me your field glasses, remember?"

"Right. I'll come with you," said Uncle Bob. "Do me good to stretch my legs. What time do you want to start?"

"Er – would ten o'clock do?" asked Nicky, remembering that he must leave himself enough time to work out a message in code, so that he could plant it somewhere for his uncle to find.

"That'll suit me fine," said Uncle Bob. "I'll unpack my field glasses after breakfast – they're still in one of my cases. Is Punch coming with us? I hope he won't race about and scare all the birds for miles."

"Of course he's coming," said Nicky, feeling a sudden little paw on his knee. He bent down to Punch, who was as usual under the table. "You heard what Uncle Bob said, didn't you, Punch? No racing about and barking – but plenty of sit, sit, sit, when you're told. Got that?"

"Wuff," said Punch, quite understanding, and lay down again.

Nicky hurriedly finished his breakfast, trying to think out what message he should write on a piece of paper.

"Please excuse me, Mother," he said. "I've a few things to do before we go."

"Well, remember that one of them is to make your bed, please," said his mother, as Nicky raced off with Punch just behind him.

He went to his bedroom and hurriedly pulled together his sheets and blankets. Then he tore a piece of paper from an old writing pad, sat down and chewed the end of his pencil. What should the message be? Perhaps he had better go and see if Ken had thought of one.

Soon he was down in Ken's shed. "Ken – I *can't* think

48

of a message!" he said. "And Uncle Bob will be ready to go with us at ten. What shall . . .?"

"Don't worry. *I've* thought of one," said Ken, proudly, and showed Nicky a piece of dirty, torn paper. On it he had written a most mysterious-looking message, which looked like this:-

UFMM KJN XFSF SFBEZ. NFFU JO DFM-MBST. TUVGG IJEEFO PO TLZMBSL IJMM. MPPL PVU GPS TJHOBM GSPN UPXFS. IBSSZ.

"What on earth does *that* mean?" said Nicky.

"It means *'Tell Jim we're ready. Meet in cellars. Stuff hidden on Skylark Hill. Look out for signal from tower. Harry.'*" said Ken, proudly. "It's an awfully simple code –all I've done is to use the next letter to the real one each time – B for A, C for B, D for C and so on. This first

49

word UFMM, for instance. All you've got to do is to think of the letter before . . ."

"Oh, *I* see – for the letter U the one before would be T – and for F it would be E, and for MM it would be LL," said Nicky. "The word 'tell' – and so on. Isn't it too simple?"

"No. Don't you think it's an *exciting* message?" said Ken. "I mean – when your uncle picks up this old dirty-looking bit of paper with such a strange code message on it, he's bound to prick up his ears! I rubbed it on the floor of the shed to make it look dirty."

Nicky began to feel excited. "Yes! It's fine!" he said "I don't know how you thought of such an exciting message. Jolly good, Ken. Look now – when Uncle Bob is training his field glasses on some bird or other, you drop the bit of paper nearby, and maybe he'll see it and pick it up. If he doesn't I'll pick it up, and pretend to be very puzzled, because of the code. I bet Uncle will decipher it at once."

"And then the fun will begin!" said Ken, his eyes shining. "We'll go exploring the cellars – we'll hunt on the hill for the stuff that's supposed to be hidden there. We'll . . ."

"We'd jolly well better buck up!" said Nicky. "It's almost ten, and I'm not ready yet. Meet me at your front gate as soon as you can. This is going to be fun! I *bet* Uncle Bob will prick up his ears and forget to be mopey, once he gets going on our mystery!"

CHAPTER 8

Up On Skylark Hill

Nicky and Punch raced off to see if Uncle Bob was ready to go for his walk up Skylark Hill. Yes – there he was, waiting impatiently in the front garden, his field glasses slung over his shoulder.

"Oh, there you are," he said. "Where's Ken?"

"Just coming – he'll be at his front gate," said Nicky. "Shall I go in and get my bird book, Uncle?"

"No. I can tell you anything you want to know," said his uncle. "For goodness' sake let's start while it's fine! Come along."

They picked up Ken at his front gate and set out happily, Ken with his glasses slung round his shoulder just like Uncle Bob. They came to Skylark Hill, and at first took an ordinary path, Punch running ahead as usual, sniffing about for rabbits.

The birds were singing madly. "There's the chaffinch, with his 'chip-chip-cherry-erry-erry-chippy-oo-EEE-ar' song," said Uncle Bob, standing to listen. "And you can hear that greenfinch – and the hedge-sparrow – and what's that now, singing so VERY loudly?"

"The wren – look, it's over there!" said Ken, pointing. "Seems funny that such a *little* bird should have such a very loud voice!"

It was lovely up on the hill. It was quite a wild part where they were now wandering, no paths at all, except for those made by the rabbits. Uncle Bob suddenly stopped.

"Listen – there's a nightingale singing in that bush over there – see, at the top of that hawthorn bush."

"I thought nightingales only sang at night," said Nicky, astonished.

"Oh no – you can hear them in the daytime too," said Uncle Bob, "though no one notices them much then, with so many other birds singing. We really ought to come up here at night-time to hear them at their best."

Nicky at once gave Ken a violent nudge. What a wonderful excuse for coming out at night! Perhaps he could make Ken go up unseen to the old tower and flash his torch, while he and Uncle Bob were listening to nightingales! Uncle Bob would never guess that the flashing light was a put-up job – he would be sure to think there was something funny going on in that old burnt out place! He'd smell a mystery at once!

They went on a little way, and soon Nicky thought it was about time that Ken dropped his dirty bit of paper with the code message on it. He nudged him again, and Ken put his hand in his pocket, and nodded.

He went on some way in front, and suddenly spotted a chaffinch's nest in a bush. Ah – now he could perhaps make Nicky's uncle find the paper for himself! That would be very much better than either he or Nicky pretending to find it. He cautiously parted the twigs, and dropped the note into the bushy part below the nest. Then he called to Nicky.

"I say – here's a nest, just newly-built. No eggs yet, though. Ask your uncle what kind of nest it is – looks like a chaffinch's to me."

"Don't disturb the bird if it's on the nest," called Uncle Bob, as he and Nicky came up the steep little rabbit path. He peered into the bush. "Yes – that's a chaffinch's nest – see how neat it is. The bird has even woven tiny bits of torn paper into it. I wonder it didn't take *this* old bit of paper too, below the nest."

And, much to the boys' delight, he picked up the note that Ken had just dropped into the bush! He saw that something was written on it and glanced idly at it, as he was about to screw it up.

"Hello – what's this? It's a note written in code!" he said, in surprise.

"I *say*!" said both boys at once, pretending to be astonished. "Code! What's it say?"

"Don't know, unless I can break the code," said Uncle Bob. "It looks a fairly simple one. See what *you* can make of it. I don't feel too bright this morning."

The boys didn't know whether to decipher it or not. Wouldn't Uncle Bob think they were a bit too clever if they did? They sat down and put their heads together, pretending to puzzle over the queer message.

"Look at that first word," said Uncle Bob. "'UFMM'! A double-letter at the end. Now what letters can be doubled at the end of words? S can, for instance. There are plenty of four letter words ending in double S – fuss, boss, toss, hiss and so on – or in double F – such as huff, muff, etc."

"Or double L," said Nicky. "Such as ball, call, toll, er . . ."

"Or TELL!" said Ken, as if he had just that very minute thought of it. "It might be 'tell', mightn't it?"

"I should think it's more likely to be 'TELL' than anything else," said Uncle Bob, taking back the paper. "Now, let's see what the next word would be, if the first is TELL – it will mean that the letters of each code word must be replaced by the *preceding* letters of the alphabet. All right – the next code-word is KJN. We'll replace those three letters by the alphabet letters immediately before – that is, K would be J, J would be I, and N would be M – making the word J-I-M- – Jim!"

"Aha!" said Ken, "that would make the first two words 'TELL JIM'! You've broken the code already! We shall be able to decipher the whole message now!"

He looked so excited that Nicky stared at him in surprise. Goodness – how clever Ken was at acting! No one would ever think that it was he himself who had actually made up the message and put it into code.

Uncle Bob looked rather startled. He stared at the message again, and stood frowning over it.

"Queer!" he said at last. "That's the code all right – a very simple one, too – listen – I'll decode the whole message."

The boys felt a great desire to giggle. This was marvellous! Dear old Uncle Bob was well and truly taken in! They listened as he slowly read the decoded message.

"Tell – Jim – we're – ready. Meet – in – cellars. Stuff – hidden – on – Skylark – Hill. Look – out – for – signal – from – tower. Harry."

He frowned down at the paper again. "Why did the writer of this message, whoever he is, use such an easily deciphered code?" he wondered. "He might just as well have written it in plain English! I wonder if it *could* be a joke – but if so, how did it come to be in that bush?"

"Perhaps the wind blew it there," suggested Nicky. "Oh Uncle Bob – it's awfully exciting, isn't it?"

Uncle Bob put the paper into his pocket. "Something funny about it," he said. "Funny and phoney! I'll have to think about it."

"Should we try and find whatever stuff it is that's supposed to be hidden on the hill?" said Ken, feeling nervous in case Uncle Bob should decide it *was* a hoax. "We might find something interesting. Stolen goods – or – or hidden money, perhaps."

"And what about looking in the cellars of that old burnt-out house?" suggested Nicky. "It says something about cellars in that note, doesn't it, Uncle Bob? It might mean the old cellars up in that place on the top of the hill. And it's got a tower, too – a fine tower to signal from!"

"Yes – anyone on the hillside waiting for a signal could easily see flashes from that tower!" said Ken, backing up Nicky valiantly. "I *say*! We can see that tower from our back gardens, you know – we ought to watch out at night, in case someone *does* signal!"

"Well – I must say it all sounds rather queer – and, as I say, I can't help feeling there's something wrong – something phoney about that note," said Uncle Bob, frowning. "It's too easy a code. I'll think about it. In the meantime, what about a little more bird-spotting."

"Let's go up to the old burnt house," suggested Nicky. "It's quite interesting, Uncle. The tower is still all right – and the cellars too, though an awful lot of walls have fallen."

"Well – we'll have a quick look round." said his uncle. "But I'm pretty certain that note doesn't mean a thing – probably some silly schoolboy joke. Still, I can see you're longing to do a little exploring, so come along!"

The two boys fell behind Uncle Bob, as he went up the hill. "Do you think he suspects us!" said Nicky, in a low voice. "You heard what he said about 'schoolboy joke'."

"Yes – but I don't believe he thinks *we* wrote that message." answered Ken. "Come along – we're going up to the old cellars – you'll love sniffing round those! You might even find a *rat*!"

Rat? Ah, that made Punch leave his rabbit hole at once, and tear after Nicky. He hadn't any interest in birds – and there didn't seem to be any rabbits about – but maybe a nice big rat would turn up in those old cellars. Wuff!

CHAPTER 9

"Loomy and Gloomy, Glowering and Towering!"

Nicky led the way up to the top of Skylark Hill, following the overgrown path that had once been used by the people who had lived in the great old building at the summit. They came to a gateway, where broken gates hung all askew on their hinges and the old drive that had led to the house was now a mass of strong-growing weeds.

"What a miserable-looking place!" said Uncle Bob. "It gives me the creeps."

"Wait till you get a good view of the burnt-out building," said Nicky. "That'll give you nightmares!"

They went up the thickly-weeded drive and past a great clump of pines. Behind these, sheltered from the prevailing wind, stood the great, blackened hulk that had once been a grand mansion, overlooking the countryside with majestic splendour.

Uncle Bob stopped. From the bottom of the hill the old building had merely looked a poor old ruin, its one remaining tower outlined against the sky – but here, at close quarters, it was rather frightening.

"It sort of *looms* at you!" said Ken.

"Yes – I know exactly what you mean," said Uncle Bob. "It frowns – and glowers – and, as you so rightly say – looms."

"It's loomy and gloomy and glowering and towering, and sulky and hulky," said Nicky, most unexpectedly.

57

Uncle Bob and Ken stared at him in amazed surprise. "Why, that's poetry!" said Ken. "Surely you didn't say that out of your own head?"

"Well, I did," said Nicky, almost as surprised as the others.

"Whether it came out of your own head or not, it just about describes this brooding, blackened old place," said Uncle Bob. "You might give us warning when you're going to break out into verse again, Nicky. I feel almost as surprised as if Punch had suddenly burst into song!"

"Wuff!" said Punch, pleased at hearing himself talked about. He ran on in front of them, his tail wagging. He had been here before, and thought it was a most exciting place.

They all went up the curving drive, and came to the great building itself. It was a sorry sight. The fire that had devoured it had swept it from top to bottom, and had left only one tower untouched, though blackened with smoke.

"Birds build in the tower now," said Ken, as they went towards the fallen archway that had once framed the great front entrance. "And once I saw a badger coming out of a hole in the wall."

"Who lived here?" asked Uncle Bob. "It must have been a wonderful place."

"Somebody foreign," said Nicky, trying to remember. "A prince from the East somewhere."

"It had a magnificent view!" said Uncle Bob. "I wonder what caused the fire."

"Nobody knows," said Ken. "All the people down in the valley awoke one night to see flames reaching up into the sky – and not a single fire engine could get up this hill to do anything to help. It just burnt to a shell. Everyone

58

in it escaped, and went back to their own country – they were nearly all foreigners. The prince never came back."

"So there it is – just a hulk of a place!" said Nicky. "Most people are scared of coming up here to it. Like to see the cellars?"

"Yes – we'd better, as the writer of that peculiar message – what was the name he signed now – Harry – mentioned something about cellars, didn't he?" said Uncle Bob. He walked into what must once have been a great hall. The floor was still paved with stone, though it was now cracked and blackened, and weeds grew up in the crevices. Nicky pointed to a burnt mass of wood hanging from one of the walls.

"That was the staircase – or one of them," he said. "But the tower had a stone stairway, so it wasn't burnt. A good many of the stone stairs have got broken, though – perhaps the heat cracked them, or something. Some of them are missing, so you have to be careful in climbing up."

He led his Uncle to a far corner of the old hall, and in at a small stone-arched doorway. "Here's the tower!" he said. "And that's the stone stair up to it, going round and round the walls – not very safe, is it?"

"Have you ever been up?" asked Uncle Bob, going up the first few steps.

"Oh, yes!" said Nicky. "There used to be an iron rail fixed into the wall – there's still some of it left – so you can hang on to that when you come to the broken-away bits."

Uncle Bob began to ascend the narrow stone stair. He went very gingerly indeed, for much of the stone was breaking away, and he didn't want to plunge downwards. The boys followed.

When they came at last to the top, and were able to look through one of the great square stone windows through which the wind blew cold and strong, Uncle Bob gave a low whistle.

"My word! WHAT a view! All round the hill, and down into the valleys for miles and miles."

"What a place to signal from, too!" said Ken, giving Nicky a nudge. "Flashes from this tower could be seen for a long way, couldn't they?"

"Oh – you're thinking of that code message," said Uncle Bob. "What was it now – 'look out for signal from tower' or something. Yes – certainly this would be a good signalling place. But I don't imagine that anyone would want to come all the way up to this windy tower to do a spot of signalling that hundreds of people could see – if they happened to be looking!"

"I say – look – there's a dead match on the floor here," said Nicky, suddenly, and picked one up. "Would that belong to some signaller, do you think?"

Uncle Bob laughed. "No! To some innocent sightseer like ourselves, ass! Anyone would think you really did believe that message! I tell you, I'm pretty sure it's phoney – just a silly schoolboy joke."

"Where's Punch?" said Ken, hurriedly changing the subject. "Didn't he come up with us?"

"No – he doesn't much like the noise of the wind up here," said Nicky. "Don't you remember how scared he was before, when we brought him up, and the wind whistled all round him! He shot down again so fast that he rolled down the last dozen steps, and then sped off down the hill at sixty miles an hour! Let's go down and find him. He'll be lonely."

So they left the magnificent view and went carefully

down the stone stairway, calling to Punch as they came near the bottom. But no answering bark came, no patter of eager feet.

"PUNCH!" yelled Nicky. "Where are you? Surely you haven't gone home without us?"

Not a sound was to be heard, except for the hoarse croaks of crows flying round the tower. Punch was nowhere to be seen!

"Where on earth has the idiot gone?" said Nicky, puzzled. "Can he have gone down the spiral stairway to the cellars? Not without us, surely?"

"Where *is* this spiral stairway?" asked Uncle Bob, looking all round.

"In the kitchen part of the building," said Ken, and led the way through a great doorway, one side of which had fallen in, through a passage, and into what must have been the kitchen.

The boys called loudly as they went. "Punch! PUNCH! Where are you?"

"Here's the cellar door," said Ken. "At least here is where it *used* to be before it was burnt off its hinges!"

A narrow stone doorway led into an equally narrow passage. Nicky produced a torch, and shone it before him. "Better go carefully, Uncle," he said. "These steps are pretty steep – and slimy, too, because they're rather damp. See how they go round and round in a spiral?"

It was indeed a curious spiral stairway, and dangerous too. Uncle Bob wished there was a handrail to hold on to! At last, after treading warily down what seemed to be at least fifty curving stone steps, they reached the bottom.

"What a horrible place!" said Uncle Bob, shivering. It was pitch-black, cold, and rather smelly. "Surely Punch didn't come down here?"

But he *was* down there! From what seemed to be a great distance, his bark came echoing up to them, sounding weird and hollow – and scared!

"PUNCH! Come here! PUNCH!" shouted Nicky.

But Punch didn't come. Only his bark came to their ears, a frightened, pleading bark. Whatever was the matter?

"Come on – I'm going to find him!" said Nicky, and flashed his torch around, to see which was the best way to go. "Something's happened to old Punch. He sounds quite lost. I simply MUST go to him!"

CHAPTER 10

A Bit Of Excitement

"Wait a minute!" said Uncle Bob. "Do you know your way about these cellars? It seems a pretty vast place down here to me, from what I can see by the light of your torch. Passages leading off everywhere! We might easily get lost."

"Once we find Punch he'll lead us back to the spiral stairway all right," said Nicky. "Listen – he's barking again."

They went along a dark, low-roofed passage and came into yet another cellar, heaped with old rubbish.

63

The fire had not reached down into the cellars, so the old boxes and junk had not been burnt. And then, just at that moment, Nicky's torch went out! They were in complete darkness.

"Battery's gone," said Nicky, in disgust. "If only Punch would come to us, and show us the way back! PUNCH! COME HERE!"

But no Punch came – and what was almost worse, he stopped barking! Not a sound came up the dark passages, and Nicky felt scared. What could have happened to make Punch stop barking?

Uncle Bob took matters in hand at once. He took Nicky firmly by the arm, and pushed him back towards the way they had come. "No more nonsense," he said. "If we go down there any farther in complete darkness, we shall lose our way, and not know how to get back."

"But I CAN'T leave Punch by himself," protested Nicky, trying to wriggle away from his uncle's firm hand.

"If he went down there, he can come up again," said Uncle Bob. "Anyway, we are ALL going back at once! I'm a bit afraid we shall miss our way even the short distance we came, it's so dark. Ken – are you there? Keep close to us."

"I'm just behind, sir," said Ken, who felt only too thankful to be going back.

At last they were up in the kitchen again, having found the spiral stairway very difficult indeed to climb in total darkness. "Whew!" said Uncle Bob, sitting down hard on the wide windowsill that ran round the great kitchen. "Whew! I don't particularly want to go down *there* again!"

Nicky was almost in tears over Punch. He spoke sullenly to his uncle.

"I think we're cowards, leaving Punch down there. What are we going to do about it?

"We'll wait here for a bit and see if he comes back by himself," said Uncle Bob. "If he doesn't we'll go home and get lanterns or more powerful torches. But I don't think we need worry. Punch will appear soon."

Uncle Bob lighted a cigarette and wandered about a little. The boys sat sulkily on the old stone sill, ears open for Punch, eyes on the entrance to the cellars.

Suddenly Nicky leapt to his feet. "I can hear Punch barking! Listen!"

Sure enough a barking was to be heard in the distance. Nicky ran to the cellar entrance – but the barking wasn't coming from there! It came nearer and nearer. Ken looked out of the open window arch, and gave a shout.

"He's coming up the drive. Look, there he is, absolutely filthy! Punch! PUNCH! Here we are!"

Punch gave a delighted volley of barks, raced into the old building, and hurled himself on Nicky, smothering him with dirt and licks. Nicky hugged him.

"Where have you been, you dirty little dog? We thought you were down in the cellars."

"He *was*," said Uncle Bob. "And as he certainly didn't return up the spiral stairway, as *we* did, how on earth did he get out?"

"Down a rabbit hole?" suggested Ken. "I never heard of any *secret* way out of the cellars. Must have been a rabbit hole! You rascal, Punch! We almost got lost for good down those cellars because of you!"

Punch was hungry. He barked and tugged at Nicky's sleeve, trying to pull him along. Nicky patted him.

"All right, all right, we're all coming. I'm as hungry as you are! What about you, Uncle Bob?"

"Well, yes – I must say that for the first time since I came to stay with you, I feel really hungry!" said Uncle Bob. "We've certainly had an interesting morning – and what with that rather strange coded message – and all the birds we saw – and exploring this gloomy old building – I feel that life has become quite exciting again"

The boys were pleased. They looked closely at Uncle Bob, and decided that he already looked more like the cheerful, amusing man he had always seemed to be.

"Our trick worked, didn't it?" said Ken, in a low voice to Nicky, as they went back down Skylark Hill. "But I wish your uncle believed more in that message of ours – don't want our plan to come to a sudden end. I'ts been fun so far."

"The thing that puzzles *me* is how Punch got out of those cellars," said Nicky. "I suppose he *did* find a rabbit warren and went through it and found a hole into the open air. But usually he's too big for any rabbit hole."

"Well, what else could he have done?" said Ken. "I didn't much like going so far down those cellars. I couldn't help being glad there wasn't *really* any mysterious "Harry" waiting down there to meet his men."

"Harry? Harry who?" said Nicky, and then remembered the made-up message, and laughed. "Oh, of course – the Harry who was supposed to sign that message! Well, Punch would have given him a bit of a fright, wouldn't he?"

Penny and her friend Winnie were standing at Ken's front gate as he and Nicky and Uncle Bob came up. "Hello, hello!" said Uncle Bob. "And what have you two girls been up to this morning? You ought to have come with *us*. My word, we've had an exciting time, what with finding a strange message in code, hidden in a bush – and exploring that great burnt building – and seeing Punch disappear down into the cellars, and . . ."

"Oh PLEASE, Uncle Bob – don't give away our secrets," said Nicky, in a low voice, horrified to think that Penny and Winnie should be told all this. They were both agog at once, of course, and to the boys' despair and disgust Uncle Bob actually took out the coded message and showed it to the two excited girls.

"Oooh!" said Winnie, her eyes big with amazement. "Is it a *real* message? Not just one made up by the boys? Once Ken did a message rather like this, and . . ."

"Shut up!" hissed Ken, and gave poor Winnie such a hard pinch that she screamed and ran straight in through the gate, holding her arm. Uncle Bob stared after her in amazement.

"What's the matter with your friend all of a sudden?" he asked, but Penny seeing Ken's grim look, decided not to say anything about the pinch. Fortunately the sound of a gong being violently struck by Mrs Hawes in Nicky's hall, brought such delicious thoughts of dinner that Nicky and his uncle at once walked smartly to the front gate, and up the path, followed by an even more hungry Punch.

"It was *mean* of you to show the girls that secret message," Nicky couldn't help saying to his uncle.

"What on earth's *secret* about it?" said his uncle, astonished. "Anyone might have found it! Anyway it's probably a hoax, so cheer up. There *won't* be any meeting in the cellars – there *won't* be any flashing of signals in the tower. There are *no* goods hidden on the hill."

67

Nicky frowned and set his teeth. "Oh, won't there!" he thought. "You just wait and see, Uncle Bob! You'll be surprised! And very soon too! I'll just pay you out for showing our secret message to those girls! You just wait!"

It was a pity Uncle Bob couldn't read Nicky's angry thoughts. He didn't even know that the boy felt so angry, or he would have been gentler to him. Poor Nicky! He had only thought of the mystery just because he wanted to *help* his uncle, and now everything had gone wrong – and those GIRLS knew about the message!

He sat rather silent at dinner time, pondering what to do next. Could he possibly persuade Ken to go and signal from the tower at night – and then he, Nicky, could wake his uncle and tell him to look at the flashes. *That* would make him sit up and take notice! "It's no good *me* going to the tower," thought Nicky. "Because someone has got to tell Uncle about the signalling – and he'd think it funny if Ken came to him in the middle of the night – and I wasn't anywhere to be found. Oh blow! I do hope this plan isn't going wrong. Ken will simply HAVE to go and do the signalling. He can take old Punch with him, if he's afraid. Yes – that's a *good* idea."

"You're very quiet this meal time, Nicky," said his mother. "What are you thinking about so deeply?"

"He's pondering over a very strange message, I expect!" said Uncle Bob, laughing. "Am I right, Nicky?"

"NO!" said Nicky, so fiercely that everyone jumped, and Punch began to bark. "You wait and see, Uncle – I bet that message was right. You just wait and see!"

CHAPTER 11

Quite A Few Things Happen!

After dinner was over Nicky disappeared. "Where's he gone?" said his mother. "He seems rather down in the dumps. What happened this morning, Bob?"

"Oh nothing much," said Uncle Bob. "We did some bird-spotting and found a strange message in a bush – and explored that old burnt-out place – and almost lost Punch in the cellars. Nicky seemed a bit cross because when we met Penelope, Ken's sister, and her friend, I told them what we'd been doing."

"How silly of Nicky to be cross about that!" said Mrs Fraser. "But he and Ken can't bear the girls knowing about their doings. Penny is a bit of a snooper, from what I hear."

Nicky was certainly feeling cross. After all their trouble in making up a super mystery, Uncle Bob had laughed at it, and almost given it away! He made up his mind to go across to Ken's and find out whether the girls had wormed anything out of him. Ken wasn't very clever at keeping things from Penny!

Ken wasn't in the shed – but *somebody* was! Nicky shushed Punch, afraid he would bark, and went to peep in at the window. Penny and her friend Winnie were there, poring over a piece of paper, and giggling.

What could be so amusing about it? Nicky longed to know. Then a horrid thought struck him. Had the two girls found the first rough copy of that coded message? Had they looked in the drawer of the old table in the shed, where Ken kept his things? He ran up to the house to find Ken, and ask him where he had left the copy. If the girls knew all about their mystery, he and Ken might as well give up their little joke on Uncle Bob.

Ken was in his room, reading. He was very pleased to see Nicky and Punch. "Hello! Anything up? You look upset," he said.

Nicky told him what he had just seen. "Those *tiresome* girls!" said Ken, in a rage. "I thought they were going for a walk, so I didn't bother to hide that first rough copy of the coded message. I felt sure they'd do a bit of snooping sometime – but they *said* they were going for a walk, so I didn't rush down to the shed to hide my things!"

"Well, we'd better give up the whole idea," said Nicky, very angry. "And I jolly well hope you'll knock their silly heads together when they come in."

"What's Punch doing under my bed?" said Ken. "He's chewing my new slippers! Come on out, Punch, and behave yourself. Go on down and chase the girls out of the shed."

Almost as if he understood what Ken had said Punch ran to the door, pushed it open with his nose and disappeared. All right – if he couldn't play with Ken's slippers, he'd go and find someone else's. *He* wasn't going down to the shed! He slipped into the room that the two girls shared and was faced with a most wonderful array of shoes of all kinds! He sniffed at a pair of fur boots, and settled down to chew them in peace and quiet.

The boys began to play a game of cards, but after a few minutes the thought of the two girls messing about in his shed was too much for Ken. "Let's go and give them a fright and turn them out," he said. "Come on." So down the stairs they went, and out into the garden. When they came to the shed it was empty!

"Blow them! Where have they gone?" said Ken. Here it is in my drawer – they'll pretend they never found it or read it!"

Punch arrived at that moment, carrying the fur boot he had been chewing. "Where did you get that, Punch?" said Nicky, sternly. Punch ran out into the garden with it, and Nicky was just going after him when the two girls came running up to the shed, pretending to be very excited.

"Ken! Nicky! What do you think we've found! A note! A secret message – just like the one you found up on the hills. See what it says – let's decode it, quickly."

"We found it under a bush," said Winnie. "Who *could* have put it there!"

"Idiots!" said Ken, angrily. "You can't spoof *us*!"

"It says we're to watch out for a man with a limp," said Penny. "And it's . . ."

"You made it all up yourselves and hid it, so don't tell such whopping stories," said Ken.

"Was *your* message true then?" asked Winnie, giggling. "Go on – do tell us. We're certain you made *yours* up!"

Penny gave a sudden shriek, and pointed at Punch. "Winnie! He's got one of your best fur boots! He's chewing it! Drop it, Punch, drop it!"

She made a dart at Punch, who picked up the fur boot and danced away with it, out of the shed. This was a lovely game! The two girls chased him up the garden and round the pond. Punch suddenly stopped and very neatly dropped the boot into the water, where it bobbed for a few seconds and then sank.

Winnie angrily picked up a stick and ran after Punch, who at once disappeared through the hedge. "If you bring that dog of yours here again I'll–I'll put him in the dustbin!" she shouted. "He's *ruined* my new boot!"

The boys decided to leave the two angry girls to themselves. They went through the hedge, grinning at one another. "Clever old Punch! The way he dropped Winnie's boot into the water – splash! Just as if he were saying, 'Sucks to you! There goes your boot!'" said Ken. "I vote we give him a jolly good bone or something."

"There are some sausages in the larder," said Nicky. "I'll get him one if Mrs Hawes is out of the way."

And a little later, a most surprised Punch was eating a really delicious sausage, and being patted and petted. Well! If dropping people's shoes into the pond produced sausages to eat, Punch was quite willing to drop any amount into all the ponds in the district!

Winnie and Penny were quite determined not to make up their quarrel with the boys. "We'll just ignore them," said Penny. "Letting Punch drop your boot into the pond like that! They'll be telling him to drop in our hats next and goodness knows what. He's a most annoying dog!"

So, much to Ken's relief, the girls ignored him and said nothing to him at all. They played a game of cards by themselves after tea, watched television until supper, and then went up to their room to read.

But that night something happened to make the girls change their minds about not speaking to Ken. They were both in bed, and had been asleep for some time, when a screech owl suddenly screamed outside. They both woke up with a jump.

"Blow that owl! It *will* sit in that tree at night below our window and screech its head off!" said Penny, crossly. She jumped out of bed to frighten it away, and it flew off on silent white wings. Penny glanced idly out into the night. Her room was at the back of the house, and looked across the fields to Skylark Hill. Penny was just about to turn back to bed when something caught her eye. What was that flashing on the top of Skylark Hill? It must be a light in the old tower!

"It's those boys!" she thought. "Ken and Nicky must be up there, playing a silly trick. That was one of the things in the silly secret message we found in Ken's drawer – signals from the old tower! Winnie – are you awake? There's a light flashing from the tower – those two boys must actually have gone up there to do what that silly message said!"

"But what on earth *for*?" said Winnie, astonished. "Anyway, it's surely too late for the boys to be out, Penelope! It's half-past eleven!"

"I'll see if Ken's in bed," said Penny and went to the room across the passage, where Ken slept. She pushed open the door and switched on the light. To her amazement Ken was in bed and asleep! Could it be *Nicky* up in the tower, then, all alone? She shook Ken awake.

"What is it? What's up? Penny, what's the matter?" mumbled Ken, sitting up, rubbing his eyes.

"Ken – there's a light signalling from the old tower on Skylark Hill," said Penny, fearfully. "Just like you said it would in your secret message. Ken, can Nicky be up there, all alone? If not – who is it?"

Ken shot out of bed and went into Penny's room. He looked through the window – and had a real shock when he saw the flashes coming from the old tower up on the hill. He stared as if he couldn't believe his eyes!

"It *can't* be Nicky!" he said, quite dazed. "He would have told me if he'd planned to do anything like that. Penny, there's something strange about this. There is really."

"That's what *I* think," said Penny. "You'll have to tell Uncle Bob in the morning. But I bet he won't believe you. *He* didn't believe that silly message of yours. It *was* a made-up one, wasn't it – all pretence?"

"Oh shut up!" said poor Ken. "I'm going to dress and go over to Nicky's. I'll throw some stones at his window and see if I can wake him. If he doesn't come I'll climb up the tree just outside and see if he's in bed. If he's not – well – he must be up in that tower. Whew! Better him than me! I'd be scared stiff. Get back to bed, Penny. I'll just drag on a few clothes, and I'll be off to Nicky's."

In a few minutes' time, Ken was letting himself quietly out of the back door, and running down the garden to creep through the hedge. Would he find Nicky in bed – or not? and if he *were* in bed, what in the world was happening up on Skylark Hill?

CHAPTER 12

An Adventurous Night

Ken was soon under Nicky's bedroom window, which was at the front of the house. He scraped about in the gravel path there, and gathered a few small stones. He threw them up one by one, missing the window with all but two, which hit the glass with a sharp click. Nicky was fast asleep, and didn't stir. As a rule not even a thunderstorm would wake him!

But someone else stirred – someone who pricked up his ears at the very first sound! Punch was on Nicky's bed as usual, and he growled when he heard the soft sound of

75

footsteps outside. He growled even more when a stone struck the window! Then he gave a sharp bark, and tugged at the blanket which was tucked in round Nicky's neck.

Nicky awoke. "Shut up, Punch! What do you think your're doing?" he said, sleepily. Punch tugged at his sleeve as he sat up, rubbing his eyes.

Click! That was another small stone against the window. Punch growled again and ran across the room, standing up with his paws on the sill.

"Is there somebody about?" said Nicky, waking up properly now. He leapt out of bed and joined Punch at the window. "Anybody there?" he called.

"Sh!" said Ken's voice from below. "It's me, Ken. I'm coming up the tree, Nicky. Give me a hand at the top, will you? I've some startling news!"

He climbed the tree carefully. It wasn't easy in the dark. Nicky took his torch and shone it down the tree to give him a little light. Ken was most relieved when he was at last on the sill.

"What's up?" asked Nicky.

"There's someone up at the old tower – flashing lights," said Ken. "Penny's bedroom faces that way, and she saw them and came to wake me. At first she thought it might be us up there on the hill – carrying out what we'd said in that code message! Who on earth can it be? I did think for a moment it might be you – but you wouldn't go without telling me, of course!"

"Ken! This is *extraordinary*!" said Nicky. "I mean – we go and make up a mystery – and put in signals from the tower – and it comes true! Look – are you *sure* that you saw flashes? I mean – you might have been half-asleep or something."

76

"Well, I wasn't," said Ken. "Nor were the girls. Look – let's go into a room where we get a view of Skylark Hill and the tower – we can't see them from your window."

"Wuff!" said Punch, annoyed because Ken and Nicky were taking absolutely no notice of him. He was delighted to see Ken in the middle of the night, but neither of the boys had even patted his head! They were too puzzled and excited to fuss over Punch!

"Now you be quiet, Punch, and don't growl or whine or *anything*," ordered Nicky, in a low voice. "Stay here for a minute. We'll be back soon."

He and Ken stole across the passage to an empty room at the back of the house – but alas, a tree was just in front!

"Blow!" said Nicky.

"Well, let's go into another room," said Ken.

"They're all occupied," said Nicky. "Uncle Bob's got the spare room. We might steal into his if he's asleep. I daren't wake up Dad."

"Come on, then," said Ken. So Nicky led him down a passage to another door. They listened outside. To their delight little snores came from inside – yes, Uncle Bob was well and truly asleep!

They turned the door handle carefully, and crept in. A lamp in the street outside gave a faint light to the room, which had its curtains pulled right back. The boys avoided some clothes on the floor and tiptoed to the window, glad that the curtains were drawn back. They pressed their noses to the glass, and looked towards Skylark Hill. Faintly outlined against the night-sky was the old tower – and as the two boys watched, they saw a sudden sharp flick of light, then another and another.

"There you are!" said Ken, in excitement. "See that –

77

and that! If that's not someone signalling I'd jolly well like to know *what* it is!"

The light from the street lamp caught some glassy surface in the room, and Nicky realized what it was.

"Look – Uncle's field glasses are over there in that corner – let's borrow them and see if we can focus them on the tower and see more clearly what's going on!"

In his haste to get the field glasses Nicky fell over some shoes on the floor, and knocked against the bed. Uncle Bob awoke at once – the bed creaked as he sat up in alarm.

"Who's there? What is it?"

"It's all right, Uncle Bob – it's only us – me and Ken," said Nicky.

Uncle Bob switched on his bedside light and stared at the boys in the greatest astonishment.

"What in the world are you doing?" he asked. "And what's *Ken* here for, in the middle of the night? Or am I dreaming?"

"Uncle Bob, listen!" said Nicky, keeping his voice low. "Someone's signalling from the tower on Skylark Hill – it looks as if he's signalling with a powerful torch."

"Now look here, my boy – don't let's have any more of this silly nonsense," said Uncle Bob, annoyed. "I'm pretty certain you and Ken made up that coded message – the look on your faces gave you away! I didn't mind playing along with you for a joke – but when it comes to you both invading my bedroom in the middle of the night, talking about someone signalling from the tower, it's just TOO MUCH!"

"Didn't you believe our message then?" said Nicky, feeling very small.

"Look – I'm a private detective in real life, as you very well know!" said Uncle Bob. "And I'm not likely to be taken in by a joke invented by a couple of silly schoolboys. Clear out of my bedroom, and don't let's hear any more of this nonsense."

"But *listen*, Uncle Bob," said Nicky, desperately. "We DID see lights in the tower – so did the two girls. Look, you get your field glasses and focus them on the tower. I bet you'll get as much of a surprise as we did."

"I simply don't believe a word of it," said Uncle Bob, reaching for his field glasses. "And I very much resent you two boys invading my bedroom in the middle of the night and telling me fairy tales!"

He got out of bed with the field glasses, and went to the window. He focussed the glasses carefully on the tower and stared for so long that the boys felt impatient.

"Can you see lights flashing?" asked Nicky, at last.

Uncle Bob lowered the glasses and turned on the two anxious boys.

"NO!" he said. "There's not a thing to be seen. Just as I thought! You both deserve a good hiding for coming into my room like this at night – you really must think I'm a bit of a fool to play such idiotic tricks on me. Now, clear out, and be your age!"

"But Uncle *Bob*," began Nicky, desperately. "I tell you we did see some . . ."

"Oh shut up and go away," said Uncle Bob, and gave the boys a hard push. Ken wriggled away and went to the window for a quick look at the tower. Alas – Uncle Bob was right – all was darkness there now. Whoever had been signalling had stopped flashing his torch or lantern. What bad luck!

"Come on, Nicky," said Ken, and the two boys went

79

out of the room, dismayed and angry. Whoever would have thought that Uncle Bob would treat them like that?

The boys sat on Nicky's bed, an excited Punch between them, and talked sorrowfully about Uncle Bob's utter disbelief.

"Anyway, there *is* something going on up there," said Ken. "And *we'll* go and find out what it's all about. We made up a mystery – and it seems to be coming true! That's strange – but strange things do happen."

"All right. We'll keep Uncle Bob out of it all," said Nicky. "We'll solve everything ourselves. We'll take Punch up to the tower tomorrow and scout round for all we're worth! We'll show Uncle Bob we're better detectives than he is! But gosh – I hope he doesn't tell Dad about all this. I'd get into trouble, I bet I would."

"Cheer up – he won't say a word," said Ken, comfortingly. "He's angry with us – but he's not mean enough to get us into trouble! I rather wish we hadn't made up that mystery now!"

"Well, *I'm* not," said Nicky. "If we hadn't thought of it, we'd never be solving this one, would we? You go back home now, Ken – we'll talk about this tomorrow."

"We'll have to tell the girls, you know, Nicky," said Ken. "I mean – it was they who saw the lights flashing from the tower. We can't keep them out of things now."

"Oh blow it!" said Nicky. "I suppose we can't. But they're not to come up to the tower with us, Ken. I won't have that! What we do, we do on our own."

"All right," said Ken, climbing out of the window. "I'll leave *you* to argue with them about that. So long, Nicky! Sleep well!"

And down the tree he went. What a truly adventurous night!

CHAPTER 13

Exciting Plans

The girls were both fast asleep when Ken crept back into the room, so he didn't disturb them – he was, in fact, very thankful not to have to explain what had happened.

He jumped into bed, puzzled about the lights in the tower for a few seconds, and then fell into a deep sleep. Penny woke him up in the morning by shaking him violently, and demanded to know whether it was Nicky who had been up to the tower and was playing about there in the night.

"No, it wasn't," said Ken. "And get out of my room.

Can't you wait till I'm dressed? I'll tell you everything then, though I don't really think you deserve to come in on this, after all your snooping."

"Oh Ken – we won't snoop any more," said Penny. "But Ken, was that secret message of yours REAL, not made-up? How did you know about the lights in the tower – I mean, you must have known *something*, to put that in the message, if you did make it up."

"You're muddling me," said Ken. "For goodness' sake stop talking and let me get up. We'll have a meeting down in the shed after breakfast."

And so, at ten o'clock when the girls had done their household jobs, they went down the garden to the shed, to join the boys. Ken was already there, cleaning out the guinea pig cage, and Nicky was just arriving with Punch.

Nicky took charge at once, determined not to let the girls get out of hand.

"Now just listen, everyone," he said. "You two girls know that Ken and I made up a mystery to interest Uncle Bob and make him forget about being over-worked. *We* wrote out that message, Ken put it into code – jolly clever of him – and we dropped it into a bush on Skylark Hill. That's where Uncle Bob found it – and he *seemed* to believe it, I must say."

"I bet he didn't really," said Winnie, with a giggle. "He wouldn't have shown it to *us*, if he'd *really* believed it."

"Shut up, Winnie," said Ken, sharply, and Winnie subsided, with a grin spreading over her plump face.

"Well," went on Nicky, "you two girls saw lights in the tower last night, and you told Ken, and he came over to me – and we *both* saw them, of course. We had to go in to Uncle Bob's room to see them, and he woke up, and . . ."

"Ooooh! Did *he* see them too?" asked Penny. "Whatever did he say? I bet he believed in your mystery then!"

"Will you PLEASE not interrupt?" said Nicky, exasperated. "He *didn't* see them! The beastly signals had stopped by the time he got to the window – and so he doesn't believe us – he thinks we made up the flashing signals, and he's so angry that he won't listen to a single word about any mystery now, real or otherwise!"

"Gosh!" said Penny. "What are we going to do, then? I mean – your pretend mystery's turned into a *real* one, hasn't it? *Someone* must have been up there in the tower last night – up to no good – and there are others in the mystery too – *the people he was flashing to*. And what was he signalling about, – and why – and . . .?"

"All right, all right, Penny," said Ken. "Just hold your tongue for a minute – if you *can* – and let Nicky get on. It's only because you saw the flashes last night, and were decent enough to tell me, that we're letting you come in on this."

"And what's more we're going to tell you any future plans we make," said Nicky. "You'll have to be in on this now that you know so much – BUT – you've got to take orders from *me*, and do as you are told, see?"

"Right," said Winnie, glowing with excitement. "Oooh, Nicky – you do sound grown up. I'll do exactly what you say! You will, too, won't you, Penny?"

"I don't know about *that*," said Penny. "I'll back up the boys – but I'm going to have *my* say in the matter, too."

"WUFF!" said Punch, sitting up straight as if he thoroughly agreed with all this.

"Now, don't *you* start airing your views, too," said Nicky, giving Punch a tap on the head. "It's bad enough coping with two girls without *you* entering into the argument as well!"

That made everyone laugh. Ken went to his cupboard and took out a packet of toffees.

"All this talk is making me hungry," he said. "Have some, girls? No, not you, Punch, old thing. Have you forgotten what happened to you last time you chewed up some toffees? You lost your bark for ages because your teeth got stuck together!"

Winnie giggled. "Oh I *wish* I'd seen him! Now do let's go on with your plans. What are you going to do about this mystery? What do you *think* is going on?"

"Well – I really haven't the faintest idea," confessed Nicky. "I've just thought of the usual things you know – thieves – or somebody captured and imprisoned up there, perhaps – or someone hiding there for some reason – perhaps an escaped prisoner . . ."

"Oooooh!" said Winnie, her eyes round with excitement. "Go on, Nicky!"

"Whatever it is, we're going to find out," said Ken, firmly. "And though we'll let you girls know what we're doing, you are NOT going to be mixed up in this."

"We'll see about that," said Penny.

Ken put the toffee bag well out of Punch's reach and sat down. "*I* think the first thing to do is to try and find out who was up there signalling last night – see if he left any traces – try to find where he was hiding – and that means that Nicky and I go up there for the day – take a picnic lunch, and do a bit of spying."

"We ought to go down into the cellars again and look round," said Nicky. "We couldn't look round properly yesteday because my torch battery went phut. There might be some very interesting clues down there!"

"Gracious – I hope you'll be careful!" said Penny. "Do you remember old Harriet, our daily woman? Well, her sister is caretaker at the local museum here, and one day when we were there, she showed us some old plans of that burnt-out place – plans made before it was destroyed, of course – and you should have seen the plans of the cellars – gosh, they seemed to go half down the hill!"

"REALLY!" said Nicky, sitting up at once. "Look, there's something you girls could do – go and have a look at the plans – perhaps copy them very simply – and see what else you can find out. There may be some secret hiding place, for instance, which might still be there. *Somebody* must be hiding up there, that's certain!"

"Right," said Penny, delighted. "We'll do that this very morning. We'll go now!"

She jumped up, and Winnie got up too. They felt very important. This was a REAL mystery now, not a silly made-up one – and they were in it!

"Right – you go straight away," said Nicky, pleased to think that the girls would not be able to track them up the hill, and follow them to the tower, as he had been half afraid they would. They would be safe in the museum. He stood up. "I'll go and get lunch packets for the two of us, Ken," he said. "Mrs Hawes will make some – she'll give us smashing sandwiches! And I'll take a bone and some biscuits for old Punch. That be all right for you, Punch, old chap?"

Punch danced round him, delighted to hear Nicky talking to him at last.

"Wuff, wuff!" he said, and Nicky patted him. Punch ran to Penny, and she patted him too. "You'd better not

85

ask *Winnie* for a pat," she said. "She hasn't forgotten how you tried to drown her shoe yesterday!"

At the word "shoe" Punch was off like lightening. Nicky groaned. "*Why* did you mention the word 'shoe'? I thought he'd forgotten all about shoes today – he hasn't dragged any downstairs at all. Now he's gone to fetch some, I bet you anything you like!"

He and Ken went back through the hedge to find Mrs Hawes, who was very pleased to make them sandwiches.

"That dog of yours shot past me at sixty miles an hour just now," she said. "Up to some kind of mischief, I expect!"

And, sure enough, by the time the boys were ready to go, and the neat packets of sandwiches were on the kitchen table, Punch had raided all the bedrooms, and brought at least six pairs of shoes into the kitchen!

"You take them back!" ordered Mrs Hawes, pointing at them with the bread-knife. "If you think *I'm* going to trot up and down the stairs with all those shoes, you'd better think again!"

"Oh you *ass*, Punch!" said Nicky, gathering them up. "This trick isn't funny any more! Ken, take the packets of sandwiches and stick them into my shoulder bag, will you? And fetch some apples and bananas from the sideboard, and take a couple of ginger beers from the larder. I'll bring some chocolate – and biscuits and bone for Punch – though he jolly well doesn't deserve them, messing about with everyone's shoes like this!"

Mrs Hawes heaved a sigh of relief when all three were safely out of the house, Punch barking his head off with joy. He was off for the day with the boys – could anything be more exciting than that? Ah well, Punch – it may perhaps be a little more exciting than any of you imagine!

CHAPTER 14

The Cellars In The Hill

While the two boys set off to go up Skylark Hill, Penny and Winnie walked in the opposite direction to the little local meuseum.

"There's Harriet's sister, look," said Penny, nodding towards a plump little woman who was dusting the glass-fronted museum cases. "Hello, Miss Clewes! How's Harriet? I haven't seen her today."

"She's in bed with a cold, miss," said Miss Clewes. "Well, it's not often I see *you* here – last time I saw you was when you came with your school class to see some old documents about our village. What do you want to see this morning?"

"Well, Miss Clewes, we're rather interested in that great old place up on Skylark Hill," said Penny. "The one that was burnt down years ago. Are there any maps of it?

"Oh, yes – plenty!" said Miss Clewes, bustling over to a cupboard. "Funny you should come about that old place – there's been quite a lot of people looking at the old plans lately. But surely nobody would want to build that awful old building up again, would they?"

"What sort of people came?" asked Penny, surprised.

"Well – not very *nice* folks, miss," said Miss Clewes, getting some enormous stiff papers out of a cupboard. "Men, you know – off-hand like – almost rude – poring over them plans, and making notes. I says to them, "What's all the excitement about, all of a sudden? Thinking of rebuilding the old place and living there in style, like in the old days?"

"And what did they say to that?" asked Penny.

"Oh, they said maybe they *were* going to do that, and maybe they *weren't*," said little Miss Clewes.

"And that it wasn't none of *my* business! Quite rude, they were."

Penny and Winnie unrolled the enormous plans and studied them. They were not very clever at making out what the plans showed. They ignored the ones of the great house itself, because the fire had destroyed all the rooms, both upstairs and down, and only the stone walls were standing now.

"Are these the plans of the cellars?" asked Winnie, poring over a curious map that showed what looked like passages and caves.

88

"Yes – the plans of the house itself aren't much use to anyone now it's burnt," said Miss Clewes, "but the plans of the passages and caves that honeycomb the hill are still more or less correct, I should think. The folk who used to live in the old place used them as cellars – but they were *natural* cellars, if you know what I mean – not man-made. Saved them the trouble of digging out cellars for the goods or the food they wanted to store!"

"Are there any old stories – old legends about the place?" asked Winnie.

"Well – a few – but I wouldn't put much belief in them," said Miss Clewes, rolling up the plans the girls had finished with. "There's the story about the golden Statue, for instance. They do say it's got magic powers, and if its feet are kissed seven times, it will grant wishes."

"A nice story – but I'm afraid no statue could grant wishes!" said Penny. "Not even a golden one. What happened when the place was burnt down? Did the statue melt and disappear? It must have been worth a lot of money."

"Nobody knows what happened to it," said Miss Clewes. "I suppose it *might* have melted, the heat was so great. Or it might have been removed to safety, and taken by the family to wherever they went. Or it *might* be just a story, you know – all kinds of tales grow up about old places."

"Yes, that's true," said Penny. "Do you mind if I quickly trace the plan of the old passages and caves in the hill just near the burnt building – the ones used as cellars? We might go exploring there today."

"No – now don't you do that," said Miss Clewes. "Since we had a great storm and a cloudburst of rain five years since, those underground places have been dangerous – fallen in, you know, or full of water. You'd much better not go exploring there."

"Well, we'll see," said Penny, putting a piece of tracing paper over the map, and running her pencil here and there. "I'll let you know what happens if we *do* explore!"

The girls left the museum at last, taking with them a very well-traced copy of the passages and caves that made up the "Cellars" of the old building.

"I don't expect it will be of any use," said Penny. "But you never know! It wouldn't *really* matter if the boys got lost in the cellars, because Punch could easily take them out. A dog always knows the way! What shall we do now?"

"Well, I'm jolly hungry," said Winnie. "Let's go home, and get some sandwiches and apples, and go up on Skylark Hill. I know the boys don't want us spying on them, but we could just have a look round. We could sit and have our sandwiches on the hill, and hear the birds singing – especially the skylarks, of course!"

So back they went and made themselves some ham sandwiches, and took some apples from the larder. Then they set off to Skylark Hill and found a cosy place at the bottom, where they could sit and munch in peace.

"Let's have a good look at our map-tracing, too," said Penny. "I've an idea it might help us a lot. If only we could find the lower entrance to the cellars! That would save us going all the way up to the old building!"

It was very pleasant sitting in the sun, munching, and poring over the map. Penny rolled it up at last. "I wonder what the boys have been doing," she said. "How I'd like to know! Well – let's have a walk up the hill, and see if we can spot anything interesting. My word, we have been a time eating our lunch!"

The boys had had a most adventurous time. They had gone up to the old tower first of all, and examined it thoroughly, trying to find some traces of whoever had been signalling there the night before.

"Here's another match like the one we found before," announced Ken, picking one up from the stone sill. "This is the window-opening that the signaller must have used last night. And here's a second match on the floor – *and* a cigarette packet – empty! All clues, Nicky! I'll put them in my pocket."

"Well, at least we know some *real* person was here, said Nicky. "It wasn't just a ghost signalling!"

They made their way down the dangerous stairway, and Ken picked up yet another match – and then, down in the great old kitchen, they found an empty matchbox, thrown near the old iron stoves. They looked at the name on the matchbox.

"Ha – the signaller uses Quick-Lite Matches!" said Ken. "And we know he smokes Splendour Cigarettes, because he left the empty packet behind. He's not very careful, is he?"

"Why should he be?" said Nicky. "He's probably only using this place to signal from, because from here any flash can be seen for miles – and he's away long before daylight, I should think."

"He could hide quite well in those old cellars," suggested Ken.

"Maybe. Yes – that's quite a thought. Or somebody might be using them as a hiding place for goods of some sort – and perhaps the time has come for whatever's hidden to be fetched in safety. You know, I think we've hit on something!"

"You mean valuables may have been stored away in those old caves and passages – maybe stolen some time ago – and the robbers arranged for a signal to be given when it was safe for the stolen goods to be fetched. A signal from someone in the know?"

"Yes – something like that," said Nicky, feeling suddenly very excited. "Gosh, this is thrilling! We certainly MUST go and explore those cellars. Thank goodness we've brought strong torches – and Punch. He'll bark like anything if there's anyone down there."

"Perhaps that's why he barked the other day?" said Ken. "Maybe there was someone down here then."

"Yes. I say – isn't this getting EXCITING! What about going down now? There's nothing more to be seen here. I've got the matches – and the cigarette packet. Come on – we'll go down the cellar stairs very quietly, and tell Punch not even to growl!"

So once again the boys went underground down the curious spiral stairway, into pitch darkness, Punch at their heels. Nicky flashed his torch cautiously around. They were in the same dark, low-roofed passage they had found themselves in the day before. They went quietly down it and came to the cellar they had seen heaped with old junk. That was as far as they had gone yesterday, for it was here that Nicky's battery had given out, and they had been forced to go back.

But now their torches shone steadily and brilliantly before them, making a path through the darkness. They stood listening, and Nicky put his hand on Punch's collar to stop him running forward. Not a sound could be heard, and Punch gave a very small whine. He wanted to go on!

92

"All right, Punch – but go quietly and carefully," Nicky warned him. "We don't know what's down here – nor do we know who may be hiding – so walk *just* in front of us, see?"

They went silently through another passage whose roof became so low at one part that the boys had to bend double to get through. Punch was very good. He stopped whenever they did, walked very slowly, and kept his nose in the air, sniffing for smells of animals or humans, all the time.

They came to three caves, all running into one another, and then another passage, a wide one this time. And then, what a surprise – they came to a cave piled with tins, boxes and cartons of all sorts and sizes! Nicky shone his torch on them.

"Tins of meat – butter – bacon – cartons of cigarettes – packets – gracious, what's all this?" he whispered. "Someone's been living here for some time – look at all the empty tins and cartons – as well as the unopened ones. This must be where that signaller lives!"

"Better go carefully then," whispered Ken. "He may be near."

They went down another passage, so narrow that it was hard at times to squeeze through. And then Punch stood absolutely still and gave a very small, deep growl!

The two boys hardly dared to breathe. What was Punch growling at? Then they knew! A long drawn-out snore came to their ears – and then another! SOMEONE was there – someone fast asleep. Who was it? Be careful now, Nicky and Ken – this may be a very dangerous moment!

CHAPTER 15

Deep Underground

The two boys stood perfectly still, Punch just in front of them, still growling softly.

"Sh!" whispered Nicky, and Punch stopped growling at once. "Take hold of Punch's collar, Ken, while I go forward a little."

Ken held Punch's collar tightly while Nicky went cautiously forward. The passage curved just there, and Nicky felt sure the snorer was just round the bend. He put his head round – and there, in a little side-cave, was an enormous man, lying on his back, snoring. Beside him were the remains of a meal, taken out of tins.

Nicky stared at him. He was dark-skinned and wore a fine beard. Nicky thought he looked as if he came from the East – was he an Indian – or perhaps a Persian? He looked pretty fierce, anyway! What on earth was he doing in the underground cellars?

Then Nicky saw tools of all kinds – spades big and small – iron bars – buckets! He was astonished. Were the men excavating, then – digging out the caves – were they looking for something?

He crept back to Ken, and pulled him farther up the passage, so as to be out of the sleeping man's hearing, should he awake.

"Something's certainly going on down in these old cellars," he said. "There are all kinds of digging tools down there – and a big, foreign-looking man with a beard is snoring away near them! What is he digging for? Who would hide anything in these caves?"

"I don't know," said Ken, puzzled. "Maybe precious things were stored here when that great old building was lived in – or taken down here for safety when the fire began, and hidden – and then perhaps forgotten."

"Or they might have been *stolen* when the fire raged," said Nicky. "Maybe someone fired the old place on purpose, so that they could run off with some of the really valuable things. After all, it was a Prince who built that place – he must have been very rich and had some wonderful treasures."

"Yes – an Eastern Prince," said Ken. "You said that snoring fellow down there looks foreign? I bet it's someone who's been told where something is hidden – hidden in this hill."

"Goodness – that's just like we put in our coded message!" said Nicky, startled. "Don't you remember –

95

we put, 'Stuff hidden on Skylark Hill'! Little did we know how true that was!"

"And we put in about the signalling from the tower, too," said Ken. "That came true, as well! What was the other thing we put? Oh yes – 'Meet in cellars'! Gosh, it looks as if that's correct, too. I say – it's all a bit queer, isn't it?"

"It is rather," said Nicky. "I mean – we only thought of our silly message just as a joke – something to amuse Uncle Bob. I don't much like the way it's all coming true. It's just as if we'd foretold what was going to happen."

"Well – we can't stop it now," said Ken. "We'd better look out for this Cellar Meeting next! Perhaps someone is coming to talk to that snoring fellow. We might over-hear something interesting."

Punch began to growl again, and Nicky tapped his head. "Shut up! No noise now, Punch. Someone else may be coming."

Nicky was right! The boys suddenly heard a scraping noise as if someone was coming up a passage to where the snoring man lay in the little side-cave. Then a man's voice spoke angrily.

"Hassan! Always you sleep! Why are you not work-ing? Have you dug out the golden urns?"

The sleeping man had awakened with a jump. He growled something in a language that the boys did not understand. Then there came the sound of metal rubbing against metal, and the boys imagined that Hassan was showing the other man what he had dug out.

"Did you find the statue?" asked the visitor.

Apparently Hassan answered no, for the second man flew into a rage, and shouted a string of words that the boys couldn't understand. Punch couldn't help growling when he heard the angry shouts.

His growl must have been heard, for the two men suddenly fell silent.

"What was that?" said the second man, in English. "Could it be Harry coming down from the passages above? He was in the tower last night, signalling for the others to meet him here, and take the stuff."

Ken gave Nicky a sudden nudge. *Harry*! Good gracious, that was the name Ken had chosen when he had signed that secret message! This was really very weird. Harry! He must be the head of this gang. Would he come?

"Hope he won't come down this way," whispered Ken. "We'd be caught then, between Harry and the others. Golly – I don't much like this!"

He fell silent – and in the silence the two boys heard another noise. Someone *was* coming down from the old building above – coming down by the very same path that they themselves had taken. The boys hurriedly squeezed into a little side-cave, pulling Punch with them. If only this fellow would go by without seeing them!

He would have done, but for Punch, who simply could *not* resist another growl – rather a loud one this time. The man stopped at once.

"What's that? Who's there?" he called, roughly.

There was no answer, of course – and then, alas, Punch growled again, a deep, angry growl that rumbled all round the little cave. The man bent down and looked into the cave. He was an ugly fellow, with a black shade over one eye. He flashed a torch on the boys and the dog.

"What's this? Who are you? What on earth are you

97

doing here?" he shouted. Then he yelled to the other two men, who were looking extremely startled. "Look! There's a couple of kids here! Didn't I tell you to keep watch, and see that no one came down here? You idiots? Just when everything's almost ready! We've only got that statue to find now! I'll knock your heads together – didn't I TELL you that . . ."

"It's all right Harry," said the second man. "If it's only kids we can shut them up in a cave, and put a stone in front of it. We'll soon be out of here – by tomorrow at the latest."

"Tomorrow will be too late," shouted Harry. "Someone may come hunting for these two kids – just when we want to take out all the stuff. We'd better go and tell the other two men to come up and help tonight."

He turned to the two frightened boys. "Well, you've got mixed up in something you didn't expect," he said, in a voice the boys didn't like at all. "Well – we shan't hurt you – but you'll just have to stay imprisoned in a cave till we're ready to go. Come on out of there – we'll find another cave for you with an entrance we can easily block."

The boys made no move, and the man lost his temper. He dragged them both out roughly – and Punch went completely mad. He flew at the man and bit him hard on the left foot, right through his shoe! The man gave an anguished yell, and pulled off his shoe at once. His foot was bleeding through his thin sock.

The other two men came running up and one of them aimed a vicious kick at poor Punch. How he yelped! He ran to Nicky at once, but he ran on three legs, because one of his hind legs was badly hurt by the kick. Nicky picked him up and ran, Ken close behind him.

The men stumbled after them. "Look – let's get into that narrow passage running off to the left – the roof's so low that I don't think the men will be able to squeeze through after us," panted Nicky.

"Right," said Ken, and he squeezed in after Nicky, who found it very difficult with Punch in his arms. In fact he had to put him down at the end of the narrow passage, because there he had to crawl on hands and knees, the roof was so low!

The men stopped – and one of them laughed. "Couldn't be better! They'll be nicely boxed up in there. We only need to roll up a heavy stone, and they'll be imprisoned! Serve them right – and that dog, too!"

The boys heard the sound of the men tugging at a stone – and then – thud – it was right up against the opening to the narrow passage, completely blocking it.

But neither of the boys worried about that. It was poor, whining Punch they were upset about. They shone a torch on to his leg, fearing that it was broken.

Thank goodness it wasn't – although it was badly bruised and bleeding. Nicky hugged Punch lovingly.

"You brave little dog!" he said. "I'm *glad* you bit that man. Does your leg hurt very much? Poor old Punch – where's my hanky? I'll bind up your leg, and hope it will be all right."

Punch licked him, and gave a tiny whine as if to say, "Don't worry! We'll be all right!" But *would* they be all right? Did the men *really* mean to leave them imprisoned? And if so, how in the world would anyone ever find them?

CHAPTER 16

An Astonishing Find

The two boys sat silently for a while, with their arms round Punch. How sickening to be caught like this! Then Ken remembered the food they had brought with them in the bag. He brightened up at once.

"Let's have something to eat," he said. "It's about dinner time, and I bet Punch would like his bone! Sandwiches will cheer us up!"

They certainly did! After the boys had eaten half the sandwiches, they felt very much better. They had a banana each too, and Punch had a biscuit. Then they drank one of the bottles of ginger beer.

"Better not eat everything now," said Ken. "You just never know how long we'll be imprisoned here."

"*Not* a very nice thought," said Nicky. "Well, anyway the girls know we've come up here, so if we don't appear for some time, they'll tell Dad, and he'll organize a search party. Wait, though – what about trying to move that stone away that they've put at the entrance of this place? We *might* be able to."

They crawled down the passage to the entrance. It was well and truly blocked with a very heavy stone indeed. No amount of shoving would move it. Punch came along and looked, too. He began to scrape round the stone with his front paws, and managed to make a small space between the stone and the rocky entrance.

But, alas, it wasn't nearly big enough for either of the boys to squeeze through, try as they would. However,

Punch managed to wriggle out, and set off cautiously on three legs down the passage where the men had gone.

"Be careful, Punch!" called Nicky. "Come back before you get into any more trouble." Punch went on very cautiously, giving a little growl every now and again. If only he could find those men, what a fright he would give them!

He came to the cave where Hassan, the sleeping man, had been. No one was there. Punch sniffed round and came across one odd shoe. It was the shoe that Harry had removed from his swollen, bleeding foot, and thrown down in the cave when he limped away to help the others in their work of shifting some goods.

A shoe! Ah – Punch simply couldn't resist picking it up in his mouth and running off with it! Back he went to the boys' cave, shoe in mouth, proud of himself. Why, even down here he could show off his latest trick!

The boys couldn't help laughing when they saw Punch with the shoe in his mouth!

"Punch, you dear old idiot!" said Nicky. "Where did you get that? Oh, of course – it must be the shoe that fellow took off when you bit his foot. Put it down, old thing – he can jolly well go without it!"

"I say, Nicky – do you suppose we could get out of the *other* end of this cave?" Ken suddenly said, shining his torch towards the back. "There must have been a fall of earth at some time – so if we dig through with our hands, we may find a passage we can go up."

"Right. Let's try," said Nicky, bored with doing nothing. So he and Ken and Punch all dug hard with hands and paws. The earth was very loose, and it was soon obvious that part of the earthy roof *had* fallen in and blocked the passage.

"We're through the fall of earth!" said Ken, suddenly, as his hand went through the last layer of soil into nothing. "Quick – we'll soon have a hole big enough for us to squeeze through. Gracious – old Punch is through already. What's the other side, Punch?"

Punch began to growl. He was on the other side of the earth-fall, and the boys could not see what he was growling at.

"There surely can't be any of the men there!" said Ken. "Here, let *me* wriggle through the hole we've made and shine my torch to see what's the other side. Punch must be growling at *something*!"

So Ken wriggled a little more, and was then able to shine his torch into the space beyond. He was silent for so long that Nicky grew impatient.

"What is it? Can you see something?"

"Yes. Yes, I can certainly see something. But I can't believe it!" said Ken, in an awed voice. "Nicky – get beside me and look. I must be seeing things! It's – it's so strange!"

Nicky squeezed beside him and looked into the dark space lighted by Ken's torch. He caught his breath in wonder and fear. Something very beautiful was there – something that looked at them out of brilliantly shining eyes, and shone brightly from top to toe.

"What is it?" whispered Nicky.

"Well – can it be the statue that one of the men spoke about?" Ken whispered back. "Nicky – it's made of *gold* – pure, shining *gold*. And its eyes are precious stones. It's a statue from one of the far Eastern lands – it must have belonged to the prince who built that burnt-out mansion. Someone must have taken it down here for safety when the fire started."

"And stuffed it right at the back of the cave – and then a fall of earth came, and it was hidden from everyone's sight!" said Nicky. "No one has found it since! We heard the men talking about finding golden urns – you remember – they must have been hidden down here, too. And after all these years *somebody* has remembered them, and sent men here to look for them!"

"But that *statue*! Did you ever see anything like it?" said Ken, shining his torch on the strangely beautiful face. "I say – we mustn't let the men know it's here!"

"They're too big to get through that narrow low tunnel to it," said Nicky. "We could only just squeeze through it ourselves. This is *our* secret, Ken! My word – it's a wonder we didn't put a statue into our coded message, isn't it?"

"I do wish we could get out of here," said Ken. "There's rock behind that statue, so the passage must end there. Let's get back into the other part – there's more room. My *word* – what a find! Come back, Punch – look, Nicky, he's licking the statue's feet to see what it's made of! It's gold, Punch, gold!"

"What do you suppose the girls are doing?" said Nicky, when they were back through the hole they had made, sitting in the cave again. "I wish I knew where they were!"

At that very moment Penny and Winnie were walking up Skylark Hill, excited because they had such a good tracing of the underground cellars in their hands. They were about half-way up when Penny stopped.

"Look – there's a strange-looking man coming down the hill!" she said. "Foreign-looking – see his very black beard. Isn't he tall!"

"And look at the man with the black eye-shade," said Winnie, "He's limping! He's wearing only one shoe, and see, his foot's bleeding! And there's another man behind him. Where in the world can they have come from? They appeared so *very* suddenly!"

"Winnie – do you think they've come from the underground cellars?" said Penny, suddenly. "You know how far down the hill they stretch – and we do know there's an entrance at this lower end, as well as through the kitchen of the old place – and you remember that the boys told us that Punch must have found a way out, too? Well – *I* think those men have come from the same outlet Punch found, when the boys missed him the other day. There's simply nowhere else on this hill for them to have so suddenly appeared from!"

"Look – I think that one-eyed man is coming up to us," said Winnie, in a fright.

Sure enough the man with the eye-shade came right up and spoke to them.

"I need a doctor," he said. "My foot is bad. It has been bitten by a dog. Can you tell me of a doctor, please?"

"Er – well – there's one down in the town there," stammered Penny, frightened, pointing down the hill. "Anyone will tell you where he lives. Er – what kind of a dog bit you?"

The man didn't answer, but went back to the others, limping. They set off down the hill again.

"I *bet* it was Punch who bit him!" said Winnie. "I bet it was. Oh, Penny – you don't think anything's happened to the boys, do you? Hadn't we better go back home for help?"

"No – we'll try to find the place where the men came out of the hill," said Penny. "I feel as if we ought to look

for the boys and make sure they're all right. Come on –
this way. That's where we first saw the men appear, over
there. Hurry, Winnie – the men may come back at any
time."

There they go, the two of them, anxious and scared.
There must be some way in, there must!

CHAPTER 17

The Girls Are Very Clever

Penny and Winnie made their way round the slope of the hill to where they had first seen the men appearing. They kept looking back over their shoulders to make sure that no one was following them.

"This is quite an adventure, Penny, isn't it?" said Winnie, in rather a trembly voice. Then she gave a loud exclamation. "OH! I *say* – I've thought of something."

"You made me jump!" said Penny, who was feeling just as scared as Winnie. "What have you thought of?"

"That tracing we made of the underground cellars!" said Winnie. "Let's have a look at it, and see if it will help us."

They sat down on the hillside and opened out the roll of tracing paper. They pored over it, frowning.

"Here's the old building, see," said Penny, her finger on the map. "And here's where the cellars begin. They go along here – down under the hill, of course – and spread out here and there – really underground passages, I suppose. But I don't see how we're going to tell where they *end* on this actual hill."

"Look – what's this on the tracing?" said Winnie, pointing to a little curving line. "Could it be a stream?"

"Well, I suppose it might," said Penny. "But what's the use of that? There's no stream here on the hill now, that I can see. It must have dried up years ago."

"But its *bed* will still be there – like a dried-up ditch!" said Winnie, jumping up. "Come on – if we can find that,

106

They pored over it, frowning.

and follow it up, we shall perhaps come across the bottom entrance to the cellars!"

The girls walked over to the place where they had first seen the three men appearing. They looked all round but at first saw nothing that could have been a stream-bed. Then Winnie gave a shout.

"Here you are! This must have once been a stream – the ditch running along this old hawthorn hedge."

"Yes – I think you're right," said Penny, excited. She looked at the traced map again. "Here it is on the map," she said. "And look – it seems to go curving up the hill, and swings off just by where the entrance to the cellars is marked. Let's follow it up the hill."

So the two girls went slowly up the hill, following the half-lost track of the old stream. But where could the entrance into the hill be found?

The old ditch took a sudden curve round – and Penny gave an exclamation.

"The entrance should be here – where the ditch curves – look on the map and see what I mean, Winnie. This is where we must hunt for the entrance, I'm sure!"

She was right. A great gorse bush barred their way, thick and prickly. The ditch curved round it – and Penny's quick eye saw a smooth patch of earth just under one side of the great bush.

"I think *that's* the way into the opening," she said. "See that worn patch of earth? The men may have gone in and out there. Good gracious – we shall be scratched to bits!"

They certainly did get well and truly scratched! Fortunately they both had coats, and were able to wrap them round their faces and shoulders as they crawled under the prickly bush. Someone had cut away the bush

in the thick middle part, so it was not so thorny there –
and what a surprise they had!

A hole went down into the ground, almost under the
middle of the bush – a hole that had rough steps cut in
one side! The girls crouched under the bush, and looked
down into the hole rather doubtfully.

"Do we go down?" said Penny. "We don't know
what's down there – or who."

"Oh, come on – let's be brave!" said Winnie, who was
not feeling brave in the least. "I'll go first."

And down she went, groping with her legs to find the
rough steps. Soon she was in an underground passage.
She switched on the torch she had brought.

"Well – that was very clever of us," said Penny,
jumping down and joining her. "Now – where do we go
from here?"

"Well – there's only one way – and that's *up*," said Winnie. "Thank goodness you took that tracing, Penny. Come on – I'll go first."

The two girls went slowly up the dark passage. They flashed their torches into little and big side-caves, marvelling at seeing so many. What a honeycombed hillside this was. There must have been many little underground streams at one time, rushing down to make such a number of caves and passages!

"Shall we shout and see if the boys answer?" said Penny. "There doesn't seem to be anyone here – no men, I mean. Let's shout."

So they shouted at the tops of their voices. "KEN! NICKY! PUNCH!"

The two boys were still far away from the girls, sitting in their tiny cave, and heard nothing. But Punch's ears were very sharp. He cocked them up and listened. What was that far-off noise? He growled.

"Oh, *don't* say the men are coming again," groaned Nicky. "I'm fed up with them. What's the matter, Punch?"

Punch heard the far-away voices once more, and stood up on three legs, holding up his hurt one. He didn't growl this time. Surely he recognized those voices! He put his head on one side and listened hard.

The girls shouted again as they came up the underground passages in the hillside – and this time Punch knew the voices. Why – that was Penny's voice – and that was Winnie's! WUFF-WUFF-WUFF!

Punch barked loudly and joyfully, almost deafening the two boys in that small place. They stared at him in astonishment.

"What's the matter, Punch, old thing?" said Nicky.

"You're barking *happily* – who's coming? It can't be the men or you'd be growling."

Punch gave Nicky a quick lick and then barked again. He could hear the girls coming nearer and nearer. They heard his bark, and knew they were near the boys. "We're coming, Nicky, we're coming, Ken. Where are you?" they yelled.

"Here! Here! Can you hear us?" shouted Nicky in delight, crawling as near as he could to the great stone that blocked the entrance. "Penny! Winnie! Here we are – imprisoned in this cave."

The girls at last came to where the boys were, and yelled to them.

"We're here! We came all the way up from the lower entrance – the one Punch must have found the other day. We saw the men – they spoke to us!"

"Gosh! Did they *see* you coming up here?" asked Nicky, as the two girls began to try and move the great stone from the entrance.

"No – they've gone down to the town to find a doctor!" shouted Winnie. "I hope it was Punch who bit that man with the black eye-shade."

"It was," answered Ken. "Look – we'll *push* this stone while you *pull*. It's such a weight that I doubt if even the four of us can move it."

To their enormous disappointment the great stone could not be moved even an inch! It had taken three strong men to put it there – and four children certainly would not be able to budge it. It was most disappointing.

Punch barked, and scrabbled frantically with his front paws, but it was no use. Everyone sat back to take a rest, and the boys told the girls about the wonderful golden statue they had discovered in the hole behind their cave.

111

"*Gracious*! Miss Clewes at the museum told us about that!" said Penny. "It's quite a legend, she said. And apparently anyone who wants a wish to come true has only to kiss the statue's feet seven times!"

"Well, *I'm* not going to kiss any statue's feet, not even to get free," said Nicky. "Gosh – what are we to do *now*? I don't like you girls hanging about in these passages in case those men come back. They'd make *you* prisoners too!"

"Would they?" said Winnie, in alarm. "Then hadn't we better go back straight away and get help? We could bring your Uncle Bob up here in no time, and your father, too!"

"Yes – I almost think you'd better do that," said Ken. "Don't you agree, Nicky? But I *bet* Uncle Bob won't believe you girls! Gosh, this mystery has come true in every detail in a most remarkable way! I'm never going to make up any more!"

"We'll go now," said Penny. "Cheer up, both of you – and pat old Punch for us. We'll be as quick as ever we can!"

And away went the two girls, very cautiously indeed. The boys sat silent, listening to the small noises made by the girls as they went down the passage. Punch listened, too, his head on one side.

"Can't hear them any more," said Ken, with a sigh. "I'm getting tired of this hole, aren't you, Nicky? Well – I just hope the men don't come back. I say – what do you suppose Uncle Bob will say when we show him the golden statue?"

"Oh – he simply won't believe it!" said Nicky, with a grin. "It's just part of the Mystery that Never Was. He – just – won't – believe it!"

CHAPTER 18

Uncle Bob To The Rescue

The two girls went down the dark passage, their ears open for any sound of the men coming back again. Penny thought she heard a noise and stopped in alarm.

"Do you think it would be wiser to go *up* the passages to the old kitchen, and get out that way – the way the boys told us about?" said Penny. "It would be so terrifying if we met the men."

"No. Let's go on down," said Winnie. "At least we *know* this way. The men won't be back yet. I expect they've not only gone to find a doctor but also to make plans for removing whatever they found in the old caves. I *am* glad that Punch bit one of them!"

They came safely to the opening under the old gorse bush. It seemed to be more difficult getting out than getting in, and the girls were in a very dirty, untidy state when at last they were safely out of the great bush, and standing on the hillside in the sun.

"My word – it's good to be out in the open air and sunshine again!" said Penny, breathing in deeply. "I'm sorry for the two boys, shut up in that horrid little cave. Buck up – let's get back as soon as ever we can, and tell everyone where the boys are. Nicky's father is home today, isn't he? He can help too, and Nicky's Uncle Bob and . . ."

"I wonder if his Uncle Bob will believe our story," said Winnie. "It does sound a bit peculiar, doesn't it – hidden men – caves – a golden statue – the boys made prisoners.

113

Still, strange things *do* happen – you see them in the papers every day."

"Well, I never thought an adventure like this would happen to *us*!" said Penny. "Usually adventures are things that happen to other people. Come on – we're nearly home."

"I've been lokking out for those men all the way back, but there hasn't been a sign of them," said Winnie. "I'd run for miles if I did meet them!"

"We're back at last! said Penny, as they came to Nicky's front gate. She ran into the house, calling for Nicky's mother and father. "Mr Fraser! Mrs Fraser! Are you in? Quick!"

"Nicky's Dad has gone to the bank, and his Mother's gone shopping, miss!" called Mrs Hawes from the kitchen. "But his Uncle's in the garden reading the paper, if you want him."

"Yes, we *do*!" said Penny, and flew out into the garden, with Winnie close behind. "Uncle Bob! UNCLE BOB!"

"Hello, hello – what's all the excitement for, Penny?" said Uncle Bob, in surprise. "And where are the boys this morning?"

"Uncle Bob, something's happened," panted Penny. "The boys went up to the old burnt building this morning to find out about that signalling, and . . ."

"Now listen – I don't want to hear any more fairy tales," said Uncle Bob, looking annoyed. "I'm TIRED of hearing what's in that silly message, I'm TIRED of the boys pretending that something's going on. The joke's OVER!"

"But Uncle Bob – the boys are prisoners in a horrid little cave," said Penny, almost in tears. "A cave with a beautiful golden statue at the end . . ."

"And if you kiss its feet and wish, your wish comes true!" said Winnie.

Uncle Bob threw down his paper in exasperation. "What next! Do you *really* expect me to believe in a golden statue that grants wishes? You must be mad. Go away."

"The men have pushed a great heavy stone in front of the boys' cave," said Penny, in a suddenly trembling voice. "And Punch is hurt. One of the men kicked him. Oh, where's Nicky's father? I MUST get someone to help Nicky and Ken. We saw those horrible men walking down the hillside, but I'm sure they'll soon be back. Winnie, let's go and find *my* Daddy. He'll tell the police, I'm sure he will."

Tears suddenly ran down her cheeks, and Uncle Bob looked at her in surprise. He took her hand. "Penny – listen to me – are you *really* telling the truth? This isn't just another idiotic bit of made-up mystery, is it? You remember the silly coded message I showed you, and told you of – about a meeting in cellars – and stuff hidden on Skylark Hill – and signals from the tower – signed Harry – that the boys made up between them? Well, are you *sure* this isn't another silly bit of nonsense?"

"It wasn't nonsense – it's all *true*!" wept Penny. "It *came* true, I don't know how, but it *did*. And 'Harry' is one of the men; Uncle Bob, if you won't come and help, I'll *have* to go and find Daddy."

"Well – this is about the queerest thing I've ever come across," said Uncle Bob. "How *could* a made-up mystery have any truth in it? All right all right, I'm coming, Penny. Stop crying. I believe you, dear, though I'm blessed if I understand what's happening. Come along – we'll all go back to Skylark Hill."

So, much to the girls' relief, Uncle Bob hurried off with them to Skylark Hill. The birds were singing there, just as they had been on the morning he had been there before, but none of them stayed to listen. The girls were anxious to get back to the boys before the men returned – and Uncle Bob was beginning to feel not only puzzled, but most disturbed. What in the world was going on?

The girls took him to the great gorse bush. "The entrance is right in the middle – there's a hole that goes underground," said Penny. "I saw the men coming from somewhere about here – and Winnie and I looked at a map we have, and it showed an entrance just about here, too – so we hunted till we found it. It's awfully prickly, Uncle Bob."

"Bless us all – what next!" said Uncle Bob, not at all liking the idea of creeping under the great thorny bush, and sliding down underground. "My word – I haven't brought a torch!"

"It's all right – we've one each," said Winnie. "Do hurry – I'm so afraid the men will be back. And they're HORRID, Uncle Bob!"

With many groans, Uncle Bob managed to get down the steps that led into the passage below. The girls switched on their torches, and at once beams of light cut through the darkness.

"This way," said Penny. "We can only go uphill. We pass lots of caves on the way."

Uncle Bob followed the two girls, wondering if he was dreaming! He saw the cave where the tools lay scattered about – he saw the hoard of tins, some opened and empty, some still untouched. And then, in the distance, he heard a noise. He stopped.

"Wait – what's that?" he said.

"It's all right – it's only Punch barking," said Penny. "We'll soon come to the cave where the boys are. Who would have thought that the hill was honeycombed with passages and caves like this, Uncle Bob?"

As soon as Punch began to bark the boys wondered who was coming. Was it the men again? Surely it couldn't be the girls back with help already?

"Wuff-wuff-wuff-wuff!" barked Punch madly, scraping with his paws at the big stone blocking the cave entrance. *He* knew who was coming – he knew those voices as soon as he heard them far away in the distance!

"Here's the cave – and there's the stone the men put in front, that we can't move," said Penny. "NICKY! KEN! We're here, and Uncle Bob's with us! You shove the stone and we'll tug it."

"Hallo, Uncle!" shouted Nicky, in delight. "Come on, now – all together!" And he and Ken shoved at the great stone with all their might, while Uncle tugged and pulled till he was out of breath. The stone moved!

"It's coming!" yelled Penny, doing her bit, too. "Shove again, boys! It's moving!"

The stone gave way so suddenly that the girls and Uncle Bob fell over. The boys crawled out at once, with Punch barking loudly, leaping round on three legs!

"Well!" said Uncle Bob, sitting on the ground, rubbing his grazed hands, for the stone was very rough and hard. "This *is* a do, isn't it! I could hardly believe the story that the girls came and told me. And what's all this about a golden statue?"

"Crawl into this cave, and you'll see a fall of earth near the end of it," said Nicky. "Poke my torch through the hole in the middle of the fall, and see what's beyond!"

Uncle Bob did as he was told, though with much

118

difficulty – and when he saw the gleaming beauty of the magnificent golden statue, he was so amazed that at first he couldn't say a word.

"Well – what do you think about our pretend mystery *now*?" said Nicky, triumphantly. "We didn't put a golden statue in it – but everything else has come true!"

"I certainly have an apology to make to you all," said Uncle Bob, wriggling out of the cave. "This is a most extraordinary find. I must get on to the police AT ONCE! Come along – let's get back to the town. We oughtn't to lose any time – those men may come back for the other things they found, though probably not till night-time."

Excited, chattering, thrilled to the core, the little party began to make its way down to the great gorse bush. They clambered up the hole one by one, and squeezed through the opening, pricked once more by the bush that guarded it.

And what should they see, as soon as they came into the open, but the three men straggling back up the hill! Harry had his foot bound up now, and was walking with a limp.

"There they are!" yelled Nicky. "LOOK!"

At his shout the men stopped in surprise – then turned tail and made off, Harry limping painfully down the hill. The boys were too stiff to go after them, and the girls too scared. Uncle Bob grabbed hold of Nicky in case he *should* take it into his head to chase them! Punch limped down the hill on three legs, barking, but soon came back.

"Let them go," said Uncle Bob. "The police will soon round them up! You've had enough for one day. My word, what a shock those men must have had, when they saw us all crawling out from their own private entrance!"

CHAPTER 19

An Exciting Finish!

Uncle Bob went down the hill at a quick pace, followed by the four jubilant children. Punch hopped along behind on three legs, his left hind one still very bruised and painful. Nicky turned round to make sure that he was following, and gave a sudden loud exclamation.

"Look! Look what Punch is carrying!"

They all turned – and how they laughed! Punch carried a shoe in his mouth – rather a large one – with a bite right through the leather!

"It's the shoe belonging to Harry, the man that Punch bit!" said Nicky. "Dear old Punch – you *had* to do your shoe trick didn't you – and bring a shoe along somehow? Drop it!"

"No," said Uncle Bob. "It might be useful. Let him carry it. Which man did it belong to?"

"Er – well, I'm afraid you'll think it's queer – but actually it belonged to a one-eyed man called Harry," said Ken. "The man whose name we put at the end of our secret message."

"How extraordinary!" said Uncle Bob. "I'm beginning to think that you and Nicky must be in league with this band of thieves – how else can you possibly know so much about them?"

Everyone laughed. Nicky turned to his uncle. "I say – we never came up at night to listen to the nightingales," he said. "What about it, Uncle? We might find something else peculiar to look into. I can hear a bird singing now – and I'm sure it's carolling something about a golden statue!"

"Ass!" said Uncle Bob. "But my word – that statue really is a marvellous find, you know. There'll probably be a fine reward for that – and you kids will get it!"

This was a most exciting thought! But there wasn't much time to consider it for they were now down in the town. Uncle Bob walked straight to the police station and asked for the superintendent. The children went with him, feeling VERY important.

The superintendent listened in amazement, for he knew Uncle Bob and his work very well. He took rapid notes, telephoned sharply to somebody, called in three of his men, and rapped out some orders.

The children listened in excitement, but couldn't quite understand what was happening. The superintendent turned to them at last, and smiled.

"You've done some very good work!" he said. "I congratulate you. We shall have to ask you to identify these men for us, I'm afraid, once we've caught them, but we will let you know when that happens."

"Yes, sir," said Nicky, thrilled. "And, er – what about the golden statue, sir?"

"Well – we'll see to that at once," said the superintendent, smiling. "I doubt if it's *gold*! I can't say I've ever heard of it myself. But there may be many other quite valuable things in those old cellars – or caves, whatever they are! There must be *something* – or those men wouldn't have gone to so much trouble, digging under the hill. It's likely that the big bearded man you heard called Hassan is one who knew about the cellars and what they might contain – he may even be a descendant of the family of the prince who built the old mansion up on Skylark Hill."

121

"He ought to have kissed the feet of the statue and wished for sucess," said Winnie. "Then he might have got everything he wanted! Only, of course, he wasn't lucky enough to *find* the statue!"

The superintendent laughed. "Did any of *you* kiss the statue's feet and wish?" he asked.

"NO!" said Nicky. "We're not so silly. But wait a bit – one of us *did!*"

"Who?" said the other three children, in astonishment.

"Punch did – I saw him licking the feet!" said Nicky. "That's his way of kissing. Punch – what did you wish for?"

"WUFF!" said Punch, at once.

"He says he wished for an enormous, meaty bone," said Nicky, in such a serious voice that the others all laughed. "All right, Punch – your wish will soon come true – granted by the magic power of the Golden Statue! We'll buy you a bone on the way home!"

"WUFF!" said Punch again, delighted.

"Well – I think that's about all for the moment," said the superintendent, smiling. "We'll let you know when we need you again – and that will be when we've rounded up the men."

"Look – Punch is still carrying that shoe he brought from the caves," said Ken, when they were outside the police station. "Uncle Bob – ought we to leave it with the police?"

"Well – let him take it home, and we'll wait till they ask us to go to the police station again," said Uncle Bob. "I don't expect it will be long before we get a call to go. I feel that the superintendent had a very good idea where to look for those men.

Uncle Bob was right. The police went at once to the

next town where they had reason to believe that a small colony of foreigners had made their headquarters a few weeks back. They looked for the men that Nicky and the others had described to them.

But no – not one of the men seemed to resemble the children's descriptions! There was no man with a long dark beard, no man with a dark shade over one eye – and all of them denied knowing anything at all about the old burnt mansion, or the caves in the hillside.

"Well – you will please come along with us for an hour or two, for questioning," said the police officer, and hustled the men into the police van. A car was at once sent to the children's homes, with a message for them to go to the police station, and Uncle Bob, too. They piled into the car in great excitement. Punch went with them, of course!

The men were paraded in front of the four children. But what a disappointment! Not one of them seemed to be like the men they had seen underground – or those the girls had met coming down the hill! Not one had a beard – or wore an eye-shade

But Punch recognized them! He growled and showed his teeth. He strained at the lead and tried to get at one of the scowling men.

"Sir!" cried Nicky to the superintendent, "I believe that man is the one called Harry that kicked Punch and hurt him. He must hav taken off the black eye-shade we saw him wearing. Punch bit right through his shoe, sir, and made his foot bleed – and he even carried home the shoe! The man couldn't wear it, because his bitten foot was bleeding and hurt him. We've brought the shoe with us – just in case it might be useful. Here it is!" And Nicky promptly placed it on the superintendent's table.

The superintendent snapped out a few words, and the man sullenly took off his right shoe and sock. The foot was red and swollen, and teethmarks could be plainly seen. Punch gave a blood-curdling growl, and the man edged away, scared.

"Put this other shoe on – the one the boy brought," ordered the superintendent. "See if it fits."

It did, of course, though the man pretended that he could not get it on!

"It's the same type of shoe that he's wearing now, sir," reported the sergeant who had been watching. "A foreign type, sir. Must be his!"

The man mumbled something angrily, and put on his other shoe again, easing it on gradually because the bite that Punch had given him was still painful. Nicky noticed that his hands were shaking.

One of his friends noticed this too, and took out a packet of cigarettes. He offered it to the big man, who took one thankfully. He was obviously in a state of panic.

Nicky stared at the cigarette packet, and so did Ken. It seemed somehow very familiar! Ken gave a sudden shout.

"*He's* one of the men too, sir – the one with the cigarettes."

"How do you know?" asked the superintendent, astonished.

"Well, look sir – the cigarettes are called Splendour Cigarettes – and we found an empty packet up in that old mansion!"

"Ah!" said the superintendent. "Got the empty packet with you?"

"Yes, sir," said Nicky, and took out the packet from

his pocket. "AND we found an empty match box, sir – and these dead matches. "Quick-Lite matches they're called. I kept them in case they were clues!"

"Well, well, WELL!" said the superintendent, surprised, and he took them from Nicky. "Search the pockets of these men, Sergeant, please."

The men stood sullenly while their pockets were turned out. Aha! Two of them had "Splendour" cigarette packets, and one had a box of "Quick-Lite" matches.

"There you are!" cried Nicky, thrilled. "This is the gang all right, sir. They were probably the signallers up in the tower – they smoked cigarettes and threw down the matches, and the empty box and packet. And the shoe belongs to *that* fellow – he's called Harry. And I'm sure that the biggest fellow is called Hassan. He has shaved off the black beard he wore!"

"You know, my boy, you should be of quite considerable help to your uncle, when you're a little older," said the superintendent, smiling broadly. "Take the men away, Sergeant. I'll deal with them later."

Uncle Bob, the children, and Punch went out feeling very jubilant. Uncle Bob stopped outside a shop.

"I think," he said, "that we should all go in here and celebrate the triumphs of that fine bunch of detectives, Nicky, Ken, Winnie and Penny – to say nothing of that remarkable sleuth, Punch, who knew when to turn a most annoying shoe-fetching trick into a wonderful CLUE. Punch – will you kindly lead the way? There cannot be another dog in the world who can catch a criminal by the simple method of stealing his shoe!"

Everyone laughed. They trooped into the shop, which sold the biggest and creamiest ice creams in the town. Uncle Bob promptly ordered two each.

"What – two for the dog as well?" said the shop girl in amazement.

"Certainly! And bring six bottles of ginger beer," said Uncle Bob.

"Ginger beer for the *dog*, too?" said the shop girl, quite dazed.

"Why not?" said Uncle Bob. "He likes ginger beer so why shouldn't he share in our celebrations? Don't you agree, children?"

"Oh, YES!" said everyone, delighted that their little dog should be honoured. Punch barked joyfully, and ran round giving everyone a loving lick. He had quite forgotten his bad leg.

The ice creams were delicious. The ginger beer fizzed and bubbled in the glasses. Uncle Bob raised his glass and spoke solemnly, with a twinkle in his eye.

"Here's to the 'Mystery-That-Never-Was,' which turned into the 'Mystery-That-Came-True'!" My congratulations to you all – and apologies for disbelieving you. And let's hope the Golden Statue brings you the good luck you all deserve!"

"Hear, hear!" said everyone. And Punch joined in too. "Wuff-wuff-wuff-wuff!" What a time he had had! *What* an adventure!

"All the same," said Ken, solemnly, "it's the very last time I'll *ever* invent a mystery. Honestly – I never *guessed* it would all come true! I'll be jolly careful in future, and so will Nicky!"

No – don't be careful, Ken! Invent another one, and do tell us what happens then!

The Secret of Moon Castle

First published in a single volume in hardback in 1953 by
Basil Blackwell Ltd.
First published in paperback in 1965 in Armada

Home From School

Two girls were standing at their front gate one sunny afternoon in July.

"The car ought to be here by now," said Nora. "I hope it hasn't had a puncture or anything. I'm longing to see Mike – and Jack too, of course."

"So am I," said Peggy, her sister. "I wonder if Paul will be with them? Is he going to spend his holidays with us – or go back to Baronia? I wonder."

Paul was the little Prince of Baronia, a great friend of Nora, Peggy, Mike and Jack. He went to the same school as the boys, and had had plenty of adventures with them.

"I expect he'll spend a few days with us first," said Nora, swinging on the gate. "He usually does, doesn't he? Then he'll have to go back to Baronia to see his parents – and all his many brothers and sisters!"

"It's a silly idea, our school breaking up two whole days before the boys'," said Peggy. "We go back earlier too – that's even more of a nuisance!"

"Here's a car – and it's bringing the boys!" said Nora, suddenly. "They've come in Paul's car – the big blue and silver one. I wonder if Ranni is driving it?"

Ranni was Paul's man, who had vowed to look after Paul from the moment when he was put into his arms on the day he was born. He was devoted to the little Prince, and had shared many adventures with him. And now here he was, driving the great Baronian blue and silver car, bringing the three boys home in state!

The girls swung the big gates open as the car came near. They yelled as the car swept in. "Mike! Jack' Paul! Hurrah! Welcome back!"

The car stopped with a squeal of brakes, and Ranni, who was at the wheel, smiled at them through his fiery red beard. Three heads were poked out of the nearest window.

"Hallo, girls! Jump in. We thought you'd be looking for us!" called Mike. The door was swung open, and the girls squeezed in at the back with the three boys making room for them.

Nora gave Mike a hug. He was her twin, and the two were very fond of each other. Except that Nora was smaller than Mike, they were very much alike, with black, curly hair and bright, merry eyes. Golden-haired Peggy was a year older, but Mike was as tall as she was.

"Hallo!" said Jack, giving each of the girls a friendly punch. "What do you mean by breaking up sooner than we did!"

Jack was not their brother. He had no parents, and the Arnolds had adopted him as a big brother for Mike, Nora and Peggy. He thought the world of them all, and grinned around happily, his blue eyes shining in his brown face.

Prince Paul never punched the girls in the friendly way that the other boys did. Baronian manners did not allow that! He bowed politely to each of the girls, smiling happily – but they hadn't the beautiful manners of Baronia, and fell on him like a couple of puppies.

"Is he still ticklish? Yes, he is! Paul, are you going to stay with us for the holidays – or just for a few days – or what?"

"Stop tickling me," said Paul, trying to push them off. "Hey, Ranni, Ranni! Stop the car and turn them out!"

The car swept up to the front door, and Ranni leapt out, grinning. He went to the back to get the school trunks piled there on top of one another.

The door flew open and Mrs Arnold stood there smiling. "Welcome back, boys!" she said. Mike ran to hug his mother. "We're home!" he shouted. "Good old home!"

Jack kissed Mrs Arnold, and then Paul followed his usual custom, bent over her hand with a deep bow, and kissed it politely. The others used to laugh at Paul's grand manners, but they had got so used to them by now that they didn't really notice them.

"Come along in," said Mrs Arnold. "We'd better get out of Ranni's way. He's bringing the trunks in. Ranni, how *can* you manage two trunks at once!"

Ranni grinned. He was big, and enormously strong. Two trunks were nothing to him! He went up the stairs with them easily.

"Mother! What a lovely smell!" said Mike, sniffing. "Buttered toast – and hot scones!"

"Quite right," said his mother. "You've probably forgotten that you asked me to have them for tea as soon as you got home these holidays – though why you took it into your head to ask for such things on a hot July day I don't know."

Jack put his head in at the dining-room door. Tea was already laid there. "My word!" he said. "Home-made éclairs too – and the biggest chocolate sponge sandwich I ever saw! When do we have tea?"

"As soon as you've washed your hands," said Mrs Arnold. "I'll get the toast and scones brought in now, so don't be long."

They weren't long. All five of them tore upstairs, laughing and shouting, glad to be together again. Prince Paul was pleased too – he loved this English family, with its friendliness and generosity.

When they came down, someone else was with Mrs Arnold. The three boys smiled at the small, grey-eyed woman sitting beside Mrs Arnold.

"Dimmy!" they said, and went to shake hands. Paul, as usual, bowed from his waist, and then unexpectedly gave the little woman a hug.

Dimmy's real name was Miss Dimity, and she often came to help Mrs Arnold, especially when the children were home. They all liked her, and teased her – and although she

133

looked so gentle and timid, she could be very firm indeed, as they had found out many a time.

"Good old Dimmy!" said Mike, and looked as if he was going to try to lift her up. She pushed him off.

"No, no, Mike – I know you're almost as big as I am now – but I'm really not going to be tossed about like a bag of potatoes! Sit down before the toast gets cold."

For a little while there was silence as the five children helped themselves from the full plates on the table. Paul gave a loud sigh.

"Now this is what I call *real* food – almost as good as Baronia. Mrs Arnold, I have been half-starved all the term!"

"Don't you believe it!" said Jack. "You should just see the whopping great parcels he gets from Baronia every week!"

"I can guess what they are like,' said Mrs Arnold. "Paul's mother often sends me one too – full of the most delicious things. I had a letter from the Queen, your mother, this morning, Paul. She sends you her love and is looking forward to seeing you."

"Oh – is Paul going to Baronia very soon?" asked Nora, in a disappointed voice. "Peggy and I haven't seen him for a whole term. Can't he stay with us for a bit?"

"Well, I have rather a surprise for you," said her mother, smiling round. "Paul's father and mother have an idea that they would like to come over here for a month or two, and get to know us all better. They want to bring two of Paul's brothers, as well, so that they may know a little of England before they come over here to school."

"Oh *Mother*! How super!" cried Peggy. "But there won't be room here for the King and Queen and servants – they're sure to bring servants, aren't they, Paul? They never travel anywhere without heaps of guards and menservants and maids. Surely they're not coming *here*?"

"No, dear – of course not," said her mother. "Don't be

134

silly! There's hardly room for you five to spread yourselves in the holidays. No – Paul's father wants us to look out for a really big place, where he can bring his wife, two boys, and about twenty servants."

"Gosh!" said Mike. "He'll want a castle!"

"That's just what he suggests," said Mrs Arnold, handing a plate of very buttery scones round.

"I say! Does he really?" said Nora. "Paul, did you know about this?"

Paul shook his dark head. His mouth was too full to speak! His eyes shone, and he tried to swallow down his mouthful too quickly, and began to choke.

There was a lot of banging on the back at this, and Paul went purple in the face.

"Do leave him alone," said Mrs Arnold. "You're making him much worse. Drink some tea, Paul."

"A castle! I say – what fun to ring up the estate agents, and say, 'Please will you send me particulars of a dozen or so castles'," said Mike.

"Mother, do they know what castle they're going to yet?" asked Nora. "Is it anywhere near here? Can we go and see it?"

"Idiot! You know there's no castle near here," said Mike.

"Let Mother answer my questions," said Nora. "Mother, what castle are they going to?"

"My dear child, I told you I only got the letter this morning," said her mother. "Paul's mother has only just thought of the idea. She has asked me to find out what I can, and perhaps go and see over any suitable place – not that I would know in the least whether a castle would be suitable to live in or not!"

"Well, I suppose they only want to rent one, not buy one," said Mike. "You'd better take Paul with you, Mother, and let him poke round a few old castles. He'll know what his mother will fancy! Anyone want this last scone? If so, say the word."

Nobody did, so Mike took it. Everyone began to talk

135

excitedly about the news Mrs Arnold had just given. Paul, recovered from his choking fit, talked more loudly than anyone. He was really thrilled.

"You will all be able to come and stay with me," he announced. "We will share this castle together. You shall know my two brothers. You shall . . ."

"Your mother may not want us," said Mike.

"She certainly won't want you for very long," said Mrs Arnold, with a smile. "A noisy crowd like you! Actually, she says in her letter that she hopes we will *all* go and stay for a little while, so it should be great fun."

"If only we can find a really *good* castle!" said Nora.

"What do you mean – a *good* castle?" said Mike. "You don't suppose we're going to look for half-ruined ones, do you? Mother, have you heard of any yet?"

"Mike – I only got the letter *today*," said his mother. "Now, finish your tea for goodness sake. We'll have any amount of castles to see by next week."

"Castle-hunting – I shall like that!" said Jack. "I wonder which we'll choose – a really exciting one, I hope!"

Choosing A Castle

The next few days were very exciting in more ways than one. For one thing it was great fun to be at home again – no lessons – no bells clanging – no prep in the evenings. For another thing it was most exciting to read through the particulars of various castles that could be rented.

There were not very many. Mrs Arnold looked through the papers that came, and quickly decided which offers were no good. Big mansions were offered as well, and it really seemed to Mrs Arnold that it might almost be better

136

to take one of those for Paul's family. The castles seemed in such remote places, or had been empty for some time, with just a caretaker in.

"Oh *no*, Mother – do let's have a castle," said Mike. "A big house wouldn't be nearly such fun."

"I'm not thinking about how much fun I can provide for you children," said his mother. "I'm thinking about the difficulties Paul's mother will have, in a big, bare castle, with very old-fashioned ways of lighting and heating."

"But Baronia isn't modern, either," said Mike. "Paul's own castle hasn't got a lot of things that a big hotel in England would have, for instance. Mother, do find a castle. It sounds so much more exciting than a big house."

"Look through these," said his mother. "Take the papers with you, and pore over them with the others. They are all ones I think are no good. You will see what I mean when you read through the particulars."

Mike carried away the papers, feeling rather thrilled. What fun to try to choose a castle. He called the other four, and they took the papers out into the garden.

"Here you are – have one or two each," said Mike. "We'll all read through them, and see what we think. Mother's turned all these down."

They read solemnly through the particulars. "Castle and fifty thousand acres," said Jack. "Whew! Do people rent fifty thousand acres as well? Oh – *this* castle's no good. It's only got twelve rooms furnished – goodness knows how many your parents will want, Paul. It must be maddening to be a King and Queen and have to have such enormous places to live in."

"I like our castle in Baronia," said Paul. "But I would rather be an ordinary boy and live the life you do, Jack."

"I don't wonder Mother turned these down," said Mike, putting down his papers. "They're no good at all. Either the owners want to live in one wing of the castle too – or they want Paul's people to rent it for a whole year – or the place

137

isn't furnished. It's a lot more difficult than I thought it would be, to get a castle for a month or two!"

"There's one here," said Peggy, suddenly. "It sounds rather thrilling. I don't quite know why Mother turned it down. Listen."

The others turned to her. They were all lying on the grass, the papers spread around them. Peggy told them about the particulars she held in her hand.

"It's called Moon Castle," she said. "That's a lovely name, isn't it? Moon Castle! And it's big, but not too big – just about right for Paul's family. It's got caretakers in, so it should be in fairly good order. It can be had immediately, because the owners don't live in it. It's high on a hill with 'wonderful panoramic views over a countryside of moorland, wood and waterways'."

"It sounds good," said Mike, sitting up. "Go on – anything else?"

"It's very old," said Peggy. "It says here, 'a castle full of myth and legend', whatever that means. And it says, 'What stories its old walls could tell – tales of violence and mystery, hate and greed'. Goodness, it's just as well that old walls don't suddenly begin to talk, if that's the kind of thing they say!"

"It really does sound rather good," said Nora. "Why did Mother turn it down, I wonder?"

"There she is!" said Mike, as his mother came out into the garden, with a basket and a pair of scissors for picking flowers. "Mother! Hey, Mother! Why did you turn down Moon Castle? It sounds super."

"Moon Castle? Well, really because it sounds so very cut off from everywhere," said Mrs Arnold. "It isn't near any town – and the only village anywhere near is an old ruined one which has the queer name of Moon. I suppose that's how the castle got its name."

"But would it matter, being cut off from everywhere?" asked Peggy.

"It's called Moon Castle."

139

"Yes, I think so," said her mother. "For a big household such as Paul's mother would bring, you would need good shops at least *fairly* near – but the nearest shops are about twenty miles away, it seems to me. It sounded such a lonely, desolate place – it really gave me the creeps!"

"Oh *Mother*! But that's the sort of castle we'd all love," said Nora. "And Paul's mother would bring plenty of cars –wouldn't she, Paul? So that shopping would be easy."

"Well – not *plenty*," said Paul, laughing. "But enough."

"Another drawback is that there wouldn't be any people to make friends with," said Mrs Arnold. "No neighbours, for instance. What the poor, wretched caretakers do with themselves I really cannot imagine!"

"They probably get in a month's stores at once!" said Jack. He turned to the others, "I say, do you remember when we ran away to the Secret Island – where there were no shops – no neighbours except the rabbits and the birds – and everything was lonely and desolate? But what a wonderful time we had!"

"Yes. We did," agreed the others. Mike turned to his mother. "Mother, do let's see what this Moon Castle is really like. Can't we just go and *see* it? Paul, what do *you* think? Would your mother mind its being so far from everywhere – and having 'old walls that could tell tales of mystery and violence' and all the rest of it?"

Paul laughed. "No. Mother wouldn't mind a bit. I expect the walls of our own castle at home are far older than the walls of Moon Castle – and could tell just as fiercesome tales. Mrs Arnold, is the castle too far away for us to go and have a look at it?"

Mike glanced down at the papers in Peggy's hands. "It's nearest station is Bolingblow," he said. "I've never heard of it! Bolingblow – where is it?"

"It's about one hundred miles away," said his mother. She took the papers from Peggy and looked at them again. "Of course, I don't know how much of the castle is furnished

– it says 'partly furnished' – that might mean only two or three rooms. And we don't even know whether the furnishings are in good repair or not – they might be mouldering away!"

"Well, Mother, let's go and *see*,' said Mike, half-impatiently. "It will save such a lot of writing to and fro if we go and have a look. I must say I like the sound of it. It sounds sort of – sort of mysterious – and lost – it belongs to the past and not to nowadays. It . . ."

"Mike's going all romantic," said Nora, with a laugh. "Mike, you'll expect King Arthur's knights to go riding out of the castle, won't you?"

"Don't be an ass," said Mike. "Mother, can't we just go and *look*? Can't you telephone and say we're coming?"

"There's no telephone," said his mother. "That is another reason why I turned it down. The Queen of Baronia will not expect a castle without a telephone!"

"Oh," said Mike, thinking that his mother was quite right there. Then Miss Dimity unexpectedly put in a word. She had come up to listen to the conversation.

"I must say that *I* thought Moon Castle would have done very well for Paul's family," she said. "Except for being twenty miles away from shops, and no telephone, it sounded ideal to me. After all, Paul's mother will have powerful cars to send for any goods she wants – or to take messages. It might be worth seeing. We've got to hurry up and find one, because the family want to come almost immediately!"

"Let's go today," said Mike. "Nothing like doing things at once. Mother, ask Ranni to bring the car round. Let's go today!"

"Yes, do let's," said Paul. "I know what my parents are like! They will change their minds about a castle and a holiday here, if they don't get news of one very soon!"

"Oh dear – you do *rush* me so!" said Mrs Arnold, laughing. "Well – I suppose we'd better make up our minds and go and see this place at once. Paul, find Ranni and tell him. We will be ready in a quarter of an hour. We won't take a picnic lunch – though I should like to – but it would take too long to get ready. Mike, find the right maps, will you – we must look out the best way to go."

After that there was an enormous amount of rushing about, shouting and excitement. It was a very hot day, so the girls put on clean, cool cotton frocks. The boys put on coloured cotton shirts and shorts, except for Jack who considered himself too big and wore grey trousers.

Dimmy was not going. Even without her it would be a tremendous squash in the big blue and silver car belonging to Prince Paul. She waved them off.

"See you some time tonight," she said. "I hope you won't give the caretakers too big a shock, arriving so suddenly out of the blue! I shall be longing to hear all about the castle when you come back."

They went off excitedly. Paul and Mike were in front with Ranni. Mrs Arnold and the girls and Jack were behind. Mike had the map in front, and was poring over it, ready to tell Ranni the roads to take.

They were soon out in the country, speeding along between hedges, with fields of yellowing corn each side. The poppies gleamed in it here and there, and blue chicory flowers shone by the wayside.

"This way now," said Mike, as they came to a corner. "Then east for a good bit till we come to a bridge. Then to the town of Sarchester – then north towards Bolingblow. After that there are only minor roads shown on the map. I hope they will be good enough for a magnificent car like this!"

"Where do we have lunch?" asked Peggy.

"I *thought* somebody would ask that in a minute or two," said Mrs Arnold. "We'll have it at one o'clock, if we are near or in a town."

"We should be at Bolingblow by then," said Mike,

reckoning up quickly. "This car goes at such a speed, it simply *eats* up the miles."

"We should perhaps ask a few questions at Bolingblow about the castle," said Mrs Arnold.

"Yes, we could," said Peggy, and broke into a funny little song that made the others laugh.

> *"O Castle of the Moon,*
> *We're coming to you soon,*
> *This very afternoon,*
> *O Castle of the Moon!"*

The others picked up the words, and the car rushed on with everyone singing the silly little song:

> *"We're coming soon,*
> *O Castle of the Moon!"*

Moon Castle

Ranni drove the car into the town of Bolingblow at just after one o'clock. It was a pretty town with wide streets, and a market-place in the centre.

Mrs Arnold approved of it. "There are good shops here," she said. "And this hotel that Ranni has brought us to looks very nice. Old and picturesque and spotlessly clean."

They were all very hungry, and delighted to find a very good lunch being served. "Iced melon – good!" said Mike. "What's to follow? Cold chicken and ham and salad. Couldn't be better. All I shall want after that is an ice-cream or two."

The little waitress smiled at the hungry children, and took

143

their orders quickly. Soon they were all tucking in, too busy to talk.

When the bill was being paid Mrs Arnold asked the waitress one or two questions.

"Is the road to Moon Castle good, do you know? And about how long will it take us to get there in a car?"

"Moon Castle!" said the waitress, in surprise. "You can't go there. It's not open to the public, you know. No one is allowed to see over it."

"I hear it may be rented this summer," said Mrs Arnold. "I want to go and see it."

"Rented!" said the waitress. "Well, I would never have thought anyone would want to take an old, desolate place like that. It's such a way to the nearest town. Good gracious, nobody's lived there for years and years."

"Oh dear – then I don't expect it's in very good condition," said Mrs Arnold, feeling that her journey would probably be wasted. "There are caretakers, I believe."

"I don't know," said the waitress. "I did hear that once a month somebody comes over in a car to take back goods – food and oil and so on – so I suppose caretakers *are* there. My word! I wouldn't live in that lonely old place for anything. I've heard that queer things go on there – very queer."

"Ooooh! What? asked Nora at once.

"I don't know," said the little waitress. "All I know is that some brainy fellow went there once to ask to see some old books in the big library there – and he was frightened out of his wits! Said the books leapt out of the shelves at him, or something."

Everyone laughed. "That's good!" said Mike. "I'd love to live in a castle where books leapt out of bookshelves. I'd say, 'Hey there – is there a good mystery story waiting for me? Well, jump out, please, and I'll catch you!'"

The waitress didn't like being laughed at. She tossed her head. "Oh well – it's a queer old place that nobody knows much about nowadays. I wouldn't go near it if you paid me."

The children went off to find the car, smiling at the waitress's indignant face. They got into the car and Ranni looked round inquiringly at Mrs Arnold.

"The Castle, madam?" he asked. She nodded, and Mike looked at the map.

"Not such good roads now," he said. "Turn right at the end of the town, Ranni."

"I must say that I don't like what I hear about Moon Castle," said Mrs Arnold, as they drove off. "If nobody has lived there for so long – except the caretakers – the place must be in a very poor condition."

"Yes – it doesn't sound too good," said Mike. "How queer people are – owning a castle and never bothering about it at all! Gosh – what a road this is!"

Ranni had to slow down because the road became very bad just there, and continued bad all the rest of the way. It was full of ruts, and was uneven and in places very stony. The car went carefully.

"We should come to a fork in the road here," said Mike. "Yes, look – there it is. We take the left-hand fork, Ranni."

"That is a good thing," said Ranni. "We could not have taken the other fork! There is hardly any road to be seen!"

It was quite true. The right-hand fork was not really a road – just a fifth-rate cart-track, unused now, and over-grown. Peggy pointed to something in the distance, about half a mile up the track.

"Look," she said. "Houses of some sort. Mother, do you suppose that's all that is left of the ruined village of Moon. Why is it ruined, do you suppose?"

"Peggy, dear, how *should* I know?" said her mother. "The people probably found it too lonely and just left it."

"I can see a few of the roofs," said Peggy. "They look all tumble-down. It might be fun to go and explore a ruined village."

"Well, everyone to his taste," said her mother. "I can think of a lot of better things to do than wander through smelly old villages with not a soul there!"

"Why should it be smelly?" Peggy wanted to know, but just then the car wheels went into such a series of ruts that Mrs Arnold was half-afraid the springs would be broken. But Ranni assured her that they were very, very strong.

"Baronian cars are built for country like this," he said. "All bumps and jumps and humps. The springs cannot break, Madam Arnold. Soon we should see the castle. There is a hill over yonder. It must be there."

They all looked eagerly at the hill coming into view. It was very steep indeed, covered with trees on the slope. Jack gave a sudden exclamation.

"There's the castle – there, right at the top – well, almost at the top! It backs into the hill for protection from the

"There's the castle – there, right at the top!"

146

wind, I suppose. Look at that one great tower! It soars up higher than the hill. Just one tower. How queer!"

"Still, it *looks* like a castle, even if it's only got one tower," said Nora. "I think it's grand. It's got all sorts of turrets and bits and pieces sticking up round it. What a wonderful view it must have over the countryside. All the same – it *would* be lonely to live there always!"

"It certainly looks grand enough for your father and mother, Paul," said Jack. "I mean – it's a *proper* castle – strong and big and *commanding*-looking, if you know what I mean."

Paul did. He was rather taken with it, from the outside. It was such typical English countryside around too – and how his mother would love the little town of Bolingblow, the market-place, the corn-fields, and the countryfolk them-selves.

"Well, commanding-looking or not, I can't believe that the inside will be worth seeing as far as furnishing is concerned," said Mrs Arnold. "I expect it has been allowed to fall to pieces! However, we shall soon see. We are nearly there now."

They were going up the steep hill now. Ranni had put the car into bottom gear, and it growled up slowly, the hill-road just as bad as the road they had left. The road wound to right and left in order to make the climbing of the hill easier.

The castle seemed even bigger and more overpowering as they came nearer. "It's watching us!" said Nora, suddenly. "It's saying: 'What is this horrible noisy thing coming to disturb my dreaming?' I'm sure it's watching us."

"Don't be silly," said Peggy, uneasily. "You do say such stupid things, Nora. My word – what a grand place it is! Towering up into the sky – its one great tower soaring up high. I like it! It belongs to the days of the old knights and their ladies, not to our days."

They came to a great gateway. The gates were shut. Jack

jumped out to open them. Ranni was afraid they might be locked, but they were not. Jack managed to open them, though they creaked and groaned as if they hated to be touched.

The car went through, and up a weed-covered drive that swept round to a great entrance. A flight of wide steps went up to a great door studded with iron nails.

"Well – here we are," said Mrs Arnold, in the sort of voice that meant she wished they weren't! She got out of the car, helped politely by Prince Paul. Ranni leapt up the steps to ring or knock – or whatever one did at a castle like this.

There was a great chain hanging down, with a wrought-iron handle on the end. "Is that the bell?" said Mike, doubtfully. "There's no knocker. Mother, look – there are cobwebs all over the door – even down the opening-crack. It looks as if the door hasn't been opened for years!"

"It does," said Mrs Arnold, beginning to wonder what they would find inside the castle – if they ever got there!

"Shall I pull this chain-thing and hope a bell rings?" said Mike. "Right – well, here goes!"

He gave the chain a big heave. Nothing happened. No sound came, no jingle, no clanging. Mike pulled again. Still nothing happened.

Then Ranni pulled it – and he gave it such a tug that the chain came off and dropped round his shoulders! He threw it down in disgust.

"So old that the rust has eaten into the chain!" he said. "I will hammer on the door."

He hammered with his great fists, and then shouted so that the echoes suddenly swept round them and made them jump.

Nobody came. The door remained fast shut. "Well," said Mrs Arnold, "this is most disappointing. I suppose we must just give it up."

"Oh *no*, Mother! We can't just tamely go back home

after actually getting to the front door!" said Mike, quite shocked. "Let's walk round a bit and see if we can see another door – a back door perhaps. Or don't castles have back doors? Has *your* castle got a back door, Paul?"

"Plenty," said Paul, grinning. "Look – we will go this way. There seems a kind of path."

They followed Paul, Mrs Arnold not at all liking the idea of trying to find another way in. She had quite given up the idea of taking the castle for Paul's parents, but she knew what an outcry the children would make if she insisted on their going back to the car at once.

The overgrown way led round the walls of the castle. They came to a small door set in the wall, but that had no bell, knocker or handle. They went on again and suddenly saw a little clearing, set within a small wall of its own.

"Look," said Peggy, and stopped. "Washing hanging out on a line! There *must* be somebody here, then! Yes, see – there's a fairly big door set in the wall there, that leads into that yard – or drying-ground, whatever it is – where the washing is. This must be the kitchen quarters. If we yell, somebody might hear us now."

Mike obligingly yelled, and made them all jump, for he had a most stentorian voice when he liked.

"HEY! IS ANYONE ABOUT?" he yelled.

Nobody answered. A few hens scuttled across the yard and disappeared under some bushes. A tabby cat streaked across and disappeared, too.

"HEY!" began Mike again, and stopped. Somebody had come cautiously out of the big door nearby – the one that led into the yard.

It was a little plump woman with grey hair. She was followed by two others, remarkably like her in face, but both tall and thin. All three stared at the visitors in surprise.

"What do you want?" said the plump woman, in a frightened voice. "Who are you? Why have you come here? No one's allowed here, you know."

Inside The Castle

Mrs Arnold stepped forward, with the estate agent's letter in her hand. "We have come to see over the castle," she said. "Is it convenient to do so now? We couldn't telephone you, of course, because the castle is not on the phone."

"But – but no one is allowed to see over the castle," said the little woman, and her two tall companions nodded their heads vigorously in agreement.

"We are not sightseers," said Mrs Arnold. "We got the particulars of the castle from the agents, who said that the castle could be viewed at any time, if we took with us this letter. It came with the particulars. It is possible that it might suit a friend of mine, who wants to rent a big place for a month or two."

"Well – my son isn't in," said the woman, looking very taken aback. "He told me nobody was to come in. He said nobody would ever want this place. Nobody has ever come to see it, to buy it, or rent it before. Nobody. I really don't know if I can let you in."

"But we have come all this way to see it!" protested Mrs Arnold. "This is ridiculous! I'm afraid you will get into serious trouble with the owners if you refuse to allow people to see over their castle with a view to renting it. You could be making them lose a great deal of money. Can't you see that? Your son has nothing to do with it!"

"Well, he said we weren't to let anyone in," said the woman, and she turned to her tall companions, not knowing what to do. They held a hurried conference in whispers. The children and Mrs Arnold waited impatiently. How unhelpful these women were!

The little plump woman turned round at last. "Well – I

don't know what my son will say," she said again, "but I suppose I must let you in! I and my two sisters are the caretakers."

"Yes – I'm afraid you *must* let us in and also take us round," said Mrs Arnold, firmly. "What does your son do here? Is he a caretaker too?"

"Oh no. My son is very, very clever," said the little woman, proudly. "He is a scientist. I can't tell you the number of exams he has passed."

"Why does he bury himself here then?" said Mrs Arnold, thinking that this mysterious son must be a spoilt and lazy fellow, living in luxury in the castle, waited on by the three women!

"He has work to do," said the little woman, speaking proudly again. "Important work that needs quiet and peace. I don't know *what* he'll say if people come to live in the castle."

"It really doesn't matter in the least what he says about it," said Mrs Arnold, getting annoyed. "The castle doesn't belong to him. If he makes this kind of trouble every time anyone comes to view it, he will certainly lose you your job! Now please don't say any more about your son, but just take us round at once."

"Yes, madam," said the little woman, looking scared. The other two remained quite silent, but followed behind the party, looking grim.

"What is your name?" asked Mrs Arnold, as they went down a passage.

"I'm Mrs Brimming, and my sisters are Miss Edie Lots and Miss Hannah Lots," said the little woman. "Er – would the person who wants the castle need the whole place?"

"Certainly," said Mrs Arnold. "Except your own quarters, of course. Why?"

Mrs Brimming said nothing in answer to that, but flashed a quick look at her two long-faced sisters. The children, finding Mrs Brimming too slow in her showing-round, went on in front, down the corridor, eager to see the castle.

They came out into a great hall, hung with magnificent brocade curtains. Suits of armour stood all round, gleaming brightly. Paul slapped one and it gave out a hollow noise. "I'd like to wear one of these!" he said. "I'd like to pull the vizor down over my face and peer through it."

"You'd be too small to wear a suit of armour," said Jack. "I could get into one nicely though!"

Mrs Arnold caught a look of alarm on Mrs Brimming's face. "It's all right!" she said, with a laugh. "They won't really walk about in these suits of armour! What a lovely hall this is!"

"Yes," said the woman, and led them to a big door. She swung it open. Inside was a really beautiful room, with graceful furniture upholstered in a royal blue, dimmed with the years. A carpet stretched the whole length of the room, its colours dimmed too, in a lovely soft pattern of blues, reds and creams. The children's feet sank into it as they trod over it.

"My mother would like this," said Paul, at once. "Oh, look at that clock!"

A great clock hung on the wall. It had been made in the shape of a church with a spire. As the children looked at it, a bell inside the church began to toll the hour. It was three o'clock.

"Look! There's an angel coming out of that door in the clock – at the bottom there!" cried Peggy. "A little angel with wings and a trumpet!"

The angel stood there with his trumpet, and then went slowly back again, and the door shut.

"I've never seen a clock like *that* before!" said Nora, in delight.

"There are many curious things here," said Mrs Brimming. "Lord Moon – the one who lived at the beginning of last century, collected many strange marvels from all over the world. There is a musical-box that plays a hundred different tunes, and—"

It gave out a hollow noise.

"Oh! Where is it?" cried Peggy, in delight.

But Mrs Arnold, glancing at her watch, saw that there was only time to look over the castle itself, certainly not to listen to musical-boxes playing a hundred tunes!

"You'll have time to set the musical-box going if we come here," she said. "We must hurry up. Will you show us all the rooms there are, except, of course, your own quarters, Mrs Brimming? My friend, who is the Queen of Baronia, will bring her own servants, and they will, of course, want the use of the kitchen."

"I see," said Mrs Brimming, looking as if she was about to remark that she really didn't know what her son would say to that! "Well, the kitchens are big enough. We use only a corner of them. I'll take you to the other rooms and then upstairs."

All the rooms were beautiful. Upstairs the bedrooms were just the same – magnificently furnished, with wonderful pictures, strange but beautiful ornaments, unusual and most extravagant curtains. Some of them made Peggy think of "cloth of gold", they shone and shimmered so.

Nothing was mouldering, ragged, cobwebby or dirty. Everything was beautifully kept, and Mrs Arnold could not see a speck of dust anywhere. Queer as these three caretakers were, they had certainly tended the castle with the most loving and thorough care.

Upstairs there was a great room whose walls were lined with books from floor to ceiling. The children gazed in amazement. Except in the big public libraries they had never in their lives seen so many books together!

"How wonderful!" said Mike, staring. "I say – what a room for a rainy day! We could never, never get to the end of all these books!"

"They're old," said Jack. "I bet they wouldn't be very interesting. What a waste – to have thousands and thousands of books – and not a soul to read them!"

"My son reads them," said Mrs Brimming, proudly. Nobody said anything. Everybody was tired of Mrs Brimming's son!

On the third storey were great attics – rooms in which were stored enormous chests, old furniture and curious junk of all kinds.

"I don't think my friend would want the attics," said Mrs Arnold, who had been counting up the rooms as they went through them. "The first and second storeys would be enough. How beautifully the whole place is kept! Do you and your sisters keep it like this – does no one else help you?"

"No one," said Mrs Brimming, proudly, and the Misses Edie and Hannah Lots shook their heads too. They led the way downstairs again, to one of the rooms there. "We have been here by ourselves for years. We love this old castle. Our family has always been here, doing some kind of work – yes, our great-great-great-grandmother was here, when the present Lord's great-great-great-grandfather was lord. That's his picture over there."

The children looked at a great portrait that hung over the fireplace of the room they were in. It showed a grim-faced man with a lock of black hair falling over his forehead, his eyes looking quite fiercely at them.

"He doesn't seem to like us much," said Peggy. "I wish he wouldn't look quite so fierce. I shan't be in *this* room much, if we come here – I should never feel comfortable with great-great-great Lord Moon glaring at me!"

The others laughed. Then Mike suddenly thought of something. "We haven't been up the tower – the one, tall tower! We *must* see that!"

There was silence. Mrs Brimming looked at her sisters, and they looked back. Nobody said anything.

"Well – what about the tower?" said Mike again, surprised at the silence. "Can't we see it? I bet your mother will like the tower, Paul! She'll sit up at the top and gaze out

155

"He doesn't seem to like us much," said Peggy.

over the countryside. What a view there must be from the top. Let's go and explore it."

"Well, I'll just stay here and discuss a few things with the caretakers," said Mrs Arnold, who did not particularly want to climb hundreds of stone steps up to the top of the tall tower. "You can wander round. I suppose the tower is in good order too, Mrs Brimming?"

"Yes, madam," said Mrs Brimming, after a little pause. "There's nothing to see there, though. Nothing. I am sure your friend will not want to use the tower – so many steps up, you know – and only small, stone-walled rooms and tiny windows – no use at all."

"It's locked," said one of the Miss Lots, unexpectedly. "Fast–locked."

"Where's the key then?" said Mike at once. He wasn't going to miss going to the top of the tower!

There was another pause. "It's lost," said the other Miss Lots.

"Lost for years," added the first one. "But there's nothing there to see."

"There's a view, surely!" said Mike, puzzled. He didn't believe all this about locked doors and lost keys. Why didn't the caretakers want them to see the tower? Had they neglected it?

"Well, you must find the key before my friend comes," said Mrs Arnold. "She will certainly like to see the view from the top of the tower. Now – I must just ask a few questions about such things as food and so on. You go off for twenty minutes, children, but keep out of mischief, please!"

"Of course!" said Peggy, indignantly. "Come on, Mike." She dropped her voice to a whisper. "Let's go and find the tower!"

An Unpleasant Fellow

They went out of the room, followed by the eyes of all three caretakers. They shut the door behind them. They were in the great hall, and the suits of armour gleamed all around. Peggy gave a little shiver.

"Now I feel as if these suits of armour are watching me!" she said. "Those two Miss Lots give me the creeps. What a peculiar family."

"The son sounds the most peculiar of the lot," said Mike. "I don't feel as if I'm going to like him somehow. But I say – what a castle! Paul, do you like it?"

"Yes, I do, very much," said the little Prince, his eyes shining. "And my mother will love it. So will my two

157

brothers. There will be plenty of room here for all of us, you too! We shall have a grand time!"

"Now – where would the entrance to the tower be?" wondered Jack. "It's on the east side of the castle. So it must be in this direction – down this passage. Come on."

They all followed Jack. He took them down a dark passage hung with what seemed like tapestry, though it was difficult to tell in the dark.

"I wish I'd got a torch," said Mike. "We'd better bring our torches and plenty of batteries, because there only seem to be a few lights in this place, and I bet they don't switch them all on each night!"

They came to the end of the passage, and found themselves in a small square room, whose walls were lined with old chests. Mike lifted up a lid and looked inside. A strong smell of mothballs at once floated out. Nora sneezed.

"Rugs, I think – or curtains or something," said Mike, letting the lid shut with a bang. "I must say those three old caretakers really *do* take care of everything! Now – what about this tower?"

"There doesn't seem to be any entrance to it from here," said Jack, looking all round. He went to a hanging of tapestry that fell from the ceiling of the room to the floor, covering a space left between the many chests. He lifted up the tapestry and gave an exclamation.

"Here's the door to the tower – at least, I should think it leads to the tower."

The others crowded over to look. It was a tall, narrow door, black with age, and looked very strong. There was a handle made of a black iron ring, and an enormous keyhole.

Mike turned the handle to and fro. He could hear a latch clicking, but however hard he pushed at the door it would not open.

"Locked," he said, in disappointment. "And no key. Do you suppose it really *is* lost, Jack?"

"No," said Jack. "I'm sure they didn't want us to use the tower. I bet their awful son uses it – locks himself away from the three old ladies!"

"To do his wonderful scientific work, I suppose," said Mike, with a grin. "Or to laze the days away without anyone knowing. I wonder what he's like. He won't like having to keep in his place when your mother comes, Paul. He'll have to clear out of the tower, if he does use it – we'll have the view to ourselves then!"

Jack took hold of the iron handle and gave the door another shake, a very violent one. Just as he was doing this, footsteps sounded in the long corridor that led to the little square room where they stood.

The children swung round to see who was coming. Jack still had his hand on the iron ring of the tower door.

A man came into the room. He stopped short at once when he saw the children, and gazed at them, astounded. He was short, burly and very dark. His eyes seemed almost black, and his big nose and thin-lipped mouth made him very ugly.

He shouted loudly. "What are you doing here? How dare you? Clear out at once, the lot of you! Take your hand off that iron ring, boy. The door's locked, and you've no business to be snooping round my castle."

The children gasped. *His* castle! Whatever did he mean?

"It's Lord Moon's castle," said Jack, who was the only one who felt able to answer the angry man. "Are you Lord Moon?"

"It doesn't matter who I am!" said the man, taken aback at Jack's words. "I've told you to clear out. How did you get in? Nobody is allowed here, nobody!"

"My mother, the Queen of Baronia, is going to rent this castle from Lord Moon," said Prince Paul, suddenly finding his tongue, and speaking in the imperious way that often made the children laugh. But they didn't laugh now. They were glad of Paul's sudden imperiousness!

159

The man stared at Paul as if he couldn't believe his ears. His shaggy eyebrows came down low over his eyes so that they seemed to be only slits.

"What fairy-tale is this?" he demanded, suddenly. "The Queen of Baronia! I never heard of her! You clear out, I say – and if you ever come round here again I'll take the lot of you up to the top of the tower and throw you out!"

Jack tried again. "But it's true!" he cried. "We're all coming to stay here and we want to look at the tower rooms so that our friend can describe them to his mother. She will be sure to want to know what they are like. You seem to be able to get into the tower, so will you please unlock it for us?"

The man exploded into fury. He stuttered something, raised his hands and came towards them, looking so fierce that they backed away. The girls fled down the corridor. The boys stood their ground a moment, and then they too took to their heels! The man was strong and could have knocked all three of them down easily. He raced after them.

The five children ran down the passage, into the hall, and then flung open the door of the room where they had left Mrs Arnold and the three sister caretakers.

"Good gracious!" began Mrs Arnold, annoyed at this sudden entry, "I must say—"

After the children came the man, muttering fiercely. He stopped in surprise in the doorway. Then he marched in and addressed his mother.

"What's all this? I caught these children snooping round the castle. Who's this woman too?"

"Guy, calm yourself," said Mrs Brimming, in a shaky voice. "This is someone with a letter from the estate agents. She – she thinks her friend, the Queen of Baronia, would like to rent Moon Castle. She has come to see it – these children belong to her. And this small boy is the son of the Queen of Baronia – Prince Paul. It's – it's quite all right. They have every right to be here."

"Didn't I tell you nobody was allowed in?" said her son,

fiercely. "What's all this about renting? I don't believe a word of it."

Mrs Arnold began to feel alarmed. What an extraordinary man! She beckoned to Mike. "Go and fetch Ranni," she said. Mike sped off into the hall and went to the great front door. They had left Ranni and the car outside the flight of steps that led up to it from the drive. How Mike hoped he would be there, waiting!

The front door was well and truly bolted, and had two great keys in the locks. Mike dragged back the bolts, and turned the keys with difficulty. The door came open with a terrible groan, as if it resented being awakened from its long, long sleep.

Ranni was down in the drive, standing patiently beside the car. He saw Mike at once, and sprang up the steps, quick to note the urgency in the boy's face.

"Mother wants you," said Mike, and ran back down the hall to the room where he had left everyone. Big Ranni followed, his boots making a great noise on the stone floor.

Guy, the son of the scared Mrs Brimming, was now examining the letter, which he had almost snatched out of Mrs Arnold's hand when she had offered it to him to prove the truth of her words. His face was as black as thunder.

"Why didn't you write to make an appointment?" he demanded. "No one is allowed in without an appointment! And I must tell you that no one has rented this castle for years – not for years! I cannot—"

"You sent for me, madam?" interrupted Ranni's deep voice. Guy looked up at once, and was astounded to see the enormous Baronian standing beside Mrs Arnold.

"Yes, Ranni," said Mrs Arnold. "I have been over this castle, and I think your master, the King of Baronia, will find it to his liking. This man here – the son of one of the caretakers – does not appear to like our coming. Do you think your master will allow him to stay here when he brings his own servants?"

Ranni knew perfectly well what Mrs Arnold wanted him to say. He looked at Guy with much dislike. Then he bowed to Mrs Arnold and spoke loudly.

"Madam, you know my master's wishes. His Majesty will certainly not allow anyone here except the caretakers. I will get His Majesty's orders and convey them to this man. He will certainly have no right to be here or to object to anything."

The children looked at Guy triumphantly. Good old Ranni! Mrs Brimming gave a little cry. "But he's only my son. He always lives here. He didn't mean to be rude. It's only that . . ."

"I don't think we need to talk about it any more," said Mrs Arnold. "Your son will have to leave the castle while my friends are renting it. He appears to think the castle belongs to him!"

Guy had gone purple in the face. He took a step forward and opened his mouth – but nobody knew what he wanted to say because Ranni also took a step forward. That was enough! One glance at the big Ranni, with his flaming red beard and steady eyes, made Guy change his mind quickly. He muttered something under his breath, swung round and went out of the room.

"I think we'll go now," said Mrs Arnold, picking up the letter that Guy had flung down on a table. "I will tell the estate agents to contact Lord Moon and arrange everything quickly. My friends would like to come in ten days' time, as I told you – earlier if possible, if it can be arranged. I shall tell them how beautifully kept the castle is – and you may be sure that the Queen's servants will keep everything just as well."

"Madam – please don't tell Lord Moon that my son – that my son – behaved rudely," begged Mrs Brimming, looking suddenly tearful. "He – well, he helps to look after the castle too, you see – and he didn't know anyone was coming to see it – or rent it."

"That doesn't excuse his behaviour," said Mrs Arnold. "But I assure you I shall make no trouble for him or for you, if he makes none either. But he must certainly leave the castle while my friend's family is here. We expect *you* to remain here, of course – but not your son or any other relations or friends. We shall make that clear to Lord Moon."

Mrs Arnold said good day and walked to the front door, followed by the children and Ranni. The caretakers did not follow them. They remained behind, gloomy and upset.

But from an upstairs window two angry eyes watched the great blue and silver car set off down the drive. Nobody saw them but Ranni – and he said nothing!

Plans

When the five children got back home again, they found Captain Arnold there. He had been away on business, and was very glad to see them. He swung Peggy and Nora up in his arms, one after the other.

The boys clustered round him, glad to see him. "Where in the world have you been?" he demanded. "I came home expecting to find a loving wife and five excited children to greet me – and nobody was here except Dimmy!"

"I did my best to give him a good welcome," Dimmy said to Mrs Arnold. "But don't fret – he's only been in ten minutes! He hasn't had to wait long."

It was eight o'clock, and everyone was very hungry. "We'll tell you our news when we've washed and are sitting down to supper," said Mrs Arnold. "We've really had a most exciting day!"

So they told Captain Arnold all about how they had been

to visit Moon Castle – its magnificence, its grandeur, its loneliness – how beautifully it was kept by the three caretaker-sisters, and all about the angry son.

"Ha! He's been frightening people away, I expect!" said Captain Arnold. "Likes to think he's King of the Castle – probably brings his own friends there and impresses them very much. If I were Lord Moon I'd make a few enquiries as to why the castle hasn't been let before – and I'd find out how many friends of that son have been staying at the castle – living there for months, I expect! He sounds a bad lot."

"He soon came to his senses when Ranni appeared, though," said Mike, with a grin. "He hardly said a word after that."

"It's a most lovely place," said Mrs Arnold. "I shall ring up the agents first thing tomorrow, and tell them to get in touch with Paul's father. The place is quite ready to go into immediately. I could order all the food and other goods that will be needed. I made enquiries about what shops to go to when I was in Bolingblow."

"Do you think we'll be there next week?" said Paul, hopefully.

"I don't see why not," said Mrs Arnold. "I imagine your people will all fly over, Paul. If only we have a good summer! It's such lovely country round about the castle – real English countryside. Your mother will love it."

"Shall we go and stay with you as soon as your family come?" asked Nora, eagerly, turning to Paul.

"No, no," said her mother, answering for Paul. "Of course not. Only Paul will go to join them at first. We must give them time to settle in a little! But we will certainly join them later."

"Paul will be able to go up the tower before we do," said Peggy, enviously. "Paul, write and tell us about everything, won't you – the tower – and if the key is produced – and if that horrid man Mr Brimming has gone, and . . ."

"Of course he'll be gone," said her mother. "I certainly

will not have him hanging round the place. He seemed to me to be a little mad. The caretakers will have to keep out of the way too, and not interfere with the Queen's servants at all. I think they will be quite sensible – especially if that man isn't around. He seemed to have them under his thumb."

"I'll explore everything and take you everywhere when you come," promised Paul.

Dimmy was very interested to hear about it all. She was not going to the castle when the others did, but Paul said that she really must come just for the day. He was very fond of Dimmy. He turned to Captain Arnold, a thought suddenly striking him.

"Sir – will you be able to come too? Are you on leave for a time?"

"I hope so," said Captain Arnold, helping himself to a large plateful of trifle. "It's not certain, though. I might be off on a very interesting job."

"What job?" asked everyone, but he shook his head. "I shan't tell you till I know," he said. "I hope it will be after we come back from Moon Castle."

Nora yawned hugely, patting her hand over her mouth. "Oh dear – sorry, everyone, but I do feel so sleepy. I even feel too sleepy to have another helping of trifle, which is an awful pity!"

"It isn't," said Paul. "It means I can have it instead!"

Mike and Paul scrabbled for the last helping and made a mess on the table. "I knew that would happen," said Dimmy. "Never mind! It's nice to see every single dish finished up – so much easier to wash! Now there's Peggy yawning and Paul too."

"Get to bed, everyone," said Mrs Arnold. "I'd like a little peace with my husband! I haven't seen him for a very long time!"

The five children went up to bed, everyone yawning now. Mike wanted to talk about Moon Castle, but as both

Jack and Paul were sound asleep as soon as their heads were on the pillow, he had to lie and think instead.

Moon Castle! Fancy there being a castle like that – so very, very old – so beautifully kept – with such strange things in it. He remembered the church-shaped clock and the angel appearing at the church door. And he must remember to look for the musical-box that played a hundred tunes – and could he *possibly* try on a suit of armour? And – and . . .

But Mike was now as fast asleep as the others. Mrs Arnold sat downstairs and talked quietly with her much-travelled husband. He was one of the finest pilots in the world. How many times had he flown round the world? He had lost count! Mrs Arnold, too, was a fine pilot, and had gone on many record flights with her husband. She knew almost as much about aeroplanes as he did.

"This new job you spoke of?" she said. "Is it important? Can you tell me?"

"Yes, I'll tell you," said her husband. "It is to fly a new plane – a queer one, but a beauty! It's a wonderplane. It can rise straight up in the air at a great speed, for one thing, and it gains height in a most remarkable manner."

"Amazing!" said Mrs Arnold. "Will you be on a test flight with it, then? When will it be ready? Do you know?"

"I don't," said her husband. "Yes, it's a test flight, all right. I shall put it through a few hair-raising tests, you may be sure! The speed it goes! I've got to wear special clothes, and some queer apparatus over my head because of the enormous speed – faster than sound again, you know!"

"I want to come and see you take off," said Mrs Arnold. "I always bring you luck, don't I? The only time I couldn't come and watch, you had an accident. I must come and see you this very special, important time, my dear!"

"Yes – you must," said Captain Arnold, knocking out his pipe. "I only hope it doesn't come at a time when you want to go to Moon Castle with the Queen and her family. You'd enjoy that so much!"

166

"Well, if the times clash, I shall come with *you*, dear – and the children can go off to the castle with Dimmy," said his wife. "I *must* come with you and bring you luck when you fly this new plane."

They went off to bed, and soon everyone in the house was sleeping. How many dreamt about Moon Castle? Certainly all the five children did.

It was their first thought in the morning too. They pestered Mrs Arnold after breakfast to telephone the agents at once. She protested. "I *must* telephone Paul's mother first! It takes a little time to get a clear line to telephone Baronia."

But at last all the telephoning was done. The Queen approved heartily. She spoke to Paul too, and the boy was excited to hear his mother's voice coming so clearly over so many miles.

"Dear Paul!" said his mother, in the Baronian language. "I shall see you soon. And your brothers are so excited to be coming to England – such a wonderful country! Mrs Arnold will arrange everything as quickly as possible."

The agents were pleased to hear that Lord Moon's castle had been let. "It's the first time for years," they told Mrs Arnold. "We've had such difficulty in letting it. We've sent a few people there to see it – but they came back with queer stories – either they couldn't get in – or things were made difficult for them. I don't really know what happened. We do hope the Queen of Baronia will like her stay there. I am glad, too, to hear that the place is in such beautiful order. Perhaps we shall have better luck with it now."

Mrs Arnold thought that Mr Guy Brimming must have been the one who had made things difficult! She did not say so, but determined that she would make things very hard for that unpleasant fellow if he did not take himself off and remain away!

"Well, we don't even need to get into touch with Lord Moon," she told the children. "Apparently if the agents are

167

"I have arranged to take the castle for your mother, Paul."

satisfied, they are the judges as to whether the new tenants may go in, and when. So I arranged to take the castle for your mother, Paul, this day week!"

"Oh *good*!" said Paul, delighted. "Only seven days to wait! Well, I suppose Mother will let those three old ladies know what she wants in the way of food and so on – or are you going to do all that Mrs Arnold?"

"Oh, I shall do that," said Mrs Arnold. "What a shock for the three old things when loads of goods arrive day after day! They will hardly know where to put them!"

"Does it cost a lot to rent a castle?" said Mike, thinking that he might like to rent one himself some day.

"Good gracious, yes!" said his mother. "Why, are you thinking of renting one, dear? Just save up a few thousand pounds then!"

"Goodness!" said Mike, abandoning his ideas of castles at once. "Mother, you will be able to come too, won't you? I did hear you say something to Dimmy this morning that you might not be able to."

"Well – there's a chance that your father might like to have me with him when he goes to his new job," said his mother. "But I shall join you afterwards – and Dimmy can go with you, if it happens at an awkward time. But Daddy will soon know, and I'll tell you immediately! I promise!"

Captain Arnold came home that night with the news they wanted. "It's all right!" he said. "I'm to go next week – and as the job will probably only take a week, your mother and I will be home in time to join Paul and his people at Moon Castle in a fortnight's time – probably on the very day we have been asked!"

"Oh good!" said Mike. "Paul will have to go next week, of course, when his family come over – and then we can all go together the week after, when they are settled in."

"Better enjoy this week here while you're all

together," said Dimmy. "You'll be all alone with me next week!"

"Can't we go and watch the new tests too, Daddy?" asked Peggy. "Why can't we?"

"Oh, they're very hush-hush!" said her father. "No sightseers allowed. Cheer up – all our plans are going well these holidays! Nothing will go wrong, I'm sure!"

But he wasn't right about that – something *did* go wrong before the week was up!

Things Go A Little Wrong

The first inkling that things were going wrong came in three days' time, when Mrs Arnold got a letter from Paul's mother, the Queen.

"Any news from my mother?" asked Paul, eagerly. "What a long letter, Mrs Arnold!"

"Yes – it is," said Mrs Arnold. "Oh dear – one of your brothers is ill, Paul dear. It's Boris, who was coming to Moon Castle with your mother in a few days' time!"

"Oh," said Paul, dolefully. "What's the matter with him? He's not *very* ill, is he?"

"No. But they are afraid it is measles," said Mrs Arnold. "Oh, what a pity! Your other brother hasn't had measles, she says – so he will be in quarantine, if Boris has it, as they've been together, of course."

"Oh, Mrs Arnold – it won't mean that my mother can't come, will it?" said Paul, full of dismay. "What about Moon Castle? What about—"

"Well, we won't begin to worry till we know for certain Boris *has* got measles," said Mrs Arnold. "Your mother says it may not be. Perhaps she will come and bring some of the other children, and leave Boris and his brother behind, if they have measles. Don't worry about it."

But Paul did worry, of course. Their lovely, lovely plans! Bother Boris! He was always getting things. Now perhaps they wouldn't be able to go to Moon Castle – and it was going to be such an adventure!

Mike and the others were very disappointed too, because if the trip to England was cancelled they wouldn't have the fun of going to Moon Castle either!

"The only person who will be pleased about this is that horrid man Mr Brimming," said Mike, gloomily. "He'll rejoice like anything!"

Two more days passed. "Any news from my mother?" Paul asked at every post-time. "Mrs Arnold, we're supposed to have the castle the day after tomorrow, aren't we? What will happen if Mother decides not to come? Do you just tell the caretakers, or what?"

"Now don't keep worrying your head about it," said Mrs Arnold. "Your mother is going to telephone today after lunch. We shall know then."

"R-r-r-r-ing!" went the telephone bell after lunch, and the children rushed into the hall. Mrs Arnold pushed them firmly away. She took up the receiver. A voice came to her ear.

"A personal call from Baronia, please, for Mrs Arnold."

"I am Mrs Arnold," was the answer, and then came a lot of clicking noises and far-off voices.

The children stood round breathlessly, trying to hear what was said to Mrs Arnold. She listened carefully, nodding, and saying "Yes. Yes, I see. Yes, a very good idea. Yes. Yes. No, of course not. Yes, I agree."

The children, who could make nothing at all of all this, went nearly mad with impatience. Paul stood as close to Mrs Arnold as he could, hoping to catch a word or two from his mother's long talk. But he couldn't.

At last Mrs Arnold said good-bye, and put back the

receiver with a click. Paul gave a wail. "Why didn't you let me speak to her? Why didn't you?"

"Because it was a personal call, and because that wasn't your mother!" said Mrs Arnold, laughing at the little Prince's fierce expression. "Now listen and I'll tell you what was being said. It's not so bad as we feared."

"Why? Tell us – quick, Mother!" said Mike.

"That was your mother's secretary," said Mrs Arnold to Paul. "Boris *has* got measles – and Gregor, your brother, developed it two days ago. But it's only very slight indeed, and they'll be up and about in no time."

"What's going to happen then? Is Mother going to leave them and come over here?" demanded Paul.

"No. She doesn't want to leave them. But she is sure she will be able to come in about ten days' time, and bring them too," said Mrs Arnold. "So what she proposes is this – as she has rented the castle from the day after tomorrow, she thinks it would be a good idea for us all to go there and settle in till they come!"

"Oh how super!" cried Peggy and Nora together. Then Nora looked solemn. "But Mother," she said, "what about you and Daddy? You're going off with Daddy soon, aren't you, to those new tests? Shall you let him go alone after all, and come with us?"

"Well, dear, I think I *must* go with Daddy," said her mother. "I do bring him luck, you know. But Dimmy will go with you – won't you, Dimmy? And you'll have Ranni as well. And it will only be for a short time – a week or so. It will be nice for your mother to find you well settled in, Paul, and Dimmy able to show the servants the rooms, and where everything is to go."

"Yes. I'd be pleased to do that," said Dimmy, who had been listening to everything with interest. "I've not seen this wonderful castle – and now I shall! But when will the servants come? I don't feel that I can manage hordes of Baronian servants, all speaking a language I don't know! Not even with Ranni's help!"

"The servants will not come until the day before the Queen arrives," said Mrs Arnold. "The children can easily look after themselves, with your help. There will be any amount of food arriving, because I can't very well cancel that. I'll give you the lists, and you will know what is there. Well – what do you say, children?"

"Lovely! Super! Smashing!" said everyone at once. Peggy gave her mother a hug. "I wish you were coming too, though," she said. "Still – you'll come and join us when the Queen arrives, won't you? The plane tests will be over by then."

"I'll do my very best," said her mother. "Now – we'll have to get busy! There are your clothes to see to – the agents to ring up – and I must write a letter to the three caretakers to tell them that our plans are altered, and only you children are coming for the time being."

"I'll see to their clothes," said Dimmy. "They won't want to take a great deal this warm weather. Now, you children, if you want to take any special books or games you'd better look them out and let me have them to pack. And please, Mike, don't imagine that means you can take your whole railway set or anything like that!"

"How many books can we each take?" said Jack. Then he remembered the big library at the castle. "Wait, though – we'll have all those books to read we saw in the bookcases that covered the walls in the library at Moon Castle. We shan't mind a rainy day one bit!"

"Well, *I'm* taking a few books of my own," said Mike. "Those old books in the library might be too dull to read. I'm taking my favourite adventure books."

"We really ought to have a book written about *our* adventures," said Nora, going upstairs with Peggy. "They would make most exciting books."

"And everyone would wish they knew us and could share our adventures!" said Paul. "I bet most children would like to visit our Secret Island – the one we escaped to the first time I knew you – do you remember?"

"Come along, chatterboxes," said Miss Dimmy, pushing the children up the stairs. "Let me look at the clothes in your chests of drawers, and see exactly how much washing and ironing and mending I've got to do. You'll have to help, Peggy and Nora, if there's too much."

"Oh we will," they promised, feeling so happy at the thought of going off to Moon Castle that even the thought of mending clothes didn't depress them.

Captain Arnold was told the news when he got home that night. "Well, it's a mercy the boys have only got a slight attack of measles," he said. "It would have been maddening to cancel the visit to Moon Castle altogether. Anyway, the children will be all right with Dimmy."

Those two days were very full. Mrs Arnold rushed here and there, looking for this and that. Dimmy washed and ironed and mended without stopping. The boys began packing books and games at the bottom of the two big cases. Peggy and Nora began singing the silly little Moon song again!

> "O Castle of the Moon,
> We'll see you very soon!"

Mike added to it, after a great deal of thought:

> "And many a happy hour
> We'll spend up in the tower!"

"I wonder if that man will have gone," said Jack, suddenly. He called to Mrs Arnold. "I say, Mrs Arnold! Did you write to the caretakers? You haven't heard from them, I suppose?"

"There hasn't been time to hear from them," said Mrs Arnold. "Yes, I wrote, of course. I wrote to Mrs Brimming. Why?"

"I was just wondering about that man called Guy," said Jack. "I was hoping he would have gone."

"Oh yes, of course he will have gone," said Mrs Arnold. "I

174

told the agents that unless he went we would not rent the castle. You needn't worry about him. You won't see much of the old ladies either. I don't suppose – unless they do any dusting or cleaning till the Queen's servants arrive."

"Who's doing the cooking?" asked Peggy. "Dimmy? Will those three old women let her use the kitchen stove?"

"I don't know," said Mrs Arnold. "When I wrote I said they could choose what they would prefer to do – cook for you and be paid for it – or allow Dimmy to cook in the kitchen. I've no doubt they would rather do the cooking and earn a little extra money. I hope so, because it will be easier for Dimmy."

"I wish tomorrow would hurry up and come," said Nora, appearing with an armful of ironed clothes.

"Can't you think of anything else to say?" said Mike. "I've heard you say that about twelve times already. What's the time? Nearly tea-time. Well, this time tomorrow we'll be in the castle of the Moon!"

At last everything was packed and ready. The suitcases were shut. Dimmy went round to make sure that everything necessary had been packed and nothing left out. Mrs Arnold and her husband were also leaving on the day following. The children had not been told their address, as the tests were not to be made known – in fact even Captain Arnold was not sure exactly where he was to go the next day.

"I vote we all go to bed early," he said at supper-time. "I want to be absolutely fresh tomorow – and you look tired out already, my dear," he said, turning to his wife. "So does Dimmy."

"*We're* not tired," said Mike. "But we'll go to bed early and make tomorrow come all the quicker! What time is Ranni coming for us in the car?"

"About half-past ten," said his mother. You can have your lunch at that hotel in Bolingblow again, if you like. And I suppose I need hardly warn you to take great care of

At last everything was packed and ready.

all that beautiful furniture at the castle during your stay – and . . ."

"Mother, we'll behave like Princes and Princesses!" said Mike, laughing. "Come on, everyone – let's go to bed. Hurrah for tomorrow – and the Castle of the Moon!"

The Castle Again

Everyone was in a great rush the next morning. The house was to be left empty for the time being. Mrs Hunt, the woman who cooked and helped in the house, was to go home, and to come in daily only to dust and open the windows. She would come and feed the hens too.

Captain Arnold had his bag ready, and Mrs Arnold had packed a small one for herself. Mike wanted to open one of the suitcases, and put in two books he suddenly longed to take at the last moment.

"You can't open them," said Dimmy. "You've done that twice already and messed everything up inside. Now I've locked the case and I've got the key safe!"

"Blow!" said Mike, and went to see if he could open Paul's school trunk, which he was taking with him. But Dimmy had artfully locked that too.

Ranni came round with the shining car at exactly half-past ten. He grinned at the excited children. "So we go back to the castle!" he said. "The poor car – she will bump herself to death!"

"Baronian cars don't mind bumps," said Paul. "You said so yourself! Anyway, I rather like them. Goodbye, Captain Arnold, and the very best of luck with your new tests."

"Thank you," said Captain Arnold. "If you hear something that sounds like a big sneeze, and it's gone almost before it's come, it'll be me in the new plane!"

Everyone laughed. Nora hugged her father. "Be careful, Daddy, won't you?" she said. "And good luck!"

Soon all the good-byes had been said and the car set off, with Captain and Mrs Arnold waving from the doorstep. They were off!

It was rather a squash in the big car again, but nobody minded except Dimmy, who said that Nora was the most fidgety person to sit next to that she had ever known in her life. But when Peggy took Nora's place Miss Dimmy changed her mind, and said that she thought Peggy was worse than Nora. Certainly none of the five children stopped talking or leaning out of windows, or stretching across one another for the whole journey.

They had lunch at Bolingblow again, and the same little waitress served them.

"We went to the castle," said Peggy. "It's WONDERFUL!"

"And we're going again now – to stay!" said Nora.

The waitress laughed. She didn't believe Nora. "No one stays there," she said. "So don't you try to pull my leg. It's got a bad name, Moon Castle has."

"Why has it?" asked Mike at once.

"Well – people say Things Happen there," said the waitress, mysteriously. "I told you before about the fellow who went to see some old books in the library there!"

"Oh yes – and they jumped out of the shelves at him!" said Peggy, with a giggle. "We do hope that will happen when *we're* there! But do please believe us – we really *are* going there to stay."

The waitress stared at them, still finding this difficult to believe. "I did hear say that any amount of goods have been ordered and sent to the castle," she said. "Any amount – food and stuff. Would that be for you?"

"Well, partly," said Peggy. "Do you know any more tales about the castle?"

178

"Noises!" said the waitress, lowering her voice as if she was half-afraid to speak. "Noises! I did hear there were very strange noises."

"What sort?" asked Mike, in great interest.

"I don't know. Nobody knows," said the girl. "Just noises. Don't you go to that castle. You go home while there's time!"

She went off with their plates. Peggy laughed. "This is very thrilling. Isn't it queer how all old places have strange stories about them? I wouldn't be a bit surprised if that man Guy put out these tales, just to keep the castle to himself and prevent people going there. I bet there aren't any Noises or Things that Happen!"

"I agree with you," said Mike. "It's just tales. Well – we'll soon find out. Personally I'd like something to happen."

"Not Noises," said Nora. "I don't like noises – queer noises, I mean – when you don't know what makes them."

"Like the wicker chair in our bedroom," said Peggy. "At night it suddenly gives a creak *exactly* as if somebody had sat down in it. But when I put my light on there's nobody there."

"Of course there isn't," said Dimmy. "It's merely the wickerwork relaxing after having to bear your big lump of a weight, Peggy!"

They were now on to ice-creams. They were so nice that Miss Dimmy ordered a second round. Nora patted her arm affectionately.

"I do like some of your habits, Dimmy," she said. "Like ordering another lot of ice-creams – and looking the other way when one of us orders a third lot."

"There'll be *no* third lot," said Dimmy. "I'm calling for the bill!"

The children grinned. They didn't really want a third ice-cream, but it was always fun to pull Dimmy's leg. The waitress came up with the bill.

"I've been talking to my friend over there about Moon Castle," she said in a low voice. "She's the niece of the grocer who sent up some of the goods. And she says the driver of the van was so scared when he got to the castle that he just dumped all the things in the drive, shouted 'Here they are!' jumped back into the van, and went down the hill as if a hundred dogs were after him."

"But why was he so scared?" said Nora, puzzled. "There's absolutely nothing frightening about the front door! The driver must be crazy!"

"I tell you, it's a scary place," said the waitress, who seemed quite determined to make the most of what little she knew. "Well – you come in here and see me when you've been there a day or two. I guess you'll have some queer tales to tell!"

The children laughed. "There are only three harmless old caretakers up there now," said Mike. "They would be more scared than anyone else if Things Happened, like you said."

"Ah – caretakers! Three of them – *that's* queer!" said the waitress.

"Why? Do they fly about on broomsticks at night?" asked Jack with a grin.

The waitress was cross. She piled the plates together loudly and walked off.

"Come on," said Mike. "Off to the castle of the Moon, we'll be there very soon – no, I've got it wrong. Anyway, come on, everyone!"

They went back to the car. Ranni was already in the driving-seat, waiting patiently. It was somehow rather comforting to see him there, big and burly and confident, after hearing the waitress's tales. They all got into the car, feeling very well-fed indeed. Now for the castle!

Ranni drove off. They followed the same road as before, bumpy and full of ruts. Ranni drove carefully. Nora and Peggy looked out for the fork that led to the ruined village.

"I meant to have asked the waitress if she knew anything about that," said Nora, regretfully. "But I forgot. I'm sure she would have had a wonderful story about it."

"Look – there's the fork to it," said Peggy. "I vote we go and explore it one day. It's only about a mile from here. I'd like to explore a ruined village."

They passed the fork and the children once more caught a glimpse of tumble-down roofs and a desolate group of houses huddled together.

And then they were on the steep road to the castle. They wound to and fro on the slope, their engine sounding loudly as they went. Not even the powerful Baronian car could go up in top gear!

The entrance gates were again shut and Mike hopped out to open them. Up the drive they went and swept round to the front door. That too was shut.

"Well – here we are," said Mike, looking up at the towering castle. "It seems awfully big when we're as near as this. Now, what happens? Do we ring the bell again? On no – you broke the chain, Ranni! I hope we don't have to go all round the back, like we did before."

"The chain is mended," said Ranni, and the children, looking towards the door, saw that he was right. "We can get in at the front this time!"

Jack leapt up the wide flight of steps and took hold of the iron handle at the end of the chain. He pulled it downwards.

This time a bell rang! A loud jangle sounded somewhere back in the castle, a cracked, harsh noise, as if the bell was big, but broken.

Ranni heaved the cases and Paul's trunk up the steps. Everyone stood patiently waiting for the door to open. Jack got impatient and rang the bell again. Then he jumped. The door was opening slowly and quietly in front of him.

But no one was there! The children stood there, expecting one of the old caretakers to appear. But no one came. Was someone behind the door?

The door was opening slowly and quietly in front of him.

Jack ran in to see. No – the hall was empty. "How queer!" said Dimmy. "Somebody *must* have opened the door in answer to the bell – but why should they disappear at once?"

"One of the Queer Things that Happen!" said Mike, with a chuckle. "Oh well – I expect one of the sisters did open it, but got so scared of Ranni and his red beard that she fled at once. It's so dark in the hall that we wouldn't notice anyone scuttling away. Shall I give you a hand, Ranni?"

Ranni wanted no help. "You go and find someone and ask if everything is ready for us," he said, standing inside the hall. Jack looked at Dimmy.

"Shall I go and get Mrs Brimming?" he asked. Dimmy nodded, and Jack sped off, trying to remember the way to the back quarters.

He came back almost immediately with Miss Edie Lots who was looking rather scared. "I've found one of them," said Jack, pleased. "She says she didn't hear the bell, and doesn't believe anyone opened the door."

"Rubbish," said Dimmy. "Miss Lots, is everything ready for us to come in? You got Mrs Arnold's letter, I expect – and the one from the agent, telling of our change in plans."

"Oh yes. Yes," said Miss Edie, sounding rather breathless. "We heard that only the children were coming and a Miss Dimity. Yes. Everything is ready. You will choose what bedrooms you want yourself. And the packages have come – dozens of them! They are all in the kitchen. Yes."

"Thank you," said Dimmy. "We'll get straight in now, then – and I'll come and examine everything in the kitchen later on. Now, children – come upstairs and show me the bedrooms. What a truly magnificent place this is!"

Up the stairs they went in excitement, talking nineteen to the dozen. What fun they were going to have!

Settling Into The Castle

Ranni followed the children upstairs with the luggage. Dimmy thought she had better follow quickly too, before the children took unsuitable bedrooms for themselves! She marvelled as she went up the broad flight of stairs – what a wonderful place this was!

"What carpets! What hangings! What magnificent pictures!" she thought, leaning over the broad banister and looking down into the great hall. The front door was still open and sunlight flooded through it, gleaming on the suits of armour, standing on their pedestals.

"Not a speck of dust anywhere!" marvelled Dimmy. "Those caretakers may be strange but they do know how to take care of things!"

Ranni had put the luggage down on the great landing, and now passed Dimmy to fetch the rest of it. He stopped beside her.

"I would like a small room not far from my little master, the Prince," he said, politely. "Or one opening out of his, if that is possible."

"Very well, Ranni. I will see to that," said Dimmy, thinking for the hundredth time how devoted Ranni was to Paul. Servant – friend – guardian; Ranni was everything!

She hurried towards the sound of chattering and laughter. Where were those children?

They were in an enormous bedroom that looked out over the countryside for miles. Nora swung round to Dimmy, her eyes shining.

"Dimmy! Can Peggy and I have this room? It's wonderful! Look at the view!"

"I shouldn't think you can for one moment," said

Dimmy, amazed at the size of the room. "This must be one of the biggest rooms. Paul's mother should have it!"

"Oh no, Dimmy – there are much bigger rooms than this!" protested Nora. "Come and see!"

Feeling quite dazed, Dimmy followed Nora into room after room, all beautifully furnished, all beautifully kept. The views were marvellous.

Finally they came to a suite of smaller rooms, leading out of one another, but each with its own door to the landing. There were three of these, two of them double rooms and one single room.

"Now these would do beautifully for you five children," said Dimmy, at once. "No, don't argue, Nora – the room you wanted was far too big. Let me tell you this – you will probably have to keep it spotlessly clean and tidy yourself, if the caretakers are not going to take on the job – and you'd do much better to have these small rooms, which will be very easy to keep tidy."

"Oh," said Nora, disappointed. "Well – I suppose you're right, Dimmy. And it *would* be nice to have three rooms all together like this." She went to the door and shouted.

"Peggy! Mike! Come here – there are three rooms all together here!"

They all came running. Jack approved at once. "Yes – Mike and I could have this middle one – and you two girls the one to the left of us – and Paul the one to the right – the single room. Couldn't be better!"

He went to the window and looked out. "I never in my life saw such views!" he said. "Never! I say – is that a bit of the ruined village we can see? I'm sure I can see roof-tops and a chimney or two!"

They all crowded together at the window. "Yes!" said Mike. "It must be. Look – you can just make out a bit of the road there, too – the fork to the village comes about there. I say, we *must* go and explore it sometime."

Dimmy had wandered off. She wanted to find a room for

herself, and one for Ranni too. She found a small room for Ranni a little way down the corridor, but alas, it looked on to the hill at the back of the castle, and was rather dark, because the walls were so near the hillside itself. The hill rose up behind the castle like a cliff.

Only the tall tower rose high above the hilltop. Dimmy thought what a wonderful view there must be from that! She looked for a room for herself, hoping to find one with a view.

She found a tiny little room at the end of the corridor. It had no bed in it, but seemed more like a little sitting-room. She decided to move a bed into it from another room, and use the little room for herself – it had such a wonderful view that she felt she would rather have it than a bigger one without a view.

She went back to the children. They had called Ranni and he had brought their luggage in. Dimmy smiled at the big, bearded fellow. "I've found a room for you, Ranni," she said. "Quite nearby. But it hasn't a view."

However Ranni, brought up in a country of high mountains and sweeping valleys, had no wish for a view. He had had plenty of those in Baronia! He was very pleased with his little room, because it was so near Paul.

"There aren't any basins with running water," said Nora, looking at the great old-fashioned washstands. "Do we have to use these enormous jugs? I shall hardly be able to lift mine!"

"Use the bathrooms," said Mike. "I counted seven on this floor already! There's one just opposite our rooms. It's got a shower and everything."

"Dimmy, isn't this fun?" said Nora. "Have you got a room for yourself – a nice one? Oh Dimmy, won't it be lovely living in a castle like this? It will take me ages to find my way around properly."

Dimmy felt rather the same – but it was amazing how quickly they learnt where all the rooms were, and the

186

quickest way here, there and everywhere! There were two main staircases, and two or three smaller ones.

"We can have a marvellous time chasing one another and playing hide-and-seek," said Mike. "All these staircases to get away on! You know, Paul, it's a very good idea to let us come here on our own, before your people come – we shan't have such fun when they're here, really, because all the rooms will be occupied, and people won't like us rushing everywhere."

"No, they won't," said Paul, thinking of the different way he would have to behave when his family came, with all their servants. "Let's make the most of it this week!"

Dimmy went down to see the three caretakers. She rang a bell from what she imagined to be the drawing-room, but nobody came. So she found her way to the enormous kitchens.

There were two fireplaces in the biggest kitchen, one with a fire, the other empty. Great cooking stoves lined the walls. Six or seven sinks showed up here and there. Dimmy paused at the door. Goodness – what a place!

Sitting at an open window at the far end were the three sisters. Dimmy had already seen the one called Edie Lots. She walked over to them.

They stood up as she came, looking nervous.

"Please sit down," said Dimmy, thinking what a queer trio they were. "I will sit with you too, and find out what is the best way to manage till Her Majesty, the Queen of Baronia, comes next week."

They all sat down. None of the three said a word. Dimmy talked pleasantly, and got Mrs Brimming to open her mouth at last.

She arranged that the three should look after the children, herself and Ranni, and should continue to clean the castle and keep it tidy until the Baronian servants came.

"Everything will go to rack and ruin then, I suppose!"

said Mrs Brimming, dolefully. "My son said it would. Those foreign servants!"

"That's not a fair thing to say," said Dimmy. "You will find that the Baronians will take a pride in the place and keep it beautifully. In any case, that is hardly your business. You may be sure that the Queen will see that nothing goes wrong. Now do please cheer up – after all, Lord Moon must try to make a little money out of a beautiful castle like this, empty for years!"

"My son says that Lord Moon wouldn't let it to foreigners if he knew about it," said Mrs Brimming. "He says it's only the agents that have let it, without consulting Lord Moon. He says—"

Dimmy began to feel as annoyed as Mrs Arnold had felt over this interfering son! "I'm afraid it is no business of your son's," she said. Then she remembered that one of the conditions Mrs Arnold had made was that the interfering fellow – what was his name – yes, Guy – should go away.

"I suppose your son is no longer here, now that the castle has been let?" she said.

"Of course he's not here," said Miss Edie Lots, in a loud voice. She glared at Dimmy, and seemed about to say a lot more – but Mrs Brimming nudged her sharply and she stopped.

Dimmy left them soon after that. "I suppose they all adore this Guy," she thought, as she went to find the children and help them to unpack. "Well, it's a good thing he's gone. He certainly wasn't in the kitchens. Now – which is the way to our rooms? Good gracious – it's a mile walk to find them, really it is!"

The children had begun their unpacking. They wouldn't let Dimmy help. "No, Dimmy – you've got your own unpacking to do," said Nora. "You always forget that we have to unpack our own things at school! We can do it all right now, honestly we can!"

"When do we have tea – and where?" called Mike. "I'm hungry already."

"I've arranged it for half-past four," said Dimmy. "And we're using the smallest room downstairs, off the right-hand side of the hall – the room where there are some queer old musical instruments on the walls."

"Oh yes – I know it," said Peggy. "It's a queer-shaped room – what do you call it – L-shaped."

"Yes – it's just like a letter L," said Jack. "With the bottom part of the L having windows all down the side. I vote we put a table there, and have our meals looking out of the window. We can see for miles then!"

They unpacked everything and arranged their things in the great drawers, leaving half of them empty, of course, because their clothes took up very little room!

"The drawers of these great chests are so enormous that I could almost get into one!" said Paul, coming into the boys' room, which was between his and the girls'. "Are you nearly ready? I had much more to unpack than you and I've finished first."

"Well, we'd have finished sooner if we'd just thrown everything higgledy-piggledy into drawers, like you have." said Mike. "Get off those jerseys, Paul. There's plenty of carpet to stand on without treading on my clothes!"

"Don't be so fussy," said Paul. "What time's tea? I could do with some."

But, like the others, he had to wait till half-past four. What should they do after that? Mike had an idea at once.

"The tower! We'll see if it's unlocked now. It jolly well ought to be!"

189

Queer Happenings

Mrs Brimming brought up a really delicious tea. The children approved of it so heartily, and said so in such loud voices, that Mrs Brimming actually smiled!

"Thank you, Brimmy," said Nora, unexpectedly. Dimmy looked at her sharply, and the others stared at Mrs Brimming, expecting her to object at once.

But to their surprise she didn't seem to mind at all. In fact, she actually smiled again. "Fancy your calling me that!" she said. "I haven't been called that since I was nurse to Lord Moon's youngest, years ago! They all called me Brimmy in those days!"

She then scurried out of the room like a frightened hen, evidently as surprised as the children that she had made such a long speech!

"What cheek to call her Brimmy when you've only seen her twice!" said Mike to Nora. "But you just hit her on a tender spot – didn't she, Dimmy?"

"Brimmy and Dimmy," said Nora, with a giggle. "I could make a nice rhyme up about Brimmy and Dimmy."

"Well, I'd rather you didn't," said Dimmy, pouring out tea. "I'm used to your silly ideas, but Mrs Brimming isn't. I'm quite sure she wouldn't like to hear you all singing a ridiculous song about her."

"All right," said Nora. "Anyway, there aren't any decent rhymes to Brimmy or Dimmy. I say – what a smashing chocolate cake. Nice and big too. Big enough for us all to have a second slice."

"You really mustn't finish that enormous cake today," said Dimmy. "I'm sure Mrs Brimming meant it to last us a whole week."

"Well, Brimy will have a whole lot of different ideas about us before the week is up," said Mike. "Where did these biscuits come from? They're not home-made."

"I looked at some of the piles of goods that have arrived," said Dimmy. "I told Mrs Brimming she could open what she thought would do for us – but she had already made this lovely chocolate cake."

"Well, I'm beginning to think she's not a bad sort, after all," said Jack. "What do you think, Paul?"

Paul thought that anyone who could make a chocolate cake as good as the one he was eating must be a good sort. Dimmy laughed. She listened to the friendly chatter of the five children, poured them out more cups of tea, cut slices of cake and sponge sandwich, and decided that they really were a nice set of children.

"What are you going to do after tea?" she asked.

"We're going to see the tower," said Mike promptly. "It ought to be unlocked now. Like to come, Dimmy?"

"I don't think so," said Dimmy. "I want to go and see that the beds are all made, and if they are aired properly. Mrs Brimming didn't know which rooms we were going to choose and I saw that she had piles of sheets airing by the fire – probably for us. I shall see to all that, and I'm sure she will help me. You go and explore the tower if you like."

"Right – we'll leave Brimmy and Dimmy to gossip together over sheets and pillow-cases," said Mike, getting up. "Everybody finished? Oh, sorry, Dimmy – I didn't see that your cup wasn't empty." He sat down again.

"Don't wait for me, please," said Dimmy. "I always enjoy a quiet cup after you've all gone! Go along now, and do whatever you want to do!"

"Dimmy's jolly glad to finish her tea in peace," said Nora, tickling the back of Dimmy's neck affectionately as she passed her chair. "She's been busy looking after us the whole of the meal. If you want any help with the beds, call us, Dimmy, and we'll come."

They trooped out of the room. Dimmy sat back peacefully, and poured out another cup of tea. They had had their meal in the curious L-shaped room as they had planned, and the table had been set in front of the windows, in the short bottom part of the L. Dimmy gazed out of the window at the view.

The room was silent. Dimmy couldn't even hear the voices of the children in the distance – she heard only the sound of her spoon stirring her tea slowly.

TWANG!

Dimmy jumped. The sound came so suddenly, and so very unexpectedly that for a minute she couldn't imagine what it was!

TWANG! There it was again. What could it be? Dimmy suddenly remembered the old musical instruments hung on the wall in the other part of the room – in the long part of the L. She smiled.

"Silly children!" she thought. "One of them has crept back to play a joke on me and make me jump. Mike, I expect! He's crept in and twanged one of the strings of some instrument. Silly boy."

She stirred her tea again, listening for a giggle.

TWANG! TWANG!

"I can hear you!" called out Dimmy, cheerily. "Twang all you like – I don't mind!"

DONG!

"Run away and play," called Dimmy. "Silly children!"

DONG!

Dimmy wondered what instrument made the "dong" noise. It was a queer sound – but then the musical instruments on the wall beyond were very queer-looking – old, foreign and most unusual. Perhaps the "dong" noise was made by that thing that looked like a drum but had stout strings stretched across it. Anyway, she wasn't going to bother to get up and see.

DONG!

"That's enough," said Dimmy. "You ought to know when a joke is played out."

She listened for a giggle, or the scuffle of feet creeping away, but she heard nothing. She began to drink her tea. No more of the twanging, donging noises came, and Dimmy was certain that whichever of the children had played the trick on her had crept away.

She went to see about the beds, and was soon in a deep discussion with Mrs Brimming about sheets and pillow-cases. She felt sure that the children were now busily exploring the tower.

But they weren't! They were all very angry indeed, because the tower door was still locked!

They had gone down the tapestry-covered corridor, and into the square-shaped room lined with great oak chests. Mike went straight to the tapestry that hung over the tower door to cover it.

He pulled it to one side, expecting to see the door.

He gaped in amazement, and turned startled eyes to the other four behind him. "It's gone!" he said. "There's no door here!"

The five looked hurriedly round the room. They could see no door at all – in fact, the whole wall was lined with chests. But about three feet from the tapestry hanging was a very tall chest, taller than the others.

"I bet it's behind that chest!" Jack said, and stepped over to it. "I *thought* that tapestry was hanging in a different place when I saw it just now. Give me a hand, Mike – we'll pull this chest away."

They tugged at it. It was astonishingly heavy, and needed all five of them to move it. Nobody thought of taking out the contents of the drawers to make the chest easier to handle!

Behind the chest, just as Jack had thought, was the tower door – tall, narrow – and locked!

"That's that awful man again!" said Jack, fiercely,

193

"It's gone! There's no door here!"

194

pulling at the ring handle. "What does he think he's doing? Fancy thinking he'd hide the door by putting a chest in front of it, and hanging the tapestry somewhere else. He must be mad. What's the point, anyhow?"

"The point is that he doesn't want anyone to go into the tower – because he's got some secret there," said Mike. The others nodded in agreement. Nora shook the handle, and then bent down and peered though the keyhole.

"I can see stone steps beyond the door," she said. "Oh how could that horrible man do such a thing! Whatever will your mother say, Paul, when she finds that this kind of thing is being done?"

"Perhaps by the time your mother's family comes, the door will be unlocked," said Jack slowly. "Maybe Mr Brimming hasn't had time to clear out of the tower – and thinks that he can stop us going in by tricks like this."

"Yes. I expect that's it," said Paul. "I bet he's made himself a kind of home in this tower – thinks of it as his own – and resents us coming. I bet he's got all his furniture in there still!"

"Well, if we suddenly find the key in the lock, and the tower is empty, we'll know we were right," said Jack. "He'll probably move out one dark night."

"It's *maddening*," said Peggy, shaking the handle in her turn, as if she thought that a little temper would make the door open. She put her mouth to the keyhole.

"Hey!" she shouted. "We know you're up there! Come down and unlock this door!"

Jack pulled her away. "Don't be so *silly*, Peggy," he said. "You wouldn't like it a bit if he came tearing down those stairs and flung the door open and glared at you out of his horrid eyes!"

Peggy looked at the door, rather alarmed. "No sound of footsteps!" she said, with a laugh. "He wouldn't hear my shouting, anyway. It wouldn't carry through that thick door and up those stone steps."

Mike was looking in the big chest they had hauled away from the door. "I'd like to know what makes it so jolly heavy," he said. "We *almost* couldn't drag it away. Look – rugs – cloth of some kind – and what's this in the bottom drawer of the chest, wrapped up in blue curtains?"

They all leaned over him as he knelt down, feeling in the big bottom drawer, He tugged at the cloth that wrapped up some great, heavy objects which could hardly be moved.

Nobody could move them an inch, and everyone grew very curious about what the heavy things could be. Jack took hold of a corner of one of the cloths and pulled hard until the heavy bundle unrolled.

"Rocks! Stones big enough to be called small rocks! My word, what a time he must have had, bringing them here to weight this chest down. I wonder the drawer didn't break – but these chests are very old and solid."

"No wonder we could hardly move the thing," said Paul. What are we going to do?"

"Leave the chest moved out of place so that Mr Guy Brimming can see we've discovered his little joke – a jolly silly one," said Jack. "He probably didn't reckon there'd be five of us to move it. Well! *Somehow* we've got to get into this tower – and it's certainly not going to be easy!"

Twang-Dong Again!

The five children left the chest where it was, pulled right away from the tower door. Guy Brimming would certainly know they had gone to explore the tower, found the door hidden, and discovered it behind the chest! Would he do anything further? They would wait and see.

They decided to go back to the L-shaped room and tell

Dimmy. She wasn't there, so they went to find her in the bedrooms upstairs, remembering that she was going to see to the beds. She was there, as they thought, just finishing Paul's room. She was alone.

"Oh Dimmy – have you done the beds all by yourself?" said Nora. "I'm sorry! I thought you'd be sure to call Peggy and me if you didn't have help."

"It's all right, dear – Mrs Brimming and one of the Lots came up to help me," said Dimmy. "I don't know which one – they're so alike, those two Lots. They've only just gone."

"We couldn't get into the tower, Dimmy," said Peggy, solemnly.

"The door was still locked," said Mike.

"And *some*body had tried to hide it by pulling a chest in front," said Paul. "What do you think of that?"

Dimmy laughed at their very solemn faces. "Well – I don't *really* think very much of it," she said. "I expect there are things in the tower that need to be cleaned, or perhaps cleared out. Maybe it's been used for storing all kinds of things in – and I've no doubt the tower will be unlocked and ready for anyone to use by the time Paul's family arrive next week."

"I think you're wrong, Dimmy," said Jack. "I think there's something *mysterious* about it. I'm sure it's something to do with that fellow Guy."

"You think a lot of foolish things," said Dimmy. "I'll mention it to Mrs Brimming – and you'll see, she'll have a quite ordinary explanation for it. Maybe the key is lost, as they said before."

"Well – but why was the door *hidden* this time?" persisted Jack. "And why was the chest that hid it weighted down with rocks so that it was almost impossible to move?"

"Rocks! Nonsense!" said Dimmy. "You're joking. And, by the way, talking of jokes – TWANG! DONG!"

She made a loud twanging sound with her mouth and

197

then a loud dong. The children stared at her in wonder. She laughed.

"Yes – you can look as inncent as you please!" she said. "But *I* know those innocent faces of yours! Aha! It was funny, wasn't it – TWANG! DONG!"

The children looked rather alarmed at this Twang-Dong speech. They stared at Dimmy, and then looked at one another.

"What exactly do you mean, Dimmy?" asked Nora at last. "Honestly, we can't imagine what you're getting at."

Dimmy looked rather annoyed. "Well, as you very well know, one of you – or maybe two or three of you, I don't know – crept back to the tea-room and twanged and donged one or two of the musical instruments on the wall," she said. "So don't deny it. It was a good joke, I agree, and the first time I jumped like anything. But don't pretend to be innocent now!"

"Not one of us went back to play a trick," said Jack, astonished. He looked round at the others. "We didn't, did we? We went straight to the tower door, and we've been there ever since. We don't know a thing about this twanging and donging."

Dimmy found it difficult to believe him. "Well, well – perhaps the instruments play a little tune by themselves," she said. "Anyway – I'd be glad to know which one of you it was, when you've made up your minds that the joke is now ended."

The five children left Dimmy and went down to the sitting-room, where they had had tea. They were very puzzled. "What on earth did Dimmy mean?" said Mike. "TWANG! DONG! I really thought she had gone suddenly dippy when she made those noises! We certainly don't know anything about them."

"Perhaps old musical instruments are like wicker chairs," said Peggy. "Perhaps their strings relax or something and make a noise."

"I never heard of such a thing before," said Mike. "Let's have a good look at them."

They stood beside the walls and looked at all the queer instruments – some were like big guitars, some like banjos, and there were tom-toms and tambourines – any amount of instruments were there, many of which the children had never seen before.

Jack touched a string, and it twanged softly. Soon they were all touching the various strings and knocking on the drums and tom-toms, so that a weird noise filled the room.

They got tired of it after a time. "I really think Dimmy must have fallen asleep or something, when we left her," said Jack. "Instruments just *don't* play themselves. Come on – let's have a game. Who says Racing Demon?"

Everyone did, and they took the cards from the cupboard where they had put their various games.

Dimmy came in, in the middle of the first game. "What a nice peaceful sight!" she said. "I'll get some mending to do, so don't ask me to play. I don't like those top-speed games!"

She got some sewing, and came to sit beside them at the window. The children were playing on the table where they had had tea. Dimmy glanced out of the window, marvelling at the wonderful view she could see for miles on miles. The sky was very blue, the distance was blue too. The sun was going down, and there was a golden light over every-thing.

Jack began to deal again. "Wait a moment before you begin another game," said Dimmy. "Look out there – did you ever see anything so lovely?"

They all gazed out of the window, and Nora began to make up a few lines of poetry in her mind. It was a very peaceful moment.

TWANG!

Everyone jumped violently and Dimmy dropped the pair of scissors she was holding.

"There!" said Dimmy. "That's the noise I heard before!"

"There!" said Dimmy, in a whisper. "That's the noise I heard before. Wasn't it one of you, then?"

"No – we told you it wasn't," said Nora. "And anyway, we're all here now. Not one of us has moved to the other part of the room, where the guitars and things are."

Nothing more happened. Jack got up and went round the bend of the L-shaped room into the long part where the walls held so many instruments. Nobody was there. The door was open and he shut it.

"Nobody there," he said, and sat down. "Maybe somebody crept in and twanged a guitar. I wonder who the joker is!"

He began to deal once more.

TWANG!

Everyone jumped again, it was so loud. Jack and Mike raced round the bend of the room. The door was still shut!

"But someone might have crept in, twanged, and gone out quickly," said Jack. "Look – there's a key in the door. We'll turn it and lock the door – then the joker will be completely done!"

He turned the key. Dimmy looked rather startled. She had quite thought that one of the children had played the joke on her after tea – but now she saw that they had told the truth. Somebody else was doing the twanging!

DONG!

Jack slapped his cards down. "This is silly!" he said. "I locked the door!"

Mike disappeared into the other part of the room. "It's still locked!" he called. "Well and truly locked. Can't be opened at all."

He took a look at the instruments on the wall, wondering which one had twanged. He looked for a quivering string, but could see none. He went back to the others, as puzzled as they were.

DONG!

"Blow it," said Jack. "*Who's* doing it?"

201

"I don't think anyone is," said Dimmy, picking up her scissors, which she had dropped again. "I think it's just one or two of the instruments doing it on their own – perhaps it's this hot weather – making them expand or something."

"Well, there doesn't seem anything else to think," said Peggy, "except—"

"Except what?" asked Jack, as Peggy stopped.

"Well – except that we heard that Queer Things Happen here," said Peggy. "Don't you remember what the waitress said at that hotel? 'Strange Noises – Queer Happenings.'"

"Don't!" said Nora. "I didn't believe it. And I don't want to believe it now."

"And do you remember she said that books jumped out of the bookshelves?" said Peggy. "Oh dear – I hope things don't begin to jump about."

"Now listen to me," said Dimmy, in a suddenly brisk voice, "this kind of talk is foolish and ridiculous. I don't want to hear any more of it. Fancy believing the silly tales of a waitress! Books jumping! Too silly for words!"

"Well – but we *did* hear a Queer Noise," said Peggy.

"I dare say we did – but we've decided that it's the hot weather making the strings of some instrument or other expand, and go twang and dong," said Dimmy.

DONG!

"Yes, just like that," said Dimmy firmly, as the curious dong noise came from round the bend of the room. "Nobody is there. The door is locked – and if the instruments like to sigh and make a noise because it's hot, what does it matter?"

TWANG!

"Well, I expect you're right, Dimmy," said Nora. "If it's only noises like that I don't mind a bit. Let's go on with the game!"

Jack began once more to deal, and they gathered up their cards, listening all the time for another twang or dong.

But none came! They began to forget about it and played with a lot of noise. Dimmy watched them, glad that they were no longer puzzled. But she was very puzzled indeed.

Was she right in thinking that the noises had been natural ones? Yes, of course she must be right. She looked out of the window at the view. The sun was sinking low.

Bang-bang!

Everyone jumped so much that half the cards slid off the table. Dimmy leapt to her feet. *Now* what was it?

A voice came from the other side of the door – a plaintive, puzzled voice.

"Please, Miss Dimity, we're bringing your supper, and the door's locked."

"Gosh – that was only Brimmy knocking at the door!" said Jack, in great relief. He ran to open it. Brimmy was there with a large tray, and behind her were the two solemn sisters, also with trays.

Nobody explained the locked door. It suddenly began to seem rather silly. At the sight of a very nice supper all six completely forgot both Twang and Dong, and willing hands took the trays and set the table!

"Aha!" said Jack. "A meal fit for a King – and certainly fit for a Prince! Dimmy – are we ready? One, two, three, begin!"

An Interesting Discovery

It was fun to go to bed that night in the little suite of three rooms. The doors between were left open so that shouting could go on between the three boys and the two girls.

Nobody felt sleepy at all. When they were all in pyjamas, the girls and Paul went to sit on the beds in the middle room to talk to Mike and Jack. It wasn't long before a pillow-fight began, of course. With shrieks and thuds the fight raged round the room, and a chair went over with a bang.

"We'll have Dimmy in if we make too much row," panted Mike. "Oh you beast, Paul – you've taken my pillow. Give it back!"

Thud! Biff! Giggles and shrieks, bare feet pattering all over the bedroom, and someone pinned in a corner! And then Nora gave an agonized yell.

"Paul! Ass! Your pillow's gone out of the window!"

There was a pause in the battle at once. Paul looked rather abashed as Mike rounded on him. "Idiot, Paul! What did you do that for?"

"It sort of flew out of my hand," explained Paul, and went to the window. He leaned out so far that Jack caught him by his pyjama trousers, afraid that he might pitch out and join the pillow. "I can see it," he said. "It's down on the grass below. I'll get it."

He ran to the door of his room and opened it. Dimmy was just coming up the corridor! She saw him and called out.

"Paul! You ought to be in bed long ago. What are you doing?"

"Just looking out," said Paul. "Are you coming to bed now, Dimmy?"

"Yes, I am – and I shall come along just before I get into bed and make sure you are all asleep," said Dimmy, firmly. "So if you have any ideas of playing catch or hide-and-seek round the castle corridors, just put them out of your head! I suppose you've been pillow-fighting or something – you look so hot and tousled."

"We've had a bit of a fight," said Paul, grinning. "Good night, Dimmy." He shut the door and went back to the others, who had leapt into their beds as soon as they had heard Dimmy's voice.

"It was Dimmy," said Paul, poking his head into the boys' room. "She's just going to bed – but she's coming along last thing to see if we're alseep. Blow! What shall I do about the pillow? I don't like to go down and hunt for it now in case she comes along."

"Wait till she's been along and I'll go with you," said Mike. "It's getting dark now – we'll take our torches and slip out when it's safe. Get into bed now, for goodness' sake. Ranni will be along next!"

Mike was right. Ranni came along in about five minutes' time and quietly opened Paul's door to make sure he was in bed and asleep. There was no sound as Ranni switched on the light and saw a curled-up heap in Paul's bed. He went out quietly and shut the door. Paul heaved a sigh of relief.

When Dimmy came at last both the girls were fast asleep – and so was Paul! Dimmy had a word with Mike and Jack, said good night, and went out.

Mike sat up in bed. "Paul!" he called in a low voice. "Are you ready?"

No answer! Paul was far away, lost in delightful dreams of towers and castles and ruined villages. Mike scrambled out of bed and went to wake him – but Jack called him back.

"Let him be! He'll probably make some noise and wake up Ranni. We two will go. Got your torch?"

Without bothering to put on their dressing-gowns the two boys crept out of the room in slippers, each with his torch. The night was so warm that they felt hot even in pyjamas! It was dark now, too, and they crept along the dim corridors, flashing their torches when they came to the stretches of darkness between the lights which glowed dimly along the corridors at intervals.

"Better go out of the front door," whispered Mike. "We might bump into Brimmy or one of the Lots if we go towards the kitchen, and we're not sure yet where any other door is."

"Do you remember how the front door opened with-

205

They unbolted the great door.

out anyone there to open it, when we came today?" whispered Jack. "I'd forgotten it till now."

"Must have been one of the Lots, I expect," said Mike. "It would be just like them to scurry away as soon as they opened the door! Here we are – isn't it enormous?"

They unbolted the great door, hoping that no one would hear them. They turned the big key, and then twisted the handle. The door opened very quietly indeed, swinging back easily on its hinges.

The two boys went down the big flight of steps outside. "Round to the right," said Jack, in a low voice. "We'll keep close to the walls, and then we are bound to come to where the pillow fell."

The walls of the castle were not built in a straight line, but bulged out into odd shapes, sometimes rounded, sometimes square, as if the builder had planned queer-shaped rooms, or had planned towers that he had not completed.

"The pillow ought to be somewhere about here," whispered Jack, and shone his torch down on to the grass. Then he looked upwards to try to make out if they were under their bedroom windows.

He caught Mike's arm suddenly, and whispered in his ear. "Mike! The tower's over there, look – do you see what I see?"

Mike looked up – and saw the enormously high tower against the dark night sky, where stars shone, giving out a faint light. He gave a sudden exclamation.

"The windows! They're lighted! Somebody's in the tower!"

The two boys gazed up at the great tower. "Three of the narrow windows are lighted," whispered Jack. "Three! Somebody's very busy in there tonight!"

"Perhaps that man Guy is clearing out, as we thought," said Mike. "Clearing out his belongings, I mean."

"I wonder if it *is* that fellow," said Jack, gazing up, and wishing he could see into one of the windows just for a minute or two.

"Let's stay and watch for a bit – whoever is there might come to the window," said Mike. So they sat down on the thick grass and watched the lighted windows of the tower. Once they saw someone passing across a window, but couldn't make out if it was Guy or not.

They grew tired of watching, at last. "Let's get the pillow and go," said Jack, getting up. Then he had an idea and caught hold of Mike's arm. "Wait! What about sneaking along to that little square room where the tower door is, and seeing if the door's unlocked? We know someone is in the tower now."

"Yes! Smashing idea," said Mike, thrilled. "We might creep up the steps, even – and see what's going on. Come on – we'll go now."

They made their way back to the front door. It was still open, for which Jack was very thankful. He couldn't help thinking that a door which could apparently open by itself might also shut by itself! However, there it was, half-open just as they had left it.

They went in, shut, locked and bolted the door again, went past the silent suits of armour and then set off to the little square room. Down the tapestried passage they went, and into the square room.

It was in darkness, and neither boy could find a light switch. They turned on their torches, and at once weird shadows leapt round the walls. The boys flashed their torches to the place where the door should be. The chest was still out of its place, where they had left it. The tall, narrow door showed up plainly, set deeply in the wall.

Mike tiptoed to it and took hold of the handle. He turned it carefully. Then he groaned.

"No good!" he said. "It's still locked. Blow! No adventure tonight."

"We were silly to hope it would be open," said Jack. "That fellow wouldn't take any chances of being discovered in the tower, I'm sure. He'd be furious if he thought we had been out and had seen the lighted windows!"

"Well – it's no good waiting about here," said Mike. "Blow that fellow! I'd like to go and explore that tower more than anything else in the world! Why is he so secretive? Has he got something up there he doesn't want anyone to see? Why does he lock himself up?"

"I suppose because he knows he ought to have left the castle by now," said Jack. "I say – let's put something against the bottom of the door, so that when he opens it he pushes the obstacle away."

"What's the point of that?" asked Mike.

"Just to let him know we're about!" grinned Jack. "He'll know we're suspicious, he'll know we think there's someone up the tower, and that we'll be watching to see if the obstacle we put here is moved. He can certainly put it back again if he goes *out* of the door – but when he goes back he won't be able to – and we'll find it out of its place, and know that he's gone back up the tower again."

"All right – we'll get a rug out of one of the chests," said Mike. They got one, folded it lengthways, and shoved it firmly against the bottom of the door.

"Perhaps the door opens inwards *into* the tower," said Jack, "and not outwards, into this room. If it does, the rug won't prove anything. He could open the door, see the rug, and step over it without moving it."

"No. The door opens into this room," said Mike, and pointed to a curving line on the stone floor. "See where part of the bottom edge has scraped the stone each time it has been opened."

"Yes, you're right," said Jack, tucking the rug even more firmly against the door. He yawned widely. "Gosh, I'm sleepy now. Let's go to bed. Got the pillow?"

"Yes," said Mike, picking up the pillow from the floor. "Well, Paul's pillow certainly gave us the chance of making sure the tower is occupied!"

They went back to their rooms, keeping a sharp lookout for Ranni, who got up several times a night, as a rule, to see that his little master was safe! They didn't want to run into him.

The girls and Paul were still asleep. Mike put Paul's pillow at the end of his bed, and then he and Jack climbed thankfully between their sheets, and snuggled down.

"Good night," said Jack. "We'll ask Brimmy about the tower tomorrow, and see what she says!"

There was no answer. Mike was asleep already!

Jack Hears A Good Many Things

Next morning the two boys told the others about the lighted windows in the tower that they had seen the night before. The girls laughed when they heard about the rug that the boys had put in front of the door. "We'll go to the square room immediately after breakfast," they decided, "and see if it's still there."

But the rug had disappeared! The door was still shut and locked. Mike stared round the room. "Guy must have come out of the tower, seen the rug, and put it away somewhere. He just didn't bother to put it back. He doesn't care whether we suspect anything or not."

Jack was opening the many chests and peering inside. "Here it is!" he called at last. "Just chucked in here, still folded lengthways."

"Well – he knows we're on his track," said Nora, thrilled.

"I wish we were," said Jack. "As long as he slips in and out without anyone seeing him and challenging him, and as long as he keeps the tower locked up, we can't possibly do anything about it."

"We can ask Brimmy," said Nora. "She's doing some dusting and sweeping in the rooms downstairs. I saw her as we came here. Let's go and ask her."

They went to find Brimmy. She was on her knees, sweeping vigorously, her face very red.

"Excuse me, Brimmy," began Mike, "that tower door is still locked. Where's the key please?"

Brimmy looked up nervously, pushing some stray hairs away from her face. "The key?" she said. "Well now, perhaps it's still lost."

"It isn't," said Jack. "Somebody's been in and out of the tower door, so we know there must be a key."

"I daresay it's been found then," said Brimmy, beginning to sweep vigorously again. "There's – er – there's things in that tower that must be cleared out before the Queen comes."

"What things?" said Jack, determined to find out *some*thing. "Do they belong to Lord Moon? Are they very precious? Is that why they are locked up?"

"Maybe," said Brimmy, sounding annoyed as well as nervous. "There's things I don't want to talk about, so please don't ask so many questions. You're only renting the castle, not buying it! Everything will be unlocked, cleaned and ready for the Queen when she comes next week. You don't need the tower, and it's not safe for children."

"Why?" asked Nora.

"Oh, these questions!" said Brimmy, pushing more hair out of her eyes and looking really harassed. "Will you please leave me to my work, or I'll complain to Miss Dimity? I'm sure she wouldn't let you go up the tower, anyway, and risk falling out of those high windows. They're really dangerous."

At that moment Ranni appeared at the door. "Miss Dimity is going to take the car into Bolingblow for some things she needs," he said. "Would you like to come too?"

"Yes!" said everyone, and went out of the room, much to Mrs Brimming's relief.

"Listen – I'm not coming," said Jack, as soon as they were out of hearing. "You go, all of you – and I'll hide around somewhere. I've an idea that Brimmy will go and warn that Guy fellow, as soon as she thinks we're all safely out of the way. I might be able to find out something."

"Right," said Mike. "Well – we'll think of you snooping around while we're having big ice-creams!"

Jack hid in his room while the others went off. When they were safely gone he went cautiously into the long corridor outside his room. No one was about. He decided to go downstairs by one of the back staircases. He might hear Brimmy telling the two Miss Lots something.

The staircase led to what seemed to be staff bedrooms on the ground floor. Not a sound was to be heard. Jack passed the open doors of the bedrooms and went down an uncarpeted passage, glad that he had on rubber shoes.

He rounded a corner and came to an entrance to one of the kitchens. And then he heard voices! He stood at the half-open door, trying to make out if they were the women's voices.

Yes – they were certainly women's voices, worried and anxious. And then came a man's voice, raised as if in anger.

"Well, I can't! It won't be finished for some days. I can't help it. You'll have to make what excuses you can. It's your own fault for disobeying orders and letting people see over the place. But that tower will be locked, I tell you – so make what excuses you like about it. You don't know what you've done, letting these people into the castle just now!"

Then Jack heard angry footsteps on the stone kitchen floor, footsteps that sounded as bad-tempered and determined as the voice! The boy slid quietly behind a cupboard.

A man went by to the back stairs down which Jack had come. Jack peered out at him. Was it Guy? Yes, it was, he was sure of it. Jack debated with himself – should he follow him and see if he went back to the tower – he might even be able to see where the key was kept! No – it would be safely in his pocket, anyway. That was no good.

Jack decided that on the whole it might be foolish to follow the angry man. He stayed where he was for a

Was it Guy? Yes, it was, he was sure of it.

minute or two and then came out from his hiding-place. He went into the big kitchen. Brimmy was at the far end, weeping, and the two Miss Lots were standing by gloomily. Brimmy gave a little cry when she saw Jack.

"I thought you'd gone out! Surely you aren't all back yet!"

"I didn't go," said Jack. "What's the matter, Mrs Brimming? Why are you crying?"

"Oh – just one of my headaches, that's all," said Brimmy, dabbing her eyes. "Do you want something to do? Why don't you go and listen to the musical-box with a hundred tunes? Or go and look round the library?"

Jack saw that she wanted to get rid of him. Perhaps she was afraid he would ask her some awkward questions. He changed the subject.

"Do you know anything about that old ruined village?" he asked. "We thought we'd go and explore it one day. Why did everyone leave it?"

There was dead silence. Jack looked at the three women in surprise. They looked as if they didn't know what in the world to say!

"What's up?" said Jack. "Anything mysterious about the village?"

"No. No, of course not," said Miss Edie Lots in a suddenly loud voice. "There used to be mines there, you know – tin mines, I believe. And then something happened and they were given up, and the people drifted away to Bolingblow. That's why it's tumble-down, all in ruins. It's a horrid, lonely place – a place that no one in their senses would go near – especially at night!"

"I see," said Jack. "It sounds *most* interesting! We'll really have to go and explore it."

"Those old mines are dangerous," said Brimmy, joining in suddenly, her voice rather shaky. "If you fell down a shaft, that would be the end of you."

"We shouldn't be so silly," said Jack, wondering why

the three women seemed so worried. What was going on here? What was that man Guy doing? If only he could get into the tower!

"Well – I'll go and find the musical-box," said Jack, thinking that it would be fun to get it out and have it ready for the others when they came back. "Where is it?"

"I'll show you," said Miss Edie Lots, in her harsh, loud voice. She led the way, and soon Jack found himself in the hall, and then going down one of the corridors that led to the rooms near their own sitting-room.

"I say," he said, as he followed Miss Lots. "I say – a funny thing happened yesterday. You know those old musical instruments hanging on the wall in the room we've taken for our sitting-room, don't you? Well – they suddenly go TWANG! or DONG! – just like that! Queer, isn't it? Have you ever heard them?"

Miss Edie clutched at him, and Jack was surprised to see that she looked terrified. "You've heard them?" she said, in a loud whisper. "No! No! Oh, what dreadful thing is going to happen?"

"I've no idea," said Jack, politely. "What's up *now*? Why should anything dreadful happen because a bit of twanging and donging goes on?"

"It's the old legend," said Miss Edie, looking over her shoulder as if she expected a Twang or a Dong at any moment. "When those instruments make noises, something awful always happens!"

"What do you mean?" said Jack, with great interest. "Do you expect the castle to fall down or something – or the tower to blow up?"

"There's a legend – written in one of the old books in the library – that none but the Moon family may live here in peace," said Miss Edie. "They say that the spirit of the old castle gets angry and restless when others come, and queer things happen."

"I don't believe it," said Jack. "Beliefs like that belong to centuries ago, not to these days! You can't frighten *me* like that, Miss Lots!"

"I'm not trying to frighten you," said Miss Edie, forgetting to whisper in her annoyance with this unbelieving boy. "I've lived here all my life – I know that what I'm saying is true. I've seen dreadful things happen to those who have come here and defied the old legend. I could tell you many tales – people who have—"

"Save them up till the others come back, and then you can tell all of us," said Jack. "We'd absolutely love to hear those crazy old tales. They're such fun."

Miss Edie glared at him. She simply could not make out this smiling boy who disbelieved all she said. Most people were scared. She lowered her voice.

"The spirit of the old castle is restless again," she said, sounding really mysterious. "I can feel it! No wonder those noises came again. Now other things will happen. They always do"

"How smashing!" said Jack, sounding delighted. "What kind of things? My word, the others will be thrilled to hear all this!"

Miss Edie had now had enough of Jack. "I am not going to tell you things just for you to laugh at," she said, looking most unpleasant. "You can wait and see what happens – but be sure that my words will come true! Those noises always come first – a warning, no doubt."

"No doubt at all," agreed Jack, cheerfully. "Awfully kind of the old spirit of the castle to warn us in such an exciting way. Well – where's this musical-box? I'd like to set it going, if the spirit of the castle has no objection!"

All Very Peculiar

Miss Edie led him into a room that seemed very dark because it faced towards the hillside behind the castle, and not to the valley below.

"Do you want the light on?" she said, sounding cross. "The switch is over there."

"No thanks," said Jack. "Oh, is that the musical-box? My word, how enormous – and what a beauty!"

He went over to a long wooden box. It was about five feet long and a foot and half wide, and stood on a pedestal. Both box and pedestal were of walnut, and were beautifully carved. Little dancing figures ran all round the box and the pedestal too, carved by a clever and loving hand.

"How do you work it?" asked Jack, lifting up the lid, and peering inside at shining brass rollers set with myriads of tiny teeth.

There was no answer, and Jack looked round. Miss Edie had gone without a word! Jack grinned. Did she really think she could frighten him with those silly old tales? He wished the others could have been there to listen to everything.

"Now how does this box work?" he thought, bending over it. "Ah – here are the instructions on the lid. It has to be wound up. I wonder who made it. It must be very, very old!"

He wound it up carefully, and pushed back the lever that set it going. The roller went smoothly and slowly round, and the musical box began to play a merry old tune.

Its sweet, melodious music filled the room and Jack

listened, quite entranced. There was something unearthly and fairylike about the tinkling tunes that followed one after another, all different. The boy recognized some of them, but others he had never heard.

A sound disturbed him. He looked round the dim room into which no sunshine ever came. He saw that it was the same room that had the portrait of a long-ago Lord Moon over the mantlepiece. The face stared down at him, dark and forbidding, the black lock falling over the forehead. The eyes seemed to be looking straight at Jack, angrily and fiercely.

"Sorry if I'm disturbing you, Lord Moon," said Jack, politely to the portrait, as another tune began to play. "Please don't look so fierce!"

The same sound came again to Jack's ears through the tinkling of the music. It seemed as if it came from somewhere by the mantlepiece. Was it a hiss?

Jack walked over to the great fireplace. He listened. Then he looked up at the big portrait above his head. Lord Moon stared down as if he could say a great many things to this stupid boy who was disturbing his peace.

And then a curious thing happened. Lord Moon's eyes seemed to become alive! They glowed angrily, and seemed to flash with anger. Then came the hiss again!

Jack backed away. He was not a timid boy, and had plenty of courage – but this was very unexpected, and very eerie too, in that dim room, with the musical-box playing its tinkling music all the time.

He backed into a stool and fell over. When he got up and looked at the portrait again, the eyes no longer glowed, though Lord Moon still looked as unpleasant as ever.

Jack stared up, surprised to find his heart beating fast. Had he imagined those eyes? Was it some sudden trick of the light? The hissing noise had stopped now too. Jack frowned and walked back to the musical-box. He suddenly looked back over his shoulder at the portrait. Were those eyes looking at him, alive again and angry?

They were looking at him, certainly, but there was no glint in them now. "Imagination!" said Jack to himself. "Well, if that's the sort of effect this castle is going to have on me, I'd better be careful! I could have sworn those eyes came alive for a moment!"

The musical-box ran down with a slowing up of the music. Jack began to wind it up again. Then he heard a voice calling loudly.

"Jack! *Jack*! Where are you?"

He jumped violently – but then laughed at himself. It was only Mike's voice – they were back from Bolingblow already!

He ran out of the room and went to find the others. "Here he is!" cried Nora's voice, and she ran to meet him. "Jack, you ought to have come with us! We had meringues and ices both together. We brought you a meringue back. Here it is."

She gave it to him. He went into the L-shaped sitting-room where the others were. Dimmy was there too, and they were helping her to sort out the shopping she had bought.

"What have *you* been doing. Jack?" asked Dimmy. "You should have come with us!"

"I've been playing that musical-box with a hundred tunes," said Jack. "In the room where that portrait of a long-ago Lord Moon is – with the horrid eyes!"

Something in his voice made Mike look up. "Anything interesting?" said Mike. Jack nodded his head towards Dimmy, and Mike understood at once that Jack had something interesting to say, but not till they were alone. Fortunately Dimmy departed from the room with an armful of shopping in a short time, and left the children alone together.

"Jack! You've got something to tell us!" said Mike.

219

"What is it? Did you hear anything? Did something happen?"

"Yes – I heard plenty – and something *did* happen," said Jack. "Listen!"

He told the others what he had overheard Guy say to his mother and aunts. He told them what Miss Edie had said about the old legend of the spirit of the castle. Everyone laughed.

"Fancy trying to make us believe that the Twang and Dong came because the castle was angry we were here!" said Mike. "How idiotic!"

TWANG!

There was a startled silence. The sound echoed through the air and then was gone.

"H'm! That was timed very well," said Jack, noting that Nora and Paul looked scared. "Now then, spirit of the castle – what about a Dong?"

"Don't, Jack!" said Nora, anxiously.

No Dong came. "The spirit of the castle's gone a bit deaf," said Jack, cheerfully. "It didn't hear my request."

TWANG! Everyone jumped again. Jack ran round the bend of the room and examined every stringed instrument there. Not one had a vibrating string to show that someone had twanged it, or that it had somehow done it of its own accord.

Jack went back. He had suddenly remembered the gleaming eyes of the portrait. He glanced at Nora and Paul again. They both looked a bit scared, so Jack decided not to say anything in front of them about the portrait. He would tell Mike – and perhaps Peggy – when they were alone with him.

"Where's the musical-box?" said Nora. "Let's go and hear it."

But it was too late to do that because at that moment the two Miss Lots appeared with the midday meal. Dimmy appeared too.

"Oh thank you," she said. "Just put the trays down, and we'll set the table as usual. What a lovely meal!"

Meringues and ices did not seem to have spoilt anyone's appetite. The children looked joyfully at the trays left on the sideboard, lifting the lids that covered the various dishes.

"Cold ham. Tongue! Tomatoes – heaps of them, look. Hard-boiled eggs in salad. Potatoes in their jackets. And an enormous trifle with cherries on the top."

"Stop fiddling about with the lids," said Dimmy. "Come along, you two girls – set the table, please. Mike and Paul, you carry everything over carefully when the cloth is on."

They were soon sitting down and tucking in. It always amazed Dimmy to see how much the five could eat. It looked as if not a single crumb or fragment would be left.

"If anyone wants a biscuit or fruit, they are both on the sideboard," said Dimmy at the end of the meal.

Only Mike could manage any, and he went to take a plum. Just as he was taking it, one of the now familiar noises came from somewhere behind him.

DONG!

"There's the Dong you asked for," called Mike to Jack, glancing round quickly at each of the instruments on the wall. He took his plum back with him to the others. Nobody said anything about the noise, not even Dimmy, and a loud chatter arose as usual.

CRASH! That *did* make them all jump!

"Whatever was that?" said Dimmy. "It sounded round the bend of the room again, where the instruments are."

They all went to look. A big blue jar lay in fragments on the floor. "Look at that!" said Dimmy, vexed. "It's fallen from that shelf. But how could it have happened? What a pity!"

"It's a good thing you were here with us, Dimmy," said Mike. "You might have thought one of us had broken it! We'll have to tell Mrs Brimming. I wonder what made the jar jump off like that – it must have been too near the edge."

Jack remembered all that Miss Edie Lots had told him, and he couldn't help feeling a bit uncomfortable. They went back into the windowed corner, where they had meals. The girls began to clear the table, and stack the dirty plates and dishes on the trays for the caretakers to take down when they came.

Miss Edie Lots appeared in a short while, followed by Mrs Brimming. They stared in dismay at the broken jar; the fragments still lay on the carpet because there was no brush to sweep them up.

"I can't imagine how it happened," said Dimmy, "but we heard a crash, and when we came into this part of the room we saw this broken jar. It must have been too near the edge of the shelf it was on, and have fallen down."

"It was *well* back on its shelf," said Miss Edie. "I dusted this room myself this morning."

"Well, I'm sorry – but none of us had anything to do with it," said Dimmy. "I can't think how it could have happened."

"It's the beginning!" said Edie Lots, in a peculiar voice that made everyone look at her in surprise.

"The beginning of *what*?" asked Dimmy.

"All kinds of things," said Edie. "You'd best be gone before worse happens. The old legend is coming true again. You ask *him* what I said!" She nodded her head towards Jack. "I tell you, it's the beginning – you shouldn't have come to this castle. Bad things will happen!"

"Please don't be so silly," said Dimmy, coldly. "I cannot imagine what you are talking about. Take the trays and go!"

The Ruined Village

Mrs Brimming looked upset, and Edie Lots pursed up her lips and looked angry and most unpleasant. Dimmy turned to the children.

"I'm going upstairs for a rest. It really is so very hot this afternoon. What are you going to do ? Go for a walk?"

"Well – we might go and explore that old ruined village," said Mike. "We passed the fork to it again this morning and we felt we really must go and see it soon."

Edie Lots stared round at him and opened her mouth as if to say something. Dimmy saw her, and was determined that she shouldn't be allowed to talk again – such nonsense as she talked too! So she began to speak herself, and went on firmly until the trays had disappeared out of the room, carried by Brimmy and Edie!

Edie had no chance to say whatever it was she had meant to say – though Jack could have guessed! She would have tried to put them off going to the mines.

"I'm going upstairs now," said Dimmy. "Don't start off for your walk for half an hour or so – not *immediately* after your enormous lunch. Have a read."

"Let's go and play that musical-box, Jack," said Nora. "I do so love those tinkly musical-boxes. Does it really play a hundred tunes?"

"Well, I counted only thirty-three, and then you called me," said Jack. "All right – we'll go and count a few more. It's a lovely box – the finest I've ever heard."

They went along to the dim room with the portrait. Jack glanced up at it, half-afraid he might see those eyes gleaming again. But they were just as usual, staring down fiercely and broodingly. The children went over to the musical-box.

Jack started it. The silvery tune tinkled out, and all the children listened in delight. Just as it ended, Dimmy came quickly into the room.

"Have any of you been into my room? Surely you couldn't have played such a silly joke on me?"

All five stared at her in surprise. "What joke?" asked Jack, at last. "You *know* we haven't been upstairs since lunch-time, Dimmy."

"Well – it's very strange then," said Dimmy, frowning.

"What's happened?" asked Jack.

"The whole room is changed round," said Dimmy. "The bed is in a different place. My clothes are put into different drawers. The photos I brought with me are lying flat on their faces – and one of the vases on the chest has fallen down and smashed."

"Just like that other one did!" exclaimed Mike. "But Dimmy – who in the world could have done such a silly thing to your room? *Your* room, too! Honestly, not one of us would do such a thing."

"No, I don't think you would," said Dimmy. "Well, it must have been done in spite, perhaps – I really don't know! I can't think that one of the caretakers could have done it, grown women as they are – it's such a silly, spiteful thing. But I suppose one of them *might* have done it, just because we've arrived here and are making more work for them."

Dimmy went out of the room. The children looked at one another. "Poor old Dimmy," said Peggy. "I don't know how anyone could possibly feel spiteful towards *her* – she's so kind."

"I bet it's Guy," said Paul. "Or the spirit of the castle, whoever he may be! But he's a nasty fellow if he likes to smash Lord Moon's vases!"

The musical-box was still tinkling on. "Has anyone counted the tunes?" said Jack. "I forgot to."

"Yes, I have," said Peggy. "We've got to forty-one now. Oh listen – here's Cherry Ripe! We had it at school last term. It's a very old tune."

They were all listening to Cherry Ripe when Jack heard a noise by the mantlepiece. A distant hiss, just as he had heard before. He looked across uneasily.

Mike had heard it too, and Paul, but the girls were too engrossed in the musical-box. Paul suddenly gave a loud cry that made them all jump violently.

"Shut up, Paul," said Nora, crossly. "You nearly made me jump out of my skin!"

Paul was staring at the portrait. Mike and Jack were doing the same.

"Its eyes!" gulped Paul. "They came alive! They looked at me."

Nora and Peggy looked at the portrait too. "Don't be so silly," said Peggy. "You're imagining things! The eyes are horrid – but they're only *painted* ones that seem to look at you. Don't be such an ass, Paul."

CRASH!

A picture fell suddenly off the wall behind them, and made them all jump again. Jack stared at it. Then he went over and looked at the picture cord it had hung on. He at once saw that the broken ends were frayed.

"It's all right!" he said cheerfully to the others. "Nothing to do with the glowering Lord Moon – just frayed-out picture cord."

"Well, I don't like it," said Paul, who looked quite pale. "I *did* see those eyes gleaming just as if they were alive. Didn't *you*, Mike? You were looking too."

Jack frowned quickly at Mike. He didn't want him to say anything in front of the girls, who had neither of them seen the eyes glowing as if they were alive.

So Mike said nothing in answer to Paul, but suggested that it was time they went for their walk. "This room is getting on my nerves," he said. "I can't bear that fellow,

Lord Moon, glowering at us, and pictures falling down. Stop the musical-box, Jack, we'll go out."

"We got to forty-three tunes," said Peggy. "Listen – what's that hissing noise?"

Everyone had heard the hiss that time, for the musical-box was now silent. Jack gave the girls no chance of finding out what usually followed the hiss, and he hustled them out of the room. "It's nothing. Let's go, or we shan't have time to get to that old village."

The girls went out obediently. Jack glanced back into the room. Yes – those eyes were gleaming again, as if they were alive. Was it a trick? What a peculiar one, if so!

They made their way to the front door and went out into the sunshine, which seemed quite dazzling after the dim room where they had played the old musical-box. Ranni was outside, doing something to the car.

"Oh Ranni! What a bit of luck you're here with the car!" said Paul. He turned to Jack eagerly. "He could take us to the fork of the road in the car, Jack – it would save a lot of time. Then we need only walk up the fork to the old village. It's so frightfully hot this afternoon."

"Good idea," agreed Jack and they all got in. Ranni was quite willing to take them. He was bored with so little to do. The car swept off down the drive and out of the gates. It wasn't long before they were down the hill and at the fork of the road.

"I'll wait here," said Ranni. "I can do a little polishing till you come back."

The five of them set off up the rough road. It had never been much more than a village lane at any time, but now it was so overgrown that in places it was like a field. Only the hedges each side showed the children that they were in an old lane.

It took them a quarter of an hour to reach the village. What a desolate sight!

Every house was empty, the windows were broken, the

Every house was empty.

227

roofs had gaps in them where tiles had fallen off. A few houses had once been thatched, and there were great holes in the straw roofs.

"This must have been the main street," said Jack, stopping. "Is that a little church? What a shame to let it fall to bits like that."

"How silent and still it is!" said Nora. "Poor old village –no one to walk down the streets, or bang a door or call out cheerily."

"What's that over there?" said Mike, pointing. "A lot of tumble-down sheds and shacks – and that looks like some kind of old machinery."

"It's the mines, of course," said Jack. "Don't you remember – we heard there were mines here once, before the people all drifted away from the village. I suppose they were worked out. They were tin mines."

Nobody knew anything about tin mines. They walked over to the shacks, and looked at the old, rusted machinery. Jack came to a shaft driven deep into the earth. He looked down it.

"Come and see – here's where the miners went down," he said. "And there's another entrance over here – a bigger one."

"Let's go down!" said Mike.

This was just what Jack wanted to do, but Peggy and Nora looked doubtful. "Do *you* want to come, Paul – or would you like to stay and look after the girls?"

"They can look after themselves, can't they?" said Paul, indignantly. "Or go back to Ranni. But don't they *want* to come down?"

"Not particularly," said Nora. "It looks so dark and horrid down there. How do you get down?"

"There's an iron ladder," said Mike, peering down. "Gosh, it's pretty rusty, though. I wonder if it's safe?"

"This one's better!" called Jack, who was looking at the bigger shaft not far off. "This is much more recent, I should think. We'll try this one. I'll go down first."

228

He climbed down over the edge of the shaft. The others peered after him, excited. Tin mines! What did one find in tin mines? Nora had a vague picture of sheets of tin neatly stacked everywhere, which was very silly, of course. Mike thought of rocks with streaks of tin in them!

Jack called out to them when he was halfway down. "This ladder's fine. Come on, Mike and Paul!"

The other two boys followed him. The ladder seemed strong and in good order, surprisingly so, considering how long the village must have been deserted. Jack was now at the very bottom and was waiting for the other two.

They jumped down beside him, one by one. A hollow, most peculiar voice came down the shaft. "Are you all right, boys?"

"It's Peggy," said Jack. "How queer her voice sounds, echoing down that shaft!" He shouted up loudly. "Yes. We're at the bottom. There are tunnels everywhere. We'll have a quick look and come back again!"

"Don't get lost!" came Peggy's voice again, hollow and full of echoes.

The boys had their torches with them. Jack had switched his on as soon as he got to the bottom of the shaft. He flashed it round.

There were tunnels, as he had said, radiating out from the shaft. They seemed quite ordinary tunnels. Nothing glinted in the walls, no metal shone anywhere. Jack shone his torch into each one.

"Which shall we take?" he said. "This is going to be quite an adventure!"

Down In The Mines

The three boys decided to take a fairly wide tunnel, and they went down it. The roof was low, and Jack, the tallest, had to walk with his head bent. They came to a cave-like room after a time, out of which two tunnels led.

"Look," said Jack, picking up a bent knife. "This must have belonged to one of the old workers – and that broken mug too."

They shone their torches round. The roof of the cave was shored up by big timbers, but one had given way and that side of the cave had collapsed.

"I hope these timbers will hold up the roof till we get back!" said Mike, shining his torch on them. "They must be very old now. Look – there's some funny old machine they must have used -- all rusty and falling to bits."

They took the right-hand tunnel and went on. "We could spend a long time exploring these old mines," said Jack. "There seem to be heaps of tunnels. Hallo, what's this?"

They had come up to what looked like a rough wall, blocking the tunnel. They shone their torches on it. "It's not a wall," said Mike. "It's a fall from the roof. Blow! We can't go any farther this way."

Jack kicked at the heap of rubble, and it fell all round him. Another lot then fell from the roof, and rubble and stones rolled round the boys' feet.

"There's a hole in the middle of all this stuff," said Jack. "I'll shine my torch through and see if there's anything to be seen."

He was just about to do so when Mike gave an exclamation. "Jack! Don't shine your torch through. There's

230

a light the other side of this rubble wall! Look – you can see it shining through the hole. What can it be?"

Jack stared in surprise. Yes – through the hole that had appeared in the fallen rubble came a dim light. He set his eye to the hole in excitement.

He saw a strange sight. Beyond the fall of rubble was a spacious cave, and from it led another tunnel. Jack could see the opening to it, dark and shadowy.

On the floor of the cave burned a fire. It burned slowly and clearly, sending up vivid green flames from its deep-red heart. What it was burning Jack could not see – nothing so far as he could make out!

The fire made a noise, almost as if squibs or small fireworks were going off in it all the time. After every little explosion a purple tinge came into the green flames, and they sent off circles of greenish-purple that floated away like smoke-rings.

Jack gazed and gazed, filled with amazement. What was all this? What was this strange fire, and why was it burning here, in the old mines? Did anyone know of it?

"Let *me* see," said Mike, impatiently, and pushed Jack aside. He put his eye to the hole in his turn, and gave a loud cry of wonder.

"Gosh! Whatever is it? A fire – a green fire, burning all by itself!"

Paul elbowed him away in excitement. "My turn to see!" he said, and then fell silent in amazement as he gazed through the hole at the leaping flames, and heard the crick-crick-crack of the constant explosions.

Jack pulled him away after a minute or two. "My turn again," he said, and gazed earnestly through the hole. The others, leaning close against him, felt him suddenly stiffen and catch his breath.

"What is it? What is it?" whispered Mike and Paul, and tried to pull Jack away so that they too might see – but Jack resisted them, and went on looking.

Then he started back suddenly, just as the others heard a deep roaring noise from behind the rubble. A curious tingling came into their arms and legs, and they began to rub them quickly.

"What did you see? Tell us!" said Mike, rubbing his legs which felt as if they had pins and needles from the top to the bottom.

"I saw a figure," said Jack, rubbing his legs too. "Gosh, why have I suddenly got pins and needles? I saw a very strange figure, with a hood right over his face so that I couldn't see it. He wore very loose things, and very big gloves, so I couldn't see his skin at all. He poured something on the fire, and it made that sudden roaring noise, and its flames changed to brilliant purple. I simply couldn't look at them!"

Mike went to peep again. But, how bitterly disappointing – the fire had disappeared! Not a flame was to be seen, although the curious roaring noise still went on. Then in the tunnel beyond, lighted by a strange glow, he saw two figures – not one, as Jack had seen, but two.

They came forward slowly with what looked like a small broom. One of them swept gently over the place where the fire had been, and a little heap of stuff appeared, gleaming and glowing in its own light. What colour was it?

Mike didn't know! He wasn't sure that he had ever seen a colour quite like that before. Was it green – purple – blue? No, none of these.

The men swept the little heap into a curious narrow shovel made of some glittering metal that seemed to make the heap of glowing dust disappear as soon as it touched it. Then one of them put a bag or sack over the shovel, and the two of them disappeared down the tunnel.

Mike told the others all this. They sat back in their own tunnel, amazed and rather alarmed. What had they seen? What was happening in these old ruined mines?

"I wish I could get rid of these pins and needles in my

He poured something on the fire!

arms and legs," said Jack, rubbing vigorously again. "As soon as I stop rubbing, the feeling gets worse."

"Same here," said Mike. "Jack – what do you make of all this?"

"Nothing," said Jack. "I'm absolutely stumped. These are only old tin mines – *tin*, mark you – quite ordinary stuff. And yet we find this queer affair going on – a strange and most peculiar fire of green flames, that cricks and crack – and roars – and sends off rings of curious colour. Then for no reason at all that we can see, it dies down – and what's left is collected by a couple of men in the strangest clothes I ever saw!"

"Do you suppose that fellow Guy has anything to do with this?" asked Paul, after a pause.

"He might have," said Jack. "But how do the men get into that cave? Not through the way *we* came, or they would have removed this wall of rubble. I wish we could find the right way in. Then we could perhaps hide and watch everything properly. Yes, and see who the men are, and where they take the shovelful of stuff to."

"Well – I don't feel inclined to wander through all these mazy tunnels and get lost for ever," said Mike. "Couldn't we get a map of the old mines? If so, we might trace out a way to the cave we've just been looking at."

"Yes. That's a good idea," said Jack. "We'll do that – and I bet I know where we could get a map from, too! In that old library! This land probably belongs to Lord Moon, and we're sure to be able to find a book – or books – about the castle and all this property, in the castle library. I've no doubt that he made a lot of money out of the tin dug from here – or some of the Lord Moons did. I expect the mines had fallen into ruin long before the present one inherited the castle."

Mike glanced at his watch to see what the time was. "Surely it's more than half-past three?" he said, astonished. "Oh – it's stopped."

To their surprise the watches of the others had stopped too. "Better get back," said Jack. "The girls will be worried. I suppose that queer fire stopped our watches – and gave us these pins and needles too!"

They each took one more look through the hole, and then, as they could see absolutely nothing at all now, except for a faint glow from the floor of the next cave, they made their way back to the foot of the shaft they had entered by.

Nora and Peggy were leaning over the top, feeling anxious. They heard Nora shouting as they came to the bottom of the shaft.

"Mike! *Jack!*"

"Coming!" yelled the three boys, and then they heard Ranni's deep voice booming down.

"It gets late. Hurry, please."

They climbed up, and were very glad indeed to find themselves in the sunshine once more. But how their pins and needles tickled and pricked when the sun fell on their arms and legs! The three boys rubbed and scratched at top speed, much to the amazement of the girls.

"You have been too long, and such a pit is dangerous," said Ranni, severely, to Paul. "I was just coming to fetch you, little Prince. I have left the car waiting at the fork."

"Our watches stopped," said Paul. He turned to the girls. "Have your watches stopped too, by any chance?" he asked.

"No," said Nora, glancing at hers and then at Peggy's. "What did you see down there? Anything thrilling?"

"Gosh, yes," said Jack. "We'll tell you when we get back to the car."

The girls listened in the greatest astonishment when the boys related their adventure. Ranni, at the wheel, heard every word, and he was horrified.

He stopped the car and turned himself round to face the children at the back. "You will not come here again," he said, sternly. "If this tale is true, this place is not for you. I will not have my little master mixed up in such dangers."

"They're not dangers," said Jack. "We weren't in any danger, Ranni, really we weren't!"

Ranni thought differently. "Something goes on here," he said. "Something secret. It is not for children to meddle with it. Jack – you must promise me never to go down those shafts again, nor to take Paul with you."

"Oh Ranni!" said Jack, protestingly. "I can't promise that, Ranni. I mean – we really must discover what all this means."

"You will promise me," said Ranni, unmoved. "If you do not, I will tell Miss Dimity, and she shall take you back home."

"You're jolly mean, Ranni," said Jack. But he knew Ranni of old. There was nothing for it but to promise!

"All right – we won't go down the beastly shafts again," he said, sulkily.

"Nor will you come to the village," persisted Ranni who was taking no chances.

"All right," said Jack again. "Anyone would think we were six years old and wanted looking after. Go on – let's get back."

Ranni drove off, satisfied. Jack made a few plans, which he outlined to the others. "Even though we've had to promise Ranni we won't go to the village, there's no reason why we shouldn't find out a bit more about the mines from old maps. We'll go to the castle library after tea!"

"And have books jumping on us from the shelves!" said Nora, with a giggle. "Like that waitress said!"

"Well, it will all add to the fun," said Jack. "I say – don't let's say anything about what we saw in that mine, when we get back to Dimmy. She *might* whisk us back home – there's no knowing what she'll do if she thinks there's something we can't cope with."

"Oh, my pins and needles!" groaned Mike. "How long will they last? Honestly, mine are worse than ever!"

"Here we are!" said Nora, as the car swept in at the gates. "You're lucky, you boys, even though you've got pins and needles – you've had a fine adventure, and we haven't!"

236

Pins And Needles – And Jumping Books!

Dimmy was wondering what had happened to them all, because they were so late back to tea. She sat at the tea-table, occasionally looking out of the window to see if the children were coming.

She was most relieved when she saw them walking into the room. "Ah – here you are," she said. "Have you had a good afternoon?"

"Yes. We went to the old village – where the tin mines are," said Mike. "Ranni took us in the car. Sorry we're late. We did quite a bit of exploring. It's a queer old place, that village."

"Yes," said Nora, who really *had* explored it with Peggy, while the boys had been down the mine. "The tumble-down houses are all covered with ramblers and blackberry sprays, and tall-growing weeds, Dimmy. It's a sad sort of place, really – not a soul there. Only birds, and one or two rabbits we saw scampering around."

"Go and wash," said Dimmy, "and then come back quickly. Mrs Brimming has managed to provide another good meal for you!"

They were soon sitting down at the table, washed and brushed. The boys had bathed their arms and legs in cold water to try to get rid of the pins and needles that still attacked them. The water helped them at first, but as soon as they sat at the table, the pins and needles came back again so fiercely that the three boys wriggled and rubbed themselves in pain.

"What *is* the matter?" said Dimmy. "Have you been stung by something?"

"No," said Mike.

"It's just pins and needles," said Jack. "It came on us suddenly in the village. But it won't stop!"

When Brimmy came to take the tea-tray, Dimmy spoke to her about the boys' pins and needles.

"Do you think they've been stung by something?" she said, anxiously. "I can't make it out. Look at them – they can't keep still for a minute. They're wriggling and squirming all the time."

"They've been near the mines!" said Brimmy, at once. "Been down into them too, I wouldn't be surprised! You can do only one thing, Miss Dimity. Put them to bed, and I'll give you some lotion I have so that you can soak bandages for their arms and legs. That will soon put them right."

"But what *is* this pins and needles?" said Dimmy. "Why should it come on them like this?"

"It's the illness that drove the people away from that old village," said Brimmy. "It came all of a sudden, they say. The men were working the mines as usual – and for some reason a great fire came. When it died down, the men went to work down in the mines again – but when they came up they all had this pins and needles."

"Good gracious!" said Dimmy. "Is it dangerous?"

"Oh no, Miss," said Brimmy. "These boys will soon get rid of it if they lie quiet with this lotion on their limbs. But when it first came to the village it soon attacked every man, woman and child in the place, and only when they got away from the place did the attacks stop."

"What caused these attacks then?" said Dimmy, most interested.

"I don't rightly know," said Brimmy. "They do say that the great fire had something to do with it – it set loose radiations or something down in the mine, and these seeped up into the air above, and gave the village people this pins and needles in their limbs – a kind of tickling and prickling that drove them nearly crazy!"

"And so they left the village, did they?" asked Jack.

"Yes. The place got a bad name," said Brimmy. "No one would work the mines, and so there was no money to be earned. In three years' time there wasn't a soul there – and it's been going to rack and ruin ever since. My, that's over a hundred years ago now! I remember my grandmother telling me how it all happened in her grandad's time. I did warn these children not to go there, Miss Dimity – but they're headstrong, aren't they?"

Dimmy wasn't going to say anything against the five children! "Perhaps you'll get that lotion you kindly said you'd let us have," she suggested. "Nora, go with Mrs Brimming and bring it back."

Dimmy thought that the three boys would be sure to make a fuss at having to go to bed at once, but they did not. "Pins and needles can be most terribly tiring when it doesn't stop at all!" complained Mike, rubbing his arms hard. "It's quite funny when you have it for a little while – but not when you've got to put up with it for hours!"

"You're right," said Jack, feelingly. "It's like hiccups – quite comical for a few minutes, but alarming after half an hour!"

They went to their rooms to undress. Dimmy said she would bring the lotion as soon as she had it. The boys opened their doors – and then stared.

Their rooms were completely changed round, just as Dimmy's had been! The beds were by the window, the clothes had been taken out of drawers and arranged on the tops of the chests, the vase of flowers was on the floor, and their shoes were on the window-sill.

"This is crazy!" said Jack, staring round. A shout from Paul told him that his room was the same. They went into the girls' room – and that was changed round too.

"Mad!" said Mike. "Who's doing it? And why?"

"If it's the spirit of the castle, he's been pretty busy!" said Paul.

"Stuff!" said Jack. "This is no spirit – this is someone spiteful. But what's the point?"

"All part of the Queer Happenings that the waitress foretold, I suppose," said Mike, taking his shoes from the window-sill. "Look here – let's change the rooms round quickly and put everything tidy. Don't let Dimmy see what's happened. If she gets the wind up we'll all be taken back home – and I'm *jolly well going* to find out a bit more myself."

"Hear, hear!" said the other two.

"Mike, go and put the girls' room right, I'll do ours, and Paul can do his," said Jack. "Buck up! Dimmy will be here in a trice."

They hurried as much as their pins and needles would let them! They had got their rooms right, and were just beginning to undress when Dimmy came in with a big bottle of green lotion and some strips of old sheet for bandages. She looked reproachfully at them.

"Oh! I did think you'd all be in bed! I suppose you've been monkeying about, as usual. I don't think you're as bad as you make out."

"We *are*," said Mike. "Look at my leg – I've scratched it almost raw already! Come on, do me first, Dimmy. I'm in bed now,"

Dimmy put the bandages soaked with the green lotion on his legs and arms, wrapping them round loosely. Mike lay back in great relief. "That's super! Oh, how heavenly! That lotion feels as cold as ice. I can hardly feel the pins and needles now."

"Mrs Brimming says you'll be as right as rain in the morning," said Dimmy. "I must say it's very extraordinary – the whole tale of the village is queer. In fact, I think quite a lot of things are extraordinary here. I've half a mind to take you all back home."

Mike sat up, shocked. "Oh *no*, Dimmy! Don't be such a spoil-sport! It's grand here. There – you've made my pins

240

and needles come back again by saying such a worrying thing."

"Rubbish!" said Dimmy, and began to bandage Jack. "Lie down, Mike, I'll leave the lotion near you, so that when the bandages dry off, you can soak them again. Do you want any books?"

"The girls will get us some from the library," said Mike, making up his mind to get Nora and Peggy to bring up some books about the castle and the mines too, if they could find them. "Ask Nora and Peggy to come up, will you, Dimmy?"

The girls came up and said yes, of course they would go down to the great library and try to find some books for the boys. So down they went. They bumped into Edie Lots as they came to the library door. She had a duster in her hand, and they imagined she must have been dusting the books.

She stood with her back against the library door as they came up, her face unsmiling.

"Oh – er – do you mind moving, we want to go into the library," said Peggy, seeing that Edie was standing there for them to pass her.

Edie stood aside and even opened the door for them. "What kind of books do you want?" she said. "There are no books for children here."

"Well – we thought we'd like to read up about the old castle – and the old village," said Nora. "Goodness – what thousands of books there are! We'll never be able to find what we want here. It would be like looking for a needle in a haystack!"

"I'll help you," said Edie obligingly. "I've dusted these books so often I almost know their titles by heart. You sit down there now, for a minute. I'll get the little ladder from the cupboard outside, so that I can climb up to the shelf where the books are that you want."

She disappeared. The girls did not sit down, they began to wander round, reading out the titles of the books at

High up on a shelf a book was tilting itself over.

random. Nora suddenly gave a cry, and Peggy turned round quickly. Nora had her hand to her head.

"Peggy! You threw a book at me!" said Nora crossly. "It hit me on the head."

"I didn't throw one," said Peggy in astonishment. They bent down to pick up the book – and immediately another crashed down beside them, hitting Peggy's foot. She swung round, alarmed. Where were the books coming from? Then she clutched Nora's arm, and pointed. High on a shelf a book was tilting itself over – then it seemed to spring from its place, and landed about two feet away from the children.

"This is just what the waitress said happened to the man who came here to see some of the old books," said Peggy in a whisper. "Look out – here's another!"

Sure enough, yet another book tilted itself backwards, and then with a spring was off the shelf and on the floor in a heap, lying wide open. It was near Nora and she glanced down fearfully at it.

On the open pages she saw a map. She picked up the book at once. A map! Would it show the mines?

She looked at the title. It was difficult to read because the lettering was old and dim. "*A History of Moon Castle and its Lands*," she read. "Gosh, this is just the book we want, Peggy!"

Miss Edie came in, carrying a small library ladder. She stopped when she saw the books on the floor. "Now don't you treat the books like that!" she said angrily. "I won't have it!"

"They jumped off the shelves themselves," said Nora, not expecting to be believed. But Edie did believe her! She threw the ladder down and ran off at top speed, looking scared out of her life! Was she pretending, or was she really scared? She certainly looked terrified!

"Let's take this book to the boys and go and tell them about the jumping ones!" said Nora. "Whatever will they say!"

Some Exciting Map-Reading

The boys were feeling very much more comfortable. As long as they kept their bandages soaked with the green lotion they had no more pins and needles – but if they got out of bed and walked about, then back came the prickling at once!

They were very pleased to see the girls. Ranni had been in, and had put Paul's bed into the middle room with Mike and Jack, so all three were now together.

"Ha! You've brought a book!" said Mike, and reached out to get it. "A history of the castle – and its lands! Good work! This is just what we wanted. How clever of you to find it so quickly."

"We didn't find it," said Nora. "We didn't even look for it. It leapt straight off a shelf and fell at our feet!"

"Don't be an ass," said Mike, opening the book. "That's only the waitress's tale!"

"It's her tale, certainly – but it's ours too," said Peggy. "Do listen, Mike. It *really* happened!"

Now the girls had the whole attention of all three boys, of course! They listened as the two girls told their strange little story. Then, in their turn, they told Peggy and Nora how they had found all three rooms changed round, with everything in a different place.

"I can't make out what's happening," said Mike. "It looks as if we're being driven away from here – but I'm not going! I'm sticking it out till Paul's family comes. If things are still odd then, well, your father can go into the matter, Paul. But I feel somehow, from what Jack overheard this morning, that it's the next few days that are important to somebody – Guy, perhaps – or the two men we saw down in the mines. We just don't know."

They began to discuss everything again – the Twang-Dong noises – the way the rooms had been upset – the books flying off the shelves – the hissing noise in the room where the musical-box was, and then Mike mentioned the gleaming eyes of the portrait, forgetting that the girls hadn't seen them. They listened, finding this difficult to believe.

"It must have been some effect of light," said Peggy.

"It wasn't," said Paul. "That room's so dark."

"Well, I give it up," said Peggy. "In fact, I give everything up. I just don't understand a thing. If the castle really had a spirit of its own I'd understand what's happened, because it might not like us, and might want us to go – but I can't believe in spirits of that kind!"

"Nor can I," said Jack, and the others said the same, except Paul. Paul had been brought up in far-off Baronia, a wild land of mountains and forests, where legends were believed in, and strange things actually happened. But here – well, here it was just impossible. And yet – what *was* happening then?

Mike was looking through the book. The pages, solid with small print, were not easy to read, so Mike was looking for maps.

He found a section of them, unexpectedly clearly drawn. Some of them opened out into big sheets, like motoring maps. Mike opened one and spread it out over his bed. Paul left his bed and clambered on to Mike's to see. Soon all the children were poring over bits of the big map.

"It's the castle," said Mike. "Here's a plan of the downstairs floor. Let's find our L-shaped sitting-room."

They found it at last – then they found the library – the room with the musical-box – the one with the clock like a church. They found the different staircases. What a maze of rooms this castle possessed!

They examined the next plan, which showed the first floor, where their own rooms were. "Here's our suite of rooms," said Mike, pointing. "One – two – three – all connected. And there's Ranni's room – and this must be Dimmy's. Look – what's this extra door shown here – opening into Paul's room? *Is* there a door there – look, it would be in the wall on the right-hand side of your bed, Paul. Did you notice a door there? I didn't."

"I'll go and see," said Paul, and leapt off the bed. He took a few steps and then hobbled back again. "Oooh, my pins and needles!" he said. "As soon as I take a step or two they come back worse than ever. Peggy, you go and look. I'm sure there isn't a door. I'd have noticed it, I know."

Peggy and Nora went off to Paul's room at once and looked at the right-hand wall. No – there was no door there. The room was panelled all round, but, except for the door that led out to the corridor and the one that led into the middle room of the suite, there was no other door to be seen.

"No door," they reported when they came back. "Either it's a mistake on the map, or else there was once a door and it's been removed and the wall panelled over."

"Where did the extra door once lead to?" asked Jack with interest. "Let me see now – if it had been in the right-hand wall of Paul's room, it would have led into that blue bathroom next to it, wouldn't it? Well, I suppose there wouldn't have been a bathroom there in the old days – so I daresay when the bathroom was built, the old door was done away with."

"You mean, the door just led into the room that was there *before* the bathroom?" said Peggy. "Let's have another look. It's marked with a T. I wonder why."

"Let me fold this map up," said Mike impatiently. "Take your hand off, Peggy. I'll shake out the next map."

He shook it out, and there was an excited exclamation at once. "It's the tower! A map of the old tower!"

So it was. The children pored over it with great interest. The tower was shown in a diagram, as if it were cut in half from top to bottom, and the children could quite clearly see how it was built, and could imagine what it was like inside.

"There's the door at the bottom – the one that's locked," said Mike, pointing. "Then the stone stairway is shown – quite big, really – then the room on the first floor, look – how strange, it's quite round. I wonder how big it looks in reality? It looks fairly small here. Then up goes the staircase again, from just outside the room – it gets wider above and then narrows again to the second-storey room."

"I rather imagined the tower was like that inside," said Paul. "It's a bit like one we have in a castle in Baronia. Look – up go the stairs to the third–floor room, and up again to the roof. What a view there would be from there!"

"These square marks in each room must be the fireplaces," said Mike, pointing. "And this line must be the chimney, connecting all the fireplaces, and leading the smoke somewhere out at the top."

Nora put her finger on a small door-shaped drawing shown in the fireplace on the second floor.

"What's that?" she said. "It can't be the door that shuts off the staircase outside the room, because that's shown here, look. And yet it *looks* like a door. What's that mark on it?"

"It looks like a letter T," said Jack.

That rang a bell in Peggy's mind at once. "T! Well, that secret door in Paul's room – the one we couldn't find – was marked with T too, when it was shown on the other map," she said. "T – T for Tower perhaps."

"Why should a door leading off Paul's room be marked with T for Tower?" said Mike scornfully.

"Well – it might have been a door that at one time *led* to the tower," said Peggy, sticking up for herself. "I mean – there might have been a passage from this suite to the tower at some time – the tower isn't so very far from this suite of rooms!"

Mike looked at her, thinking hard. "You know – she

might be right," he said to the others. "Wait now – let's see the other maps."

There were no other big maps, except one for the attics, which was not very interesting. But there was a curious little map, marked ALL COMMUNICATIONS, which puzzled the children for some time.

"'All communications' – that *might* mean such things as stairways, passages, corridors and so on, connecting one part of the castle to the other," said Mike. "This is rather a muddled map if it means those though. I can't make out any of the staircases, for instance."

"Communications might mean *secret* ways," said Paul suddenly. "All old castles have secret ways and secret doors. Ours has in Baronia. They were once used for all kinds of things – hiding-places – escape routes – ways to get in by when the castle was surrounded by enemies. I expect Moon Castle has got its own secret communications too!"

"You're probably right," said Mike, looking suddenly excited. He pored over the map again, and then traced a curving line with his finger. "This line is marked with T at this end – and T at the other," he said. "It might be showing the two doors and the connecting passage between Paul's room and the tower. I *say*! Wouldn't it be super if we could find a secret way into the tower?"

There was a hush of excitement, and then Paul pounded on the bed. "We must find it! We must! We could creep in on Guy then, and see what he is doing. We *must* find it!"

"Well – look at this," said Jack, pointing to the map again. "It looks as if the passage from that secret door in Paul's room leads inside the walls somewhere, and then comes out to another door – or perhaps an opening of some kind – *inside the chimney* of one of the tower rooms. What does everybody think?"

Everybody was only too anxious to think that Jack was right!

"I know how we can tell if we're right," said Mike. "We

could measure the width inside of Paul's room, and the width of the bathroom, and see what they come to, together – and then we could measure the walls of both, *outside*, in the corridor – and if that measurement is bigger than our first one, we'll know it includes a secret passage in between the two rooms!"

"Gosh – what a super idea!" said Peggy. "I'll get a tape-measure out of my work-basket this very minute!"

She soon found one, and she and Nora measured Paul's room from wall to wall – exactly fourteen feet. Nora popped her head into Mike's room. "Fourteen feet exactly," she said. "Now we're going to measure the bathroom."

They measured it carefully, and came back to report. "Eight feet," said Nora. "Eight and fourteen make twenty-two. Now we'll measure the walls *outside* the rooms, in the corridor, and see what we make the length there."

Carefully they measured the walls that stretched along the corridor, outside Paul's room and then the bathroom. They counted in excitement – and then raced back into Mike's room.

"The measurements are different! The inner walls measure twenty-two feet – but the outer ones measure twenty-four! What do you think of *that*?"

Mike looked excited. "Two feet missing! Just the width for a secret passage. Good work, girls. There *is* a passage that starts somewhere in Paul's room, goes between his room and the bathroom – and then curves away behind walls to the tower!"

"Shall we go and find the secret door now?" said Paul excitedly, and leapt out of bed again. But he was soon back groaning. The boys had forgotten to soak their bandages when they had got dry, and now their pins and needles were coming back badly. Poor Paul had started his up again at once by jumping out of bed.

"We'll have to leave the secret door for tonight," said Mike dolefully. "No, Peggy – you're not going to look for secret doors without us, so don't think it. It'll be something to do tomorrow. My word – we'll have some fun!"

In The Middle Of The Night

All the five children felt really excited that night when bedtime came. Nobody could sleep. As for Paul, he tossed and turned, wondering where in the world the secret door could be in his room – if there still was one!

"But there must be!" he thought. "Because we know there is a space in the walls between this room and the bathroom next door."

He had, of course, not been able to stop himself from tapping his wall, and banging it here and there to see if there *was* a door in the panelling! It certainly sounded hollow – there was no doubt about that!

He had to get into bed before he had really examined the right-hand wall properly, because his pins and needles came back again with a rush. Mike heard the tapping and called from the next room.

"Paul! No probing about for that secret door now! You just wait till everybody can hunt for it!"

"Right!" said Paul, safely in bed, stretching his tingling legs out straight and rubbing his arms. Ranni had moved his bed back into his room again, though Paul had wanted to stay in Mike and Jack's room for the night.

"I shall come in two or three times, little master, to see that you are all right," said big Ranni, who had been most concerned about Paul's legs. "Do not be frightened if you see me standing by you."

"I wish you wouldn't fuss so, Ranni," said Paul. But it was of no use to say that. Paul had been put into Ranni's care, and the big Baronian was by his side as much as possible.

Everyone went to sleep at last, the girls first, because they had no pins and needles to bother them. Paul tossed and turned for some time and then he too went to sleep.

He woke very suddenly, some hours later, and sat up wondering what had awakened him. In his dreams he thought he had heard a loud click.

He saw a figure over by the window, and lay down again. "Bother you, Ranni," he murmured. "You woke me up!" He lay watching Ranni, and then his eyes began to close. He wondered if Ranni would come and fuss him about his bandages, and decided to pretend to be asleep.

He heard no further sound for a minute or two and then opened his eyes again. He could not see anyone now – perhaps Ranni had gone. Good!

Another loud click made him open sleepy eyes again – that must be Ranni going out of the room. He thought he saw a shadow moving high up on the wall, and tried to wake himself up enough to see more clearly. No – he couldn't – he was too sleepy. Clicks and shadows and Ranni all merged into a muddled dream.

He didn't hear low voices in the next room. It was Mike and Jack talking. They too had awakened suddenly, though they didn't know why. Mike thought he heard a sound in the room, and strained his eyes to see where it came from. The room appeared to be very dark indeed – not the slightest light came from the window, and Mike couldn't see even one star in the sky.

Jack spoke in a low voice. "You awake, Mike? How are your pins and needles?"

"Not too good," said Mike. "I'm awfully sleepy and I don't want to get out of bed – but I simply *must* get that lotion and soak my bandages again."

He saw a dark figure over by the window.

"Yes, I must too," said Jack. "Blow these pins and needles. It's most peculiar to get them like this, just because we went down those mines."

There was a creaking of the two beds as the boys sat up. Mike felt for the torch he always had by his bedside. He couldn't find it.

"Put *your* torch on," he said to Jack. "I can't find mine."

"Right," said Jack, and fumbled about for it. But he couldn't find his either! "Where on earth did I put it?" he grumbled. "Oh for a bedside lamp to put on! Living in a castle is great, but I do miss some things we have at home. *Where's* my torch?"

"It's most awfully dark tonight!" said Mike. "Surprising, really, because when we went to sleep it was such a starry night – no moon, but millions of stars. It must have clouded up."

Jack got out of bed, determined to find his torch. "I may have left it on the window-sill," he said. "Ooooh – my pins and needles!"

He went towards the window and fumbled for the window-sill. He couldn't find it! Something thick and soft and heavy hung over it.

"I say!" said Jack suddenly, "who's pulled the curtains over our windows? No wonder we couldn't see a thing! These great heavy curtains are pulled across, making the room as black as pitch and frightfully stuffy. No wonder I was so hot in bed!"

"Well, *I* didn't pull them!" said Mike. "You know I hate sleeping with a shut window or pulled curtains. I suppose Dimmy came in and did that."

"But whatever for?" said Jack. "She's just the one that's all against it! Well, I'm going to pull them back again and get a bit of air. I bet it's a beautiful starry night."

There was a soft rattle of curtain rings as the heavy curtains were pulled across the window. Jack leaned out, taking deep breaths of the warm night-air. The sky was full of stars.

253

"That's better," said Mike, getting out of bed. "I can breathe now. Why, the room's quite light, there are so many stars!"

He leaned out of the window with Jack. It was really a beautiful night. The boys soon felt, however, that they must get some more lotion on their bandages – the pins and needles were beginning to prickle unbearably! They turned to find the bottle.

"We can see by the starlight, really," said Jack. "But I do wish I could find my torch. I *know* I put it by my bed!"

They got the sponge, soaked it with the lotion, and dabbed the sponge over their bandages. "That's better already," said Jack.

They went to the window for one last look out at the lovely night. Both boys at once saw something that made them stare and draw in their breath quickly.

"Look! What is it!" said Jack, startled.

"A light – a sort of glow – shimmering over the ruined village!" said Mike, amazed. "What colour is it? It's the same colour as that little heap of stuff we saw that the men swept up after the roaring fire!"

"Yes," said Jack, his eyes on the soft, shimmering haze that hung over the rooftops of the village far below. "My word – this is really very peculiar, Mike. What *is* going on here – and down in those mines? I'm sure it's something that man Guy is mixed up in."

"Some experiment, perhaps," said Mike. "If so, that's the reason why he doesn't like people renting the castle or even coming to look over it. And now that he knows the Baronians are coming here in a few days, he's got to finish up whatever this experiment is, and clear out. No wonder he's angry!"

The strangely coloured haze began to fade, though it still shimmered beautifully. The boys watched till it completely disappeared. "What a sight!" said Mike, going back to bed. "I bet he would be annoyed if he thought we'd seen that!

It's a thing he can't hide – something that would make people enquire into it if they saw it – and then his little experiments, or whatever they are, would be found out!"

"Gosh – of course – he *didn't* want us to see it!" said Jack. "That's why the curtains were drawn across the window, so that if we woke we shouldn't see a thing! That's why our torches are gone, so that if we woke we couldn't put them on and discover the curtains blocking out the light!"

"Well, of all the cheek!" said Mike, sitting up indignantly in bed. "Coming in here – drawing our curtains – hiding our torches! I say – do you suppose he did the same in the girls' room – and Paul's?"

"I bet he did," said Jack. "I'm going to look." He soon reported that Mike was right. The curtains had been carefully pulled across in each room! "I've dragged them back again," said Jack. "I expect you heard me. What's he done with our precious torches? If he's taken them away with him I *shall* be wild!"

"Well – we've seen what he didn't mean us to see," said Mike, pleased. "We're one up on him! I say – he must be quite scared of us, mustn't he – trying to stop us discovering what he's up to!"

"He knows we're snooping round," said Jack, getting into bed and lying down. "He must have found that rug we put against the tower door to see if he came in and out – he saw we'd moved the chest there, when he put it to hide the tower door."

"Fancy him daring to come along here in the middle of the night, and take our torches and draw our curtains." said Mike. "He would have to pass Ranni's door – and Ranni sleeps like a dog, with one ear always open."

"He may have come through that secret door – the one we haven't found yet," said Jack, sitting up straight again. "Down the secret passage, straight from the tower! He wouldn't need to pass anyone's door then – or bump into anybody. I bet that's what he did!"

"Gosh! I shall never get to sleep tonight now," said Mike. "What a place this is! Twang-dongs, breaking vases, jumping books, gleaming eyes, secret doors, peculiar mines – well, we've had a good many adventures, Jack – but this beats the lot!"

"And we're only just in the middle of it so far," said Jack. "Come on – we really must go to sleep, Mike. We *must* find that secret door in Paul's room tomorrow. It will be very, very well-hidden, I'm sure – but we'll find it!"

They settled themselves down to sleep. Their pins and needles had subsided again. They lay and looked through the uncurtained window into the starry sky, puzzling out this and that, feeling little surges of excitement now and again.

They went to sleep at last, and woke late in the morning. The girls were already up and about. Peggy heard Jack speaking to Mike and went in. "Hallo, sleepy-heads!" she said. "We're just going down to breakfast. How are your legs?"

"Well – they feel absolutely all right," said Jack, getting out of bed and trying them. "Not a twinge! Not a pin, not a needle! Good!"

"Then you don't want to stay in bed for the day or anything?" said Nora, pleased.

"Good gracious, no!" said Mike, leaping out too. "We're quite all right. I say – anyone lost their torches?"

"Yes," said Peggy and Nora together. "Ours have both gone. We thought you'd borrowed them."

Paul poked his head in at the door. "Are your legs all right?" he asked. "Mine are. Did I hear someone ask about torches? Mine's gone too!"

"Blow!" said Mike. "Not one of us has got a torch then. All right, girls, don't look so puzzled. Jack and I have got a bit of news for you – something that happened in the night, while you were snoring your heads off!

We're in the very middle of an adventure – the strangest one we've ever had. Just wait till Jack and I are dressed, and we'll tell you all about it – and we'll have to Make Plans. Aha, Plans! We're going to be very, very busy today!"

Where Is The Secret Door?

Dimmy was pleased to find that the boys' legs and arms were better. She told Brimmy so when she and Edie Lots came to collect the breakfast trays.

"That lotion is very good," she said. "I've never heard of anyone keeping a lotion for pins and needles before! How did you hear of it? Do you suffer from pins and needles yourself?"

"No. But my son does," said Brimmy, and Mike nudged Jack at once. "I bet he does," he said, in a low voice, and Jack grinned. "I bet he gets it every time he goes down those mines!"

"It's a pity it's raining," went on Brimmy. "It'll keep the children in."

"We've got plenty to do," said Jack at once, and winked at the others. They laughed. They knew what Jack's wink meant – they were going to hunt for that secret door in Paul's room. The girls and Paul had now heard of all the happenings of the night before, and were feeling very thrilled.

"Where are you going to play?" Dimmy asked the children after breakfast. "You can be in here, if you like, now the breakfast is cleared."

"Well – we rather thought we'd just go up to our suite of rooms and look for something we've lost," said Jack. "So you can sew here in peace, Dimmy. Anyway, we've got a game or two up there, so there's no need to disturb you with our shouts and yells!"

"You don't disturb me," said Dimmy. "But if you want to go up to your rooms, you can. But wait till they are dusted and cleaned. And by the way, you must put that book back into the library that you borrowed last night."

"Oh yes – I'll fetch it now," said Jack. "You four go and wait for me in the library." He sped off, and the others went to the library.

"I hope some books do a bit of jumping," said Nora. She looked up at the shelves. "Books – we're here!"

But, most disappointingly, nothing happened. The books that had fallen out the day before had been picked up and put away in their places. Only one gap showed in the shelves, and that was where the *History of Moon Castle* had leapt from!

Jack came in with the big book. He shut the door and looked round the room. "Any circus performances yet?" he said. The girls shook their heads.

"No. Most boring," said Nora. "The books are behaving just like books!"

There came a knock at the door. "Come in!" said Jack. The door opened and Edie Lots looked in. "I thought I heard you," she said. "Will you please not throw the books about as you did yesterday. Some are very valuable."

"We didn't throw them, you know we didn't," said Nora. "We told you what happened and you rushed off looking scared!"

Edie said nothing to that. She noticed the big book in Jack's hand. "Oh, you've come to put that back," she said. "I'll fetch the ladder for you – it belongs to that high shelf there."

She went off and in a minute or two came back with the ladder. She set it up against the shelves, and then went out again.

"She's a misery," said Mike. "I don't like her. I don't like any of them much. Well – does anyone want to have a squint at this book again before I put it back?"

"Let's not talk too loud," said Peggy, suddenly. "I have a feeling that Edie may be listening at the door. I'd like to have one more look at the book – where that secret passage to the tower is." She dropped her voice at the last words, so that no eavesdropper could hear her.

They all pored over the maps once again. "It's a pity it doesn't show the mines too," said Jack. "I'd like a book about those mines."

CRASH! They all jumped. A book lay near them, half-open, on its face. "Welcome, dear book!" said Jack. "Are you by any chance a book about the mines?"

He picked it up – but it wasn't. It was called *Rolland, the Duke of Barlingford. A History of his Horses*.

"Sorry, Duke Rolland," said Jack, "but your horses don't really interest me. Nice of you to throw yourself at my head, though!"

"Jack – look," whispered Mike, and Jack turned quickly. He saw that Mike and the others were staring at a picture over the mantelpiece. It was swinging slowly to and fro! It was a dark picture, of mountains and hills, of no interest at all – except that it was swinging to and fro like a pendulum!

Jack walked up to it and took hold of it. It stopped swinging immediately.

"I don't like it," said Nora. "It's worse than jumping books!"

THUD! CRASH!

The children swung round. Two more books lay on the ground – and then Jack caught sight of another one tilting up on the shelf. Over it went and down it came!

He took the ladder, put it below the shelf where the book had fallen from, and climbed up. He could see nothing that could cause the books to jump out.

"All the books have come from the same side of the

room, and from the same shelf-level," said Paul. "That's queer, isn't it?" Oh my goodness, there goes the picture again!"

Sure enough it had begun to swing, though more slowly than before. Jack stood on the ladder and watched it. What was the point of all these silly happenings? "Pass the books back to me," he said to Mike. "I'll put them in their places."

He put the last one in its place, and climbed down again, expecting more to fall out immediately.

"Let's get out of here," said Nora. "I really don't like all these happenings."

"Come on then – we'll go upstairs. Our rooms will be done by now, I expect," said Mike. So they left the library and went up to their suite of rooms. Mrs Brimming was just coming out of them with a duster and a brush and pan.

"I've finished them," she said. "Now I'm going to do Miss Dimity's."

The five children went into the rooms. Jack locked the outer doors of all three rooms. "If we're going to hunt for a secret door, we don't want anyone bursting in just as we've found it!" he said.

They all felt excited. They went into Paul's room and looked at the right-hand wall. It was panelled from floor to ceiling. At first sight it seemed impossible that there should be a door at all.

"I wonder you didn't hear the fellow coming through the secret door into your room last night," said Jack to Paul.

"Well – I did hear a click once or twice," said Paul. "But I thought it was Ranni coming into my room and going out again. He stood over there by the window – I saw his outline."

Jack thought for a moment. "Well, perhaps that *was* Ranni, Paul. The man who came in by the secret door drew all our curtains across the window, as you know – so you wouldn't have been able to see his outline there, if the curtains were drawn. The man must have come after Ranni had been."

"Or else Paul saw him by the window just *before* he drew the curtains," said Nora. Jack nodded.

"Yes – that might be," he said. "Now come on – let's find this door. And mind – we don't give up till we've got it."

They each went to a portion of the right-hand wall, and began to search the panelling carefully. They pushed this panel and that. They pressed, they tapped. They leaned against the panels, they tried to shove them sideways.

"Well – we're not very successful," said Jack, at last. "I've examined my portion of the wall as high as six feet – but as far as I can see it's all ordinary panelling – no secrets anywhere. Let's change over places and try our hands at each other's bits of wall."

So they changed places, and began all over again. What a probing and tapping and pressing there was! The smallest knot of wood was examined, the tiniest crack!

In the middle of it all somebody tried the handle of the boys' door, and then tapped sharply on it. The five children, intent on their search, jumped in fright.

But it was only Dimmy, bringing up biscuits and plums for their elevenses. She was cross because the door was locked. Peggy flew to open it.

"What do you want to lock this door for?" demanded Dimmy.

"To keep out Brimmy and the Lots," said Jack, truthfully. "They're always snooping about. Oh thanks, Dimmy. You're a brick – chocolate biscuits and plums – I could do with those."

Dimmy went, and the children took a rest from their labours and ate all the biscuits and the plums, sitting on Mike's bed. They were very disappointed.

"We've been over an hour looking for that wretched

door," said Jack. "We *know* it must be there! It's pretty certain our night-visitor came through it from the tower passage. Why can't we find it then?"

"We'll try again," said Mike. He hated giving up anything. "Come on. I bet we'll find it this time."

But they did not. They had to give it up at last. "There's not a single inch we haven't examined," said Jack, with a groan. "It's beaten us. I really don't feel that I can possibly look panelling in the face again – I'm fed up with it!"

Everyone was. "Let's go out," said Nora. "It's stopped raining, and the sun's out. I hope to goodness nobody comes along while we're out and changes our rooms round again. That's such a silly trick."

"We'll lock the doors," said Jack, "and take the keys with us."

So when they left their rooms they locked each of the three corridor doors, though they left the ones connecting them wide open. Off they went into the sunshine, and wandered all round the enormous castle, exploring it thoroughly from the outside.

"It's almost lunch-time," said Nora, at last. "We must go in. Gosh, I'm filthy! Let's go straight up and wash, as soon as we get in. Dimmy will have a fit if she sees us like this."

They went up the stairs and came to their rooms. Jack took the keys out of his pocket. He unlocked the girls' room door and they all went in.

"Everything's all right," said Jack, pleased. "No change-round this time. Whoever the joker is, he or she couldn't get in today, because the doors were all locked. Good!"

"Look – my torch is back!" said Nora suddenly, pointing to the table beside her bed. "So is Peggy's."

"So's mine!" said Mike, running into the middle room, "and Jack's. But – the doors were all locked, weren't they?"

"They were," said Jack. "So – whoever brought back the torches came through the secret door – the one we couldn't find. There's no other way in. It *is* there! It *is*! And he came through it. Oh, why can't we find it? Paul – can't you think of *anything* that might help? You're the one that heard the clicks, and saw a man. Think hard – tell us everything you heard or saw."

"I have," said Paul, frowning hard, trying to remember the least detail. "I just remember a last click, that I thought was Ranni going out of the room – and a sort of shadow high up on the wall – and—"

"A shadow! High up on the wall! That's it, that's it!" cried Jack, his eyes shining. "This entrance must be high up, of course – higher than we looked – that shadow must have been the secret visitor going back through the door – but a door that is set high up in the wall! We'll find it now – we will!"

A Strange Night Journey

The children could not stop then and there to look for the door, because it was past their lunch-time already. Dimmy would be coming to look for them, not at all pleased. In excitement they flew to the bathroom, washed their hands, and then rushed back to brush their hair.

Downstairs they went, to find Dimmy just about to set out to fetch them, looking most annoyed. Peggy caught her round the waist and gave her a sudden hug, which stopped Dimmy's scolding at once. She couldn't help laughing, as Peggy nearly swung her over.

"Don't be so violent," she said. "And please set the table quickly. The meal has been here for ten minutes."

All the children longed to discuss the secret door, and longed even more to set to work and find it, but, of course.

they did not want to discuss it in front of Dimmy. They would have to answer so many, many questions if they did. It was their secret, and they hugged it to themselves all lunch-time.

"I've told Ranni to be here with the car at two o'clock," said Dimmy, dropping a sudden bombshell. "Mrs Brimming has told me of a glorious bathing-pool about six miles from here, and, as it's so very hot today, I thought you would all enjoy a really good bathe. We're taking our tea with us, and our supper too!"

To her great surprise nobody seemed at all pleased. She did not know their tremendous impatience to get back to hunting for the secret door, now that they thought they knew where it was! She looked round, surprised at the lack of excitment.

"Don't you *want* to go?" she said. "What funny children you are! I thought you'd love it. I suppose you had made other plans. Well, never mind, your plans can wait till tomorrow. I've ordered the picnic tea and supper now. Fetch your bathing-things quickly after lunch, because I don't want to keep Ranni waiting."

Jack saw that Dimmy was disappointed because they didn't seem pleased. He was kind-hearted enough to pretend that he was thrilled, and he kicked the others under the table to make them follow his lead.

They played up valiantly, and soon Dimmy was thinking that she had been mistaken – the children really did want to go! Actually, when they went to fetch their bathing-things, they began to feel excited about the unexpected treat. A bathe would be heavenly this hot weather – and a picnic tea *and* supper would be heavenly too!

"The secret door won't run away," Jack said. "It will still be there, waiting for us this evening. We'll find it all right, now we are sure it's higher up in the panelling than we searched. I never thought of that. Let's enjoy ourselves, and look forward to a good hunt this evening!"

So they went off happily, and had a really wonderful time, bathing in a pool as blue as forget-me-nots, lying to dry themselves in the hot sun, and then bathing again and again. The picnic was better than they had hoped – and as for the supper, even Dimmy was amazed to see what Mrs Brimming had provided. They all enjoyed themselves thoroughly.

They were very tired when they got back. They had done so much swimming that their arms and legs ached all over! "You must go straight to bed," said Dimmy, seeing them yawn one after another. "You've had a lovely day – so have I – and we're all burnt a deeper brown than ever!"

They said good night to Dimmy and went upstairs. Their enthusiasm for the secret door was not quite so high as it had been. In fact, only Jack and Mike seemed able to hunt for it!

"We'll get into bed," said Peggy. "Nora and I can hardly stand. Do you mind looking for the door by yourselves, you and Mike, Jack? I'm sure Paul won't want to stand on chairs with you and tap the walls above his head! He can hardly keep awake."

"You get into bed, and Paul too – and Mike and I will tell you as soon as we've spotted the door," said Jack. "Good thing we've got our torches back. We can see what we're doing now."

The girls got into bed – and so did Paul, although he felt he really ought to go and help the two boys. He lay and watched them put chairs against the wall, and then, quite suddenly, fell fast asleep.

"Blow," said Jack, looking at him. "I meant to have asked him if there was a chair standing close to the wall when he woke up this morning; because it seems to me that whoever climbed back through the high-up door would certainly have to have a chair to stand on!"

"Yes, you're right," said Mike. "I remember seeing one, Jack – just about here, it was! Let's stand on one here and see if there's anything queer high up on the panelling above."

They put one of Paul's chairs in the place Mike pointed out, and Jack stood on it. He felt round the panelling there, and was lucky, almost at once!

"I've got something!" he said, in a low, excited voice. "A knob! I'm pressing it – gosh, this whole big panel is moving!"

Mike shone his torch up from below, his heart beating in excitement. Yes – a big panel had moved with a loud click to one side, and a dark gap showed in the wall. They had found the secret door! What a well-hidden one! Who would think of looking high up in the panelling for an entrance?

"Mike! See if the girls are awake," said Jack. "We'll tell them. Don't wake Paul. He's absolutely sound asleep. We'd have to yell the place down to wake him."

Mike went into the girls' room with his torch and came back immediately. "Sound asleep too," he reported. "I shook Nora, but she didn't even stir! We'd better go exploring alone, Jack. Anyway, it's probably better there should be only two of us!"

"Right," said Jack. "I think we'd better get a couple of our suitcases to put on this chair, to stand on. I don't see how we can climb into this hole unless we get a bit nearer to it!"

Mike fetched two suitcases and put them on the chair. It was easy to clamber into the hole then! Jack went first, making quite a noise, but Paul didn't even move!

"There are steps this other side," said Jack, feeling with his foot. "That's good! Pass me my torch, Mike. I've left it down there."

Mike passed it to him and Jack shone it into the passage. "Yes – it's a proper passage," he said. "About eighteen inches wide. I'll go down the steps. You get through and follow."

Mike clambered through the queer high-up door, and

Jack went first.

followed Jack down the steps into the passage. The steps were more like a ladder clamped to the wall, but were quite easy to get down.

Now the two boys stood one behind the other in the passage. They both felt exultant. They had found the way! Now where would this lead to? To a chimney of the tower? And if so, what would they find there? A way out into a room? And who would be in the room?

They began to make their way along the passage. It was

hot and stuffy. It ran straight for a little way and then bent sharply to the right. "I think we're walking behind the walls of some of the rooms on this floor," said Jack. "Hallo, we go downwards here – there's a slope."

They went downwards, and then very sharply upwards. The passage wound in and out, just as had been shown on the plan. And then, quite abruptly it stopped!

It came to an end against a stone wall. Up the wall some iron staples were set, evidently meant for climbing. "We go up here," said Jack, in a low voice, flashing his torch upwards.

They went up a little distance and then Jack stopped. "Can't go any farther up," he said. "There's a stone roof. But there's a grille or something here, just at the side of the iron staples. It's got a kind of handle. I'll pull it back. I hope it doesn't make a noise!"

He pulled it slowly back. It made not the slightest sound, and Jack guessed that it was well oiled. No doubt this was the way that the night-visitor used whenever he wanted to visit the three-room suite, or any other of the rooms on that floor, for any purpose!

Jack looked through the opening left by the sliding grille. He could see nothing but utter blackness. Was he looking into the chimney-piece of the room in the tower, which had been marked with a T door on the map? He must be! He listened. He could not hear a sound nor see a light.

"I'm climbing through the opening," he whispered to Mike, below him. "I think it's safe. Stay there till you hear a low whistle, then come up."

Jack climbed through the opening and felt about for some way to get down. His feet found some stone ledges, and he stepped down cautiously, not daring to put his torch on yet. He put out his hands and touched cold stone in front of him, at the back of him and at the sides! He decided to flick his torch on and off quickly.

When he did so he saw at once that he was standing

upright in a big chimney, his feet in the empty stone fireplace. He had only to bend down, walk forward, and he would be out in one of the tower rooms!

He bent down. There was pitch darkness in the room, but in a short time Jack made out a small strip of starry sky! He knew he was looking at one of the narrow tower windows, with the stars shining through it.

He gave a low whistle, and heard the sounds of Mike climbing up, then scrambling through the grille and down the stone ledges. Soon the two boys stood together in the dark room. Jack switched on his torch. The room was a sitting room – very comfortably furnished indeed. Nobody was there.

"What a lot of armchairs!" whispered Jack. "Guy believes in making himself comfortable. What do we do now?"

"Find the stone tower-stairway and go up it," whispered back Mike. "There are more rooms above. We know that from the map. Come on. The stairway will be outside that door over there."

They went carefully to the door and opened it. Outside was a dim light, evidently for lighting up the stairway. Jack fumbled round the curved stone wall until he found a switch, and turned off the light. "We shan't run so much risk of being spotted if we go up in the dark," he whispered. "Be careful, now. We don't know what we might come up against!"

They went silently up the stone steps in their rubber shoes. The stairway appeared to wind round and round the inside of the tower walls. They came to a door, which was a little ajar. The room beyond was in darkness.

Jack listened but could hear nothing. He pushed the door open, and looked in. He was sure nobody was there. He flashed on his torch quickly, and stared in astonishment.

"A bedroom!" he whispered to Mike. "But look at the beds – heaps of them! Whoever lives up here? Goodness, it

He flashed on his torch.

isn't only that Guy fellow – it's a whole lot of people. What *can* they be doing in this tower?"

"There's another room above this," whispered Mike, whose heart was thumping like a piston. "Perhaps something will be going on there."

They left the bedroom and went up the stone stairs again. Before they came to the next door, they heard loud voices!

They stopped at once, and pressed close together, hardly breathing. Some kind of quarrel was going on in that top room of the tower.

There were angry shouts in a foreign language. Then came the sound of something being flung over – a table perhaps?

"Who are they?" whispered Jack. "There sounds to be quite a lot. I vote we creep up and listen! Come on!"

A Truly Adventurous Time

The two boys crept up the few remaining stone steps and came to another door which, like the rest, was a little ajar. There was a small platform outside this door, and from it a narrower stairway led upwards.

Jack put his mouth to Mike's ear. "We'll scoot up these steps if anyone comes rushing out. They're not likely to think there's anyone up there at this time of night. I expect it only leads to the roof of the tower."

Mike nodded. He set his eye to the crack of the door, and so did Jack. The crack was wide and gave the boys a very good view of the whole room. They were astonished to see so many men.

Half of them were in the curious garb that the boys had seen being worn by the figures in the mine. Their heads

271

were hidden in a hood which had eye-holes covered by some stiff, transparent material. Jack thought it was probably to protect their eyes from the heat.

The other half were in ordinary clothes, but wore overalls over them. Jack gave Mike a nudge as he recognized Guy in overalls. There was no mistaking that ugly face with its fierce eyes!

It was plain that everyone was angry with Guy. They shouted at him in strange tongues. They shook their fists and threatened him. He stood there, glowering.

"You told us we were safe here, and could do our work in secret. You told us no one ever came to this castle, or to the mines. And now, before our work is finished, you say we have to clear out of this tower!"

Someone yelled something in a foreign language and Guy scowled.

"I've told you it's no fault of mine," he said. "We've been here, unseen, for nearly two years now – thanks to the help my mother and aunts have given me – ever since I first discovered the priceless metal in that old mine. I put you on to it, didn't I? I've helped you with my knowledge. But I tell you, if we stay here in this tower now, everything will be discovered. The place has been let – and the tower has got to be opened."

More yells. Then a quiet-looking man spoke up. "What you suggest, then, is that you take the stuff that is ready, and hide it away. And we leave this tower and go to live down in the mines, working there till the castle is empty of its tenants, and we can come back again and live in the tower while we finish our work?"

"Yes. And that's the only sensible thing to do," said Guy. "You know that. Lord Moon owns the castle – and the mines and everything in them, valuable or not. He thinks they are only tin mines – we know better. Because of that strange fire years ago, which drove the miners away and gave them that curious tingling disease, a new metal was formed. We've called it 'Stellastepheny', and it's going to be one of the most powerful and valuable in the world . . ."

More shouts, and someone pounded on a table.

"And you want us to let you go off and sell it, while we go down and live in the mines!" shouted one of the men in the hoods. "We don't trust you, Guy Brimming. We never did. You're not straight."

Guy looked round at them bitterly. "Not straight? And which of *you* is straight? Not one! Well, either you trust me, and we save something out of this – or you don't trust me, and all our work will be lost forever."

There was a heated discussion in all kinds of languages. Then the quiet-spoken man gave the verdict.

"All right. We *have* to trust you. Let's finish the last lot of stuff, and you can take it with the other. Then we'll take the secret way to the mines and stay there, at work, till we hear from you that things are safe. We've plenty of food down there."

"You're wise," said Guy, his face surly and unpleasant. "Get cracking, then. I want to go tonight. I'd hoped to scare the fools who want the castle – but they won't be scared. I daren't stay any longer."

"Right," said the quiet man. "We'll finish off this last lot of stuff, and you can take it and go. Then tomorrow we'll heave all the beds down into the cellars underneath the tower, so that no one suspects anything when they see the room. The other furniture won't matter. Then we'll clear up here. But tonight we must go to the mines. We all saw that light over the ruined village after we'd left last night. There will be many things to do there at once."

There was a good deal of muttering, but it was plain that everyone was now agreed. Jack and Mike watched the next proceedings in the greatest wonder.

One of the men put what looked like a glass cylinder in the middle of the floor. He clamped it down, and attached some glass tubes to it. Then the men in the loose robes and hoods brought up two or three narrow shovels covered in bags of some kind.

"Stand back," they said to the men in overalls. "Cover your faces."

Everyone stood back. Some of the men turned round to face the wall, and crouched down. Jack and Mike felt rather frightened, but they could not stop watching.

The hooded men uncovered their narrow shovels quickly and emptied the curious, shining, misty stuff on them into the wide opening at the top of the glass cylinder. Another man poured some colourless liquid into the tubes as the shimmering material slid into the cylinder.

And then the whole room seemed to disappear! A shimmering radiance came instead, that blotted out every single thing – a radiance that was of the same strange, unknown colour that the boys had seen hanging over the ruined village the night before.

Mike and Jack gazed through the crack, fascinated and entranced. What was this? They could see nothing at all in the room but this unearthly light. Men, chairs, floor, walls – everything was gone.

Jack's eyes began to hurt him. So did Mike's. They put their hands over them and stumbled away from the door and a little way up the stone steps. They sat down, unable to see for some time. No wonder the men had been told to cover their eyes!

"If that radiant stuff makes 'Stellastepheny' or whatever they called it, it's really wonderful," whispered Jack, at last. "I've never in my life seen anything like it."

"Listen – somebody's coming to the door," said Mike, clutching Jack's arm. "It must be Guy, with the stuff he wants to get away with tonight."

Somebody stumbled out of the open door and down the stone steps. The boys saw vaguely that he carried a metal box under his arm. Was the precious "Stellastepheny" in that? It must be.

"Let's follow and see if he goes out of the tower door at the bottom," whispered Jack. So they followed, and when they came to the bedroom, they saw that a light was there. Guy must have gone into that room. Perhaps he was getting a few of his clothes?

And then Jack did something so quickly that Mike could not at first make out what he was doing. He ran down the two steps to the door, shut it firmly, and turned a key that stuck out from the lock! There was a startled cry from inside, and an angry voice shouted:

"Who's that? What are you doing?" Then footsteps could be heard running over to the door. The man inside pulled at it violently, shouting again when he found it locked.

"Oh Jack! You've caught him! You've got him prisoner!" said Mike, in amazed delight. "He can't get out of that room. He can't even be heard in the room above."

"It won't matter if he is," said Jack. "I'm taking the key!" He took the key and put it into his pocket!

"What do we do now?" whispered Mike, his voice shaking with excitement.

"Shall we follow the men to the mine?" said Jack.

"No. Let's lock them into the top room, like you've locked Guy into this one," said Mike, almost choking over his brilliant idea.

"Come on, then!" said Jack, quite beside himself with all these sudden thrills. They raced up the stairs and came to the top room again. They peered cautiously through the crack.

The men were there, evidently getting ready to go, for all of them now had on the loose, hooded clothes. Jack saw that he must lock them in at once or they would be coming out. He banged the door, and felt for the key.

There wasn't one! Angry shouts came from inside, and Jack caught Mike's arm. "We must hide! There's no key!"

He pulled Mike up the steps that ascended to the roof, just as the door was wrenched open, and a man came out, looking very weird in his hooded garb.

"Who's that?" shouted the man. "Who's monkeying about with the door? Is it you, Guy?"

A murmur came from behind him, and he was pushed forward. "Of course it's Guy. Who else could it be? What's he doing, staying on here still? Come on, let's go down after him and see what he's up to."

Then the whole crowd of men poured down the stairs, never dreaming that two scared boys were on the stone steps just a little way above them!

They made a great noise, clattering down the stairs – such a noise that when Guy shouted to them as they passed the locked bedroom door, not one of them heard him. The boys, following down cautiously afterwards, heard him clearly, and grinned.

The men clattered right down to the foot of the tower, and then stopped. "He's not here. He's gone through the tower, after all," said one of them. "It must have been the wind that banged that top door shut! My, we must be scary to act like this!"

Another man produced a big key and fitted it into the tower door. He unlocked it and went out into the little square room beyond. The others followed.

One man gave a sudden exclamation. "I've forgotten to get my notes out of the sitting-room. I'll go and get them and catch you up. Give me the key and I'll lock the tower door behind me when I've got my notes."

He was given the key. Jack and Mike fled back up the steps, as silently as they could. If that man was coming to get something from the room above they would be caught if they did not get out of the way!

The man came up the stairs, slowly and heavily. He had not heard the boys. They shot past the door of the sitting-room and stood on the steps above, shaking with excitement. The man went into the room and switched on a torch. They heard him opening a drawer.

"Come on – we'll go down," said Jack, in a sudden

whisper. "It's our chance to get out of the tower before he locks it – and watch where he goes. There must be a secret way to the mines, as we thought!"

They ran silently down the steps to the very bottom, went out of the tall, narrow tower door, and crouched at the side of a chest, waiting.

Soon they heard footsteps and the man came down again. He pushed through the doorway, lighting his way with a torch, shut the door and locked it carefully. The boys watched breathlessly. What was he going to do?

He went to the side of the little square room, fumbled behind a chest and pulled at something there. In the very middle of the floor a big stone slid quietly downwards, as silently as if it had been oiled. The boys stared at the gap in the floor lit by the light of the man's torch. They were really amazed. Why, they had trodden over that stone a dozen times!

The man went over to the hole, sat down on the edge of it and let himself down carefully into the gap. He disappeared. After a few seconds the boys came out from their hiding-place and switched on a torch. Just as they flashed it they saw the stone rising slowly and silently back into place!

"Look at that!" said Jack. "I'm not sure we aren't in some peculiar kind of dream, Mike! What are we going to do now?"

"Follow that man!" said Mike promptly. Jack shook his head. "Too dangerous," he said. "I'd like to – but we might get lost underground trying to find where the man has gone. He's got too good a start. I know what we'll do!"

"What?" said Mike.

"Help me pull a heavy chest right over the stone that goes up and down!" said Jack. "Then none of the men will be able to get out. They'll be caught! If they lower the stone it won't provide a way out – because the chest will be on top! We'll have got them properly!"

So the two boys hauled one of the biggest chests right

over the stone trap door, and then stared at one another in delight.

"We've got Guy locked up in the bedroom of the tower –and we've blocked the way out for the others – unless they like to find their way through that wall of rubble we found in the mines, and come up the shaft. But I bet they won't do that!" Mike rubbed his hands in glee.

"*Now* what do we do?" said Jack. "Go to bed? Everyone is a prisoner, so we might as well! We'll tell Dimmy and Ranni in the morning – what a surprise for them, and the others, too! Come on."

"I hope we shan't wake up and find it's all a dream," said Mike. "Honestly, it's been one of the most adventurous nights we've ever had!"

An Exciting Finish

Next morning Mike and Jack were still sound asleep when the others were fully awake. It was Paul who woke them.

He came running into the boys' room. "I say, what happened last night? You found the secret entrance and never woke me! It's still open in my room. *I say*!"

The girls joined him, thrilled to hear his news. Mike and Jack woke up with a jump. Jack immediately remembered the happenings of the night before, and gave Mike an excited punch.

"I say, Mike, I wonder how all our prisoners are!"

Mike grinned, remembering everything in a rush. Goodness! What a night! Then Paul and the girls began to clamour to know all about the secret door, and if the boys had gone into the passage, and *what had happened*?

They could hardly believe their ears when the boys told

them. They listened, their eyes nearly falling out of their heads. All those men! Living in the tower too! and Guy finding out about that precious stuff, whatever it was – and getting men to work the mines for it, keeping it a dead secret.

"And he's locked up in the tower bedroom, you say!" cried Nora, with a squeal. "How *did* you think of such a thing! And all those men imprisoned underground! Quick – let's find Dimmy and Ranni!"

Dimmy was surprised to find five such excited children descending on her, as she sat waiting for them to come to breakfast. "Dimmy, Dimmy! Listen to what Jack and Mike have found out!" shouted Nora.

"I'm fetching Ranni," said Paul. "He ought to hear all this too," and he sped off, coming back with the big Baronian, who looked very puzzled at this sudden call.

Breakfast was forgotten as the children poured out their tale. Dimmy listened, almost speechless with astonishment. Ranni listened too, nodding his great head from time to time, and finally bursting into a great guffaw of laughter as he heard how Guy had been locked up in the tower bedroom.

He laughed still more when he heard how the two boys had put a heavy chest over the entrance to the underground passage to the mines. Then he looked grave.

"I should not laugh," he said apologetically to Dimmy, who looked very serious, and felt it. "There has been danger here for us – great danger. I can see that. Many things are clear to me now which puzzled me before."

"And to me too," said Dimmy soberly. "Well – the children seem to have managed everything very well without our help – but I think we should get the police in now, Ranni."

"Yes," said Ranni. "This is a serious busniess. Lord Moon must be told. He must fly back from America, or wherever he is."

"I had better ring for Mrs Brimming and the Lots," said Dimmy. "I am sure they knew all about this."

They did, of course. They were three frightened women as they stood before Dimmy and Ranni, and answered their stern questions.

Mrs Brimming wept bitterly and would not stop. Her two tall sisters were frightened, but Edie Lots was defiant as well.

"Don't blame my sister, Mrs Brimming," she said. "She never wanted her son to do this. But I urged him on. He's clever! He should be one of the greatest scientists in the world. He should—"

"He won't be," said Dimmy. "He has done wrong. The mines are not his, and he had no right to bring all those men here and put them into the tower like that. What will Lord Moon say when he knows all this?"

Mrs Brimming sobbed more loudly. The children felt sorry for her. Edie Lots spoke loudly.

"Lord Moon never comes here. He has no use for his castle or for the mines. Why shouldn't my nephew use them?"

"It is foolish to talk like that," said Dimmy. "Don't you realize that all of you will get into serious trouble over this?"

"I suppose all those queer happenings were caused by you three?" said Jack. "The jumping books – and Twang-Dong noises and so on. You wanted to scare us away, didn't you?"

"Yes," said Edie Lots, still defiant. "But I was the only one who worked them. My sisters wouldn't. My nephew Guy invented them – I tell you, he's a genius – and he showed me how to work them. The front door opening by itself – that's done by a wire. And the jumping books – there's a little passage behind the library bookcases, and Guy made some small holes in the back of one of the shelves; so that when I went into the passage behind I could poke my finger into a book, and send it leaping off the shelf."

"Very simple!" said Jack. "We didn't look for small holes at the back of the shelf! What about the Twang-Dong noises? How did the instruments on the wall make *them*?"

"They didn't," said Edie Lots, sounding quite proud. "There's a mechanical device up the chimney. When it goes off, it makes those two noises at intervals."

"Gosh! So that's why we could never spot who did it – even when the door was locked!" said Mike. "Oh – and what about those gleaming eyes in Lord Moon's portrait?"

"The canvas eyes have been scraped very thin, and then painted again, and a hole made in each," said Edie Lots. "And there is a light behind each eye that can be turned on from outside the room. I waited ouside when you were inside, and kept turning the light on and off. And the hissing noise was made by a bellows worked at the same time. My nephew thought of all those things."

"And did you change the rooms round – and break the vases?" asked Dimmy, entering suddenly into this extraordinary conversation.

"I did everything," said Edie, proudly. "I made the picture swing too. Guy arranged that." Her tall sister hung her head, and Mrs Brimming still sobbed, heart-broken. But Edie was proud and glad. She had helped her beloved nephew, and that was all she cared about!

"Oh well – it's rather disappointing – everything has got quite a reasonable explanation!" said Peggy. "But goodness me, some people would have been very scared!"

"Some people were," said Edie, and the children thought of the man who had gone to the library to look at the old books. How pleased the sisters must have been when he spread the tale of Queer Happenings about!

Nobody seemed to want any breakfast at all! Dimmy dismissed the three caretakers, and began to pour out the tea. Ranni sat down to join them, his arm round Paul. He seemed to think that Paul had escaped great dangers and must now be guarded every minute!

They talked soberly for some time. "I think you should take the car and go and inform the police, Ranni," said Dimmy. "I don't see that this will make any difference to Her Majesty the Queen of Baronia coming here, as arranged – but we must get this business settled up before she comes."

"Yes. Guy will have to come out of the tower bedroom, for instance!" said Nora.

Ranni got up to go. The children made a very poor breakfast, they were so excited and so eager to talk. They watched for Ranni to come with the police, and were thrilled when they heard the car hooting below to tell them he was back.

Things happened very quickly after that. Ranni had told the police most of the strange story. Two men were dispatched to get the angry Guy from the tower bedroom. They forced the tower door easily enough, and went up the stone stairs, having been presented with the bedroom key by Jack. Soon a very dishevelled Guy was being hustled into a police car, angry, astonished and bewildered.

His weeping mother and two aunts were not allowed to speak to him. Nothing was being done about them for the time being. Lord Moon would decide everything when he returned the next day, called back from America. He was flying over, most astonished at what the police had told him on the telephone.

As for the underground miners, they were soon rounded up by a most formidable posse of police. Jack and Mike got permission to go down the secret passage to the mines, behind the police, provided they stayed close to Ranni. Much to Paul's anger Ranni would not allow him to come.

The heavy chest was moved away from the stone trap door. Mike went to the side of the room and fumbled behind the same chest he had seen the man go to. He found an iron lever sticking a little way out of the wall. He pulled it – and lo and behold, the stone in the middle of the floor slid downwards, and exposed the opening to the secret passage!

Down they all went. The underground passage was not a pleasant one, for most of the way it was narrow, low-roofed and dripping wet. It led down the hill, meandering about. Ranni thought it must have been the bed of an underground stream, which had more or less dried up and left its bed as a tunnel.

They came into the mines at last, and at once the passage became dry and the roof rose high. The boys soon found themselves in a little tunnel near the place where they had seen the wonderful, roaring fire. It was just opposite the wall of rubble from behind which they had watched such a strange sight.

The men were all gathered together in the main cave, puzzled and anxious. They had been back to the trap door entrance, and had moved the stone trap door, to get out and back into the tower. But, of course, they had found the way blocked by the heavy chest, and had not dared to try to move it. In fact, they had no idea what it was! They had closed the stone trap door again and retreated into the mines.

When they saw the uniforms of the police, a murmur went up from the miners, who looked very strange in their queer hooded garments. Ranni was quite startled to see them!

The men had been expecting something like this ever since they had found the trap door blocked. They felt sure that Guy was at the bottom of it, and were ready to give away everything, to get even with him! It was not until they had told the police every single bit of information they knew that they were told that Guy was a prisoner too – and had been locked up all night in the tower bedroom!

"If only the men had known, they could have escaped

that way," said Jack, pointing to the wall of rubble on the opposite side of the cave. "They could have knocked down the rubble and escaped up a shaft. We knew that – but they didn't!"

"The things you kids know just don't bear thinking about," said a tall policeman, with a grin. "Keep behind your red-bearded friend, now – we don't need your help in front."

The prisoners were all taken away in police cars. Ranni and Dimmy sighed with relief. Goodness gracious – to think of all the secrets that had been going on in Moon Castle!

"I think we'll take the car and go into Bolingblow for lunch," said Dimmy, heaving an enormous sigh. "I'm sure Mrs Brimming and her sisters won't be able to provide anything like a lunch today!"

"Yes, let's go," said Nora, at once. "We can tell that waitress she was quite right. There *were* Queer Happenings and Noises in Moon Castle. Do let's."

"You're not to say a single word to her," said Dimmy. "It's nothing to do with her. We don't want the news all over the town, exaggerated and garbled – we'd never hear the last of it!"

"Dimmy – come and see the tower," begged Jack.

"No, thank you," said Dimmy, firmly. "I don't feel strong enough today to tackle that awful tower – though I *would* like to see the view from the top."

"My mother is still coming, isn't she?" said Paul anxiously. "You haven't put her off, have you, Dimmy?"

"On the contrary," said Dimmy. "I had a letter from her this morning – which, in all the excitement, I forgot to mention – and as your brothers are quite well again, they're all coming tomorrow! What do you think of that?"

"Smashing!" said Mike, at once. "It was going to be dull, now this adventure is over, waiting and waiting for them to come. Now we'll have hardly any waiting at all. Couldn't be better!"

"In fact, we've cleared up all the mysteries at exactly the right moment," said Jack. "Aren't we clever, Dimmy?"

Dimmy wouldn't say they were. She laughed and ruffled Jack's hair

TWANG!

"Oh, my goodness – don't say that awful Twang-Dong is still going!" cried Dimmy. "I can't bear it!"

DONG!

The children roared with laughter. Jack went round the bend of the L-shaped room and looked up the chimney, shining his torch there.

He put up his hand and pulled down a curious little contrivance of metal, springs and tiny hammers.

"There you are," he said, putting it on the table. "The Twang-Dong itself. One of the mysterious secrets of Moon Castle!"

"Hurrah for Moon Castle!" said Nora. "And hurrah for all its secrets, Twang-Dongs and everything!"

The Twang-Dong made a curious noise. Its mechanism seemed to be running down. It slowly raised one of its little hammers and struck the metal beneath.

DONG!

"It's finished," said Jack. "Finished – like this adventure. Well, it was GRAND FUN while it lasted!"